Dark Annie

Joseph J. Christiano

Dark Annie

By Joseph J. Christiano

Published by

Tell-Tale Publishing Group, LLC
P.O. Box 90112
Burton, MI 48509
www.tell-talepublishing.com

Nightshade
Imprint

3

For Kim

"The past is not dead.

It's not even past."

--William Faulkner

Chapter One

Should Have Knocked It Down

Anderson found himself, quite against his will, pulling into the parking lot of Deacon's Landing Magnet School. He had had no intention of even driving down this particular street. It was, after all, a few blocks outside his assigned patrol area, and God knew Captain Lange had a hard-on for him as it was. He should have simply driven past the Seven-Eleven instead of making that right at Piedmont Street, but something inside him had wanted a look. *Just a look, nothing more,* the something inside him had said in a soothing, seductive voice that sounded suspiciously like Jen's. He had been powerless against that voice when it came from a living woman; it appeared he was equally powerless against it even after its owner had taken up permanent residence in Lichgate Cemetery.

His patrol car continued its slow progress up the driveway. The brand new blacktop was smooth beneath the tires and appeared darker than the night sky in his high beams. No dips or potholes in the driveway, not even the feel of gravel crunching beneath the radials. *As smooth as silk,* Jen's voice whispered in his ear. And she was right. Like the rest of the school, this, too, had received a complete makeover. The new first selectman was thorough if nothing else and he kept his promises. Too bad. This was one time Anderson would have been happy to hear of a politician breaking a campaign promise.

He reached the turn in the driveway. The poplars vacated his line of sight and for the first time in twenty-six years he got his first look at DLMS. He had seen the place many times before, of course, had in fact spent almost two months as a student in that very building. But that was a long time ago when it was known as Deacon's Landing Elementary School and he had limited his involvement with the building to whenever some reporter with nothing better to do decided to write a piece about it and splash its picture in the *Sentinel.* He had had his share of calls within the neighborhood, as well, but he had always managed to keep a fair distance between himself and the school. He was thankful the line of duty had never forced him to venture onto the property, because he was honestly uncertain he would have been able to do it. *So why now?* he asked himself. This time Jen had no answer for him. He frowned and goosed the patrol car forward.

He intended to bypass the horseshoe that led by the front doors, the area where school busses would begin dropping off kids in a few weeks. He found himself making the turn anyway and he cursed himself as he did so. He saw the newly-planted trees and shrubs that followed the curve of the driveway, the lawn neatly mowed and the wild flowers someone had planted along the side of the building. They stood in contrast to the clean red bricks that made up the façade. It should have looked beautiful, especially in contrast to how the building had appeared for the previous three decades. As far as Anderson was concerned, the only way to make the building prettier was to knock it down to its foundation and then bury that. But no one had sought his opinion, and it would have made no difference, in any case.

His high beams reflected off the chrome bumper of the car parked in the center of the horseshoe. He recognized the blue Chevelle with the white SS stripes immediately. He did not wonder what had brought the muscle car's owner out at this time of night or to this particular location. He knew the answer. And he was relieved to have the company.

The car's owner leaned against the passenger side door, arms folded across his chest and facing the school's front entrance. His long hair whipped across his face when he looked over his shoulder at the approaching patrol car. It was probably not often Brian Murphy had such a nonchalant reaction to the approach of a police car, but this was one of those times. He seemed to know it was

Anderson even before they locked eyes through the windshield. He resumed his stance and went back to staring at the front entrance of Deacon's Landing Magnet School.

Anderson pulled up alongside the old Chevelle, put his unit in park and stepped out. Murphy did not turn, but he said, "I knew I wouldn't have the place to myself, but I have to admit, I'm glad it's you and not that asshole Bradley."

Anderson walked around the front of Murphy's car and took a spot next to him. He leaned against the Chevelle's fender and planted his hands on his hips. "Bradley's not so bad." It was a lie; Anderson's opinion of his fellow officer was the same as Murphy's. "He just has a habit of pulling you over when you're holding. How many times are you gonna get caught with simple possession, anyway? Isn't it getting old by now?"

Murphy shrugged his shoulders and laughed. "The day it's legalized I'm gonna blow a big cloud of that shit right in his face." He turned his head slightly but did not look at Anderson. "Just FYI."

Anderson nodded. "Duly noted." He regarded the front entrance of DLMS and could not believe he had allowed himself to get this close. The set of glass doors with their gleaming silver handles seemed to beckon to him and warn him away at the same time. It should have been an improvement. The old front entrance had consisted of double doors which had always made Anderson think of oblong eyes that seemed to watch him as he approached. It was ridiculous, of course, and he had realized it even then. But there seemed to be some credence to the adage, *What scares you as a child scares you as an adult.* He nodded in the direction of the entrance. "Looks different, doesn't it?"

"Not nearly different enough."

"Can't argue with that."

Murphy pointed to the right of the new doors, a corner of the building obscured by shrubs sitting in a bed of red mulch. "Right over there is where Kenny Atkins ripped Holly's sweater and I clocked him in the mouth. Remember that?"

Anderson grinned in spite of himself and nodded. "Like it was yesterday. The little shit had it coming for any number of reasons, believe me. You know, I saw him a few days ago. In town to see his father would be my guess. I don't think he recognized me."

"Some people change," Murphy offered.

"He didn't," Anderson said. "Long, greasy hair, fingernails blacker than black. Looked like he hadn't had a bath or done laundry in months."

"Typical Atkins."

They stood in silence for a few more moments. Anderson's eyes moved slowly around the front of the building. He did not know what he was looking for, if anything; nor did he know if he would be able to spot something out of the ordinary if he did see it. It had been years, decades since he had allowed himself this close to the school, let alone seen it. It all looked new, but he knew from one of the newspaper articles that much of the existing structure had been left in place. *Some cleaning crew earned their pay,* he thought. *Although they should have asked for double time just for having to go inside that fucking building.*

"I'd offer you a beer," Murphy said, "but you're on duty."

"And you're driving," Anderson replied. "You've already defied expectations and not run this beast into the reservoir." He patted the Chevelle's hood. "Don't blow it now."

"Yeah, yeah, yeah," Murphy said. He sighed loudly and put one hand on the door handle. "They never should have renovated this place. Should have knocked it down when they had the chance. You know I'm right."

"You hear me arguing?"

"I'm just glad I don't have any kids. Saves me the trouble of having to worry about them coming here every day." He turned to Anderson. "Seriously, you think parents are happy about sending their kids here?"

Anderson had been considering that very question since the announcement the school would be rebuilt and reopened. "Maybe the ones who weren't here back then and don't know much about it beyond the basics are okay with it." He swallowed. "I wouldn't be."

They stood in silence for several more moments. The night air was warm but Anderson could feel the gooseflesh on his arms. He had spent too much time here and he wanted to leave. *Besides*, he reasoned, *no need to get caught out here and give Lange an excuse.*

He patted the Chevelle's hood again and turned toward his patrol unit. "Have a good night, Murph. Don't do anything stupid here. You know what I'm talking about."

Murphy nodded in his direction and mumbled his agreement. He continued to lean against his car and look at the school.

Anderson walked around to his driver's door and opened it. He had one foot inside the car when he paused and looked at the school again. The breeze picked up momentarily and ruffled the leaves in the trees that bordered the horseshoe. It made the hair on his arms stand at attention and all at once he felt cold.

It was simply his imagination and he knew it. August in Connecticut was not cold by any stretch of the imagination, even in the dead of night. Still, he wished he had brought his jacket along.

He climbed into the car, started the engine and closed the door. He put it in drive, waved to Murphy (who did not see the gesture) and exited the horseshoe. He turned on the car's heater before he made it off the property.

****

Murphy heard the police car recede into the distance. *Just you and me again*, he thought, looking at the school. *But not for long.* Two weeks before the school year began and Deacon's Landing's newest, and oldest, school reopened for business. What that business would be, exactly, was something of a mystery. Murphy suspected (and he was not alone in this) that more than the basic curriculum would be taught here when once again the sounds of children echoed in the hallways and the playground.

He looked again at the spot where, a thousand years before, Kenny Atkins had decided to get a little payback from the girl who had turned the tables on him in gym class and left him squirming on the hardwood and clutching his balls while his friends gasped and laughed. Kenny had figured Holly would be an easy target if taken by surprise, and in this, at least, he had been correct. Had Murphy not happened to walk by at that precise moment, Atkins may well have taken his revenge on the little blonde girl with the braces and her hair in pigtails.

But he *did* happen to walk by, and Kenny Atkins had paid the price, and not just in front of his friends this time. He had picked the right moment but the wrong location. Most of the school saw what happened and it was the main topic of conversation for days afterward.

Until Dark Annie made her presence known.

In point of fact, until he pulled up to the front doors of Deacon's Landing Magnet School and his eyes fell upon the fateful corner, he had forgotten completely about Kenny Atkins and how much blood had spurted from his nose after Murphy landed the first of many haymakers on the little shit.

Holly, on the other hand, had never left his mind. It was not simply because she had been his first crush, although that was probably part of it. He saw her from time to time if some of the guys at the shop wanted to hit

Lucky's after work. Holly did not dance too often these days, apparently preferring to pour drinks and play hostess to hitting the stage herself. It was not that she lost her looks; far from it, in fact. Murphy believed she was more gorgeous now than she had been in her twenties. But the lowlifes who populated Lucky's on a Friday or Saturday night wanted more than a forty-one year-old dancing to "Pour Some Sugar On Me." That was just fine with Murphy. One of these days she'd say yes to him where she had said no so often. On that day she would say good-bye to Lucky's for the last time. Or so he hoped.

He walked around the front of his car and opened the door. Much like Anderson had some moments before, Murphy paused and looked again at the school. The wind had died down but the night air still felt cold to him. He grimaced and spat on the new asphalt. Murphy held his position a moment longer and looked at the building as if it were about to retaliate for his transgression. It did not. He slid behind the wheel of the Chevelle and turned the key.

The 396 fired right up and the Flowmaster duals produced the familiar, pleasant growl. Murphy shifted the transmission into first and was easing off the clutch when he hesitated for one last glance at the school.

He tried, quite honestly, to picture Deacon's Landing Magnet School's newest students running from the bus to the front doors on the first day of school. The teachers on bus duty trying to get them to slow down, birds squawking as they took flight from their nests in the poplars, the sun shining on smiling faces.

What he got instead was an image of Deacon's Landing Elementary School's final day of classes in 1985. There were no teachers yelling for the kids to slow down as they exploded out of the front doors. Not that day. In the distance was the sound of Engine Forty-Two from Canal Street exceeding the speed limit in its dash to the school. Smoke billowed into the blue sky and kids cried and teachers took head counts.

He also remembered the look in Mr. Ruiz's eyes, and, despite the noise and the chaos, he heard what the man said to one of the other teachers: "Dark Annie." He did not know the meaning of the name then, but he would learn more and more details over the years. Not that such knowledge would have mattered then.

He released the clutch and the Chevelle eased out of the horseshoe. Murphy tried his level best not to look into the rearview as he left the property.

He failed miserably.

****

Anderson was well within his assigned patrol area when the call came in, a ten-thirty-one and only three blocks away. He activated the red-and-blues right away and gunned the engine. He waited until he was a block from the location before he hit the siren as well. There was no traffic at this hour, a fact for which Anderson would be grateful. The last thing he needed was a bunch of rubberneckers getting in his way, or for some well-intentioned passer-by to try to lend a hand and instead make matters worse. He knew Ellis was on patrol on the opposite side of town, which would make Anderson the first on scene. He preferred it that way.

He took the turn onto Leffingwell Avenue and saw the accident scene. A single vehicle lay on its side. It was an SUV of some kind, and dark in color, but Anderson could not tell more than that at first. A Camaro sat parked perhaps twenty feet beyond the SUV. A pimply kid stood half-outside the Camaro jabbering on his cell. He waved frantically at Anderson and pointed to the left of the SUV. A girl who looked no more than sixteen years-old sat in the Camaro's passenger seat; she likewise had her cell to her ear. Beyond them, the street was deserted, no fire or medical and no Ellis. Anderson grabbed the microphone from its cradle and hit the button. "Dispatch, three-three-seven."

It took a moment before Peschel's voice came back. "Three-three-seven."

"I'm at the scene. Send fire and rescue."

"Three-three-seven, fire and rescue."

He replaced the mic in its slot and stopped the patrol car twenty feet from the wounded SUV. He stepped out and activated his flashlight. His first sweep revealed the body lying fifteen feet from the vehicle, to which the kid in the Camaro still pointed. It also illuminated the smoke drifting lazily from the underside of the SUV. He made his way to the vehicle quickly and shined the light along the undercarriage. He was relieved to see and smell the motor oil which smoked up from the muffler. He double-checked to be certain there was no fire danger anywhere else around the SUV (it turned out to be a Jeep Cherokee) before he bolted for the prone body on the blacktop.

"We saw him coming down the road," the kid in the Camaro told him. "He was swerving all over the place."

The kid remained half-inside the Camaro and Anderson was grateful for that. The girl remained in the front seat and talked excitedly on her cell phone.

Anderson said, "Stay back, both of you," as he approached the body.

The man lay on his stomach. One arm was beneath the body, the other stretched out in front of him as if he were trying to fly. His t-shirt, most likely green when he slipped it on, was nearly black with blood. A deep abrasion on his head bled profusely and matted his thinning hair to his scalp. He groaned when Anderson knelt beside him.

"Easy, sir, don't try to move. Emergency services are on the way." The man groaned and his arm twitched, the only signs he was still among the living. Anderson placed his flashlight on the ground and reached for the man's outstretched hand. He picked it up as gingerly as he could and placed two fingers on the inside of his wrist. There was a pulse, but it felt weak. He looked again at the Jeep and was relieved to see the smoke had lessened in intensity. Not much, but it made him feel better. The Jeep's driver, on the other hand, looked worse by the moment.

Anderson picked up his head when he heard the sirens in the distance. The hospital was in the opposite direction so Anderson assumed, correctly, the call had come through when the ambulance jockeys were stopped for a bite. He hoped it would not be Lyons and Ferguson; they complained enough as it was. Damned good paramedics, professional as anyone, but complainers. Especially when they were hungry.

"Ambulance is close, sir. Just lie still. They're almost here."

The man groaned again and this time the sound gurgled in his throat. Anderson knelt down until his cheek nearly rested on the asphalt and he looked at the man's face. Bubbles of blood puffed from his lips with each ragged breath. One of his teeth lay on the ground an inch or two from its former home. A second seemed imbedded in the corner of his mouth. His nose bled and the skin on his forehead was scraped away, revealing the skull beneath.

Anderson looked down the street in the direction of the sirens. He could see the headlights and roof lights of the ambulance perhaps a half mile distant. Behind the ambulance he could just make out the outline of the fire truck. "C'mon, c'mon," he said and looked at the prone man again.

He had stopped breathing. Anderson quickly grabbed at the man's wrist and checked for a pulse. He found none. He put his head down again on the road and watched the man's lips. A thin layer of blood coated his lips but it no longer bubbled. He could hear no sounds of breathing and the man's back did not rise and fall with respiration.

"No, no, no. Shit!"

"Is he dead? He's dead, isn't he?" the kid from the Camaro asked.

Anderson stood and waved his flashlight in front of him, the universal signal for *hurry the fuck up.* The ambulance jockeys saw him and did indeed step on the gas. Anderson could hear the ambulance's motor rev as it drew nearer.

He started to run toward them, as if that would somehow get them to the crash victim sooner. He was stopped when he felt the hand wrap itself quite powerfully around his ankle. He yelped and spun.

The man holding his ankle, the man who showed no sign of life a moment earlier, looked up at Anderson. His face was a wreck. The right half of it, obscured by the pavement earlier, revealed itself to be torn and pitted. It was much more than road rash; Anderson could see the man's teeth through the ragged holes in his cheek. The man opened his mouth to speak and several teeth fell out and pattered on the asphalt. He drooled blood and saliva onto the roadway. His eyes, however, were clear and focused. It made Anderson want to rip his ankle out of the man's grasp and to put as much distance between them as was possible.

Instead, when the man reached up with his free hand Anderson bent down and took it. He knelt beside the man again and held his hand. "Just hang on. They're here now. They'll take care of you."

"She's still in there," the dying man said. Blood bubbled again from his lips. "She's still in there. You have to find her."

Anderson's head snapped to the side and he looked again at the Jeep. "There was someone inside the vehicle with you?" Christ, he had been so fucking stupid. He had not even checked for additional passengers. He started to stand but the man squeezed his hand with enough force to make Anderson draw a sharp intake of breath.

"Find her. Find her before it happens again." He said something after that, a single word that sounded like *Danny.*

He looked again at the SUV and was about to pull himself free of the man when it proved to be unnecessary. The man's grasp on Anderson's hand and ankle weakened and a moment later his arm fell on the roadway. He looked from the dead man to the two approaching paramedics (who did indeed turn out to be Lyons and Ferguson).

"Wassup, Matt?" Lyons asked.

Anderson ignored him. He walked away from the dead man and approached the Jeep again. He shined his light through the windshield, but it was cracked and he could see nothing inside. He walked around to the undercarriage and pulled himself to the top of the vehicle. The passenger's window was shattered and afforded him a perfect view of the vehicle's interior.

There was quite a bit of broken glass; the little beads of it caught the flashlight beam and the red-and-blues of the emergency vehicles and threw them in every direction. The affect reminded Anderson of his days at the local roller rink and its mirrored ball. To complete the image, Katrina and the Waves were still walking on sunshine, even if the Jeep's radio's lights were dark. The driver's airbag had deployed and lay draped like a shroud across the steering wheel. Litter that included crushed soda cans, McDonald's bags and empty cigarette packs were all over the place. There was a child's car seat strapped to the back seat and Anderson had a terrible moment when he was certain he would find a dead child somewhere amid the garbage. But there was no one. The Jeep's interior was devoid of anything alive or recently-dead.

He heard another siren and poked his head up. Ellis' unit stopped a few feet behind the fire engine and he stepped out and made his way to the wrecked Jeep.

Anderson waved him off. "There might have been a second person inside the vehicle, possibly a child. Start looking."

Ellis said, "You got it," and pulled out his flashlight and went to work.

Anderson scanned the area around the Jeep but came up empty. They would need more eyes out here. He got on the radio and called dispatch.

Chapter Two

Mr. Blue Business Suit

Holly stepped through the side door at Lucky's and removed her sunglasses. The contrast between the early-afternoon sunlight outside and the characteristic semi-darkness of the strip club was quite pronounced, and it took her eyes a few moments to adjust. The second striking difference was the relative fresh air of Deacon's Landing and the perpetual smoky fog that made up the air inside Lucky's. Charles "Lucky" Luccino had little use for the statewide indoor smoking ban, and most of his customers and employees agreed with him. Holly herself had not had a problem with Lucky's disregard for the law until she quit smoking two years before, after incessant nagging from Cassandra. She hated to admit it, even to herself, but she had become one of those people; the kind of person about whom she had complained and ridiculed, an ex-smoker who nagged those who still indulged their habit. It had not been her intention to join that much-maligned group but it had turned out that way nonetheless.

Vince was at the door, as he always was. He greeted her in his customary manner of throwing his bear-crushing arms wide and widening his smile. "Hey, gorgeous!" he said and wrapped his arms around her.

Holly squeaked as she always did when Vince forced all the air from her lungs. His long biker's beard scratched at her cheek and neck. She hugged him back as best she could, which meant her hands wound up on his sides, the most she could extend her arms around his girth. When he relaxed his grip and she was once again able to breathe, she stepped back and patted his large and muscular chest.

"Hey, Vince. Looks a little slow in here today."

The giant bear of a man said, "Not even noon, yet. It'll pick up. Don't worry, I'm sure Cassandra's college fund will grow today."

Holly smiled. "I'm sure it will."

She walked past him and entered the main area of the club. The bar took up most of the south wall. It was the darkest section of the building's interior, with only a few smoke-stained ceiling lights providing illumination. Holly counted four customers, all men, seated there. Max, Lucky's son, stood behind the bar and chatted and laughed with one of the regulars. He nodded in Holly's direction and she nodded back.

Beyond the bar's ten foot perimeter the tables began. Small and round and big enough only for three patrons at a time, each table nonetheless was ringed by four chairs. They were old and sticky, regardless of how many times they were cleaned or scrubbed. The wood veneer on most of the tables was either stripped away or close to it. What little remained was stained with ancient beer rings and cigarette burns.

To the left of the tables the stage began. A long oval poked out into the club from the main stage where the girls would make their entrance from behind the curtain. The stage was ringed by rope lights of every color. The old mirrored ball spun slowly from its place on the ceiling, and a few pin spot lights most likely installed when Holly was still in elementary school somehow hung on to life.

Gina (stage name: Dakota) had the stage. There were only four men seated around the stage, and none of them together. She danced to a hip hop song Holly could not name. She worked a wave to Holly into one of her moves and did her best to keep her customers' attention. She did not appear to be succeeding, but it was hardly her fault; Holly noted with some irritation the dazed look in the men's eyes. *Not even noon and they're drunk off their asses.* It was both sad and typical.

Holly entered the staff area through the door on the side of the stage. She walked down the short, dark corridor until she came to the employee's dressing room. She pushed through the door and had to get used to the bright lights all over again.

The dressing room was nearly as large as the main bar area and much better lit. There were dressing tables and counters, each with its own mirror. Two of the girls, Luciana and Carrie (stage names Mysteria and Autumn, respectively), sat at the counters and applied their makeup. Holly waved to them on the way to her locker.

Her schedule was waiting for her when she opened the locker. It was stuffed inside one of the small, thin louvers, as was Lucky's *modus operandi*. She hung her jacket and pocketbook on the two hooks and looked over her schedule as she closed the door. She stopped when she got to Saturday.

"What the fuck?" She sighed and leaned back against her locker.

"He got us, too," Luciana said from the other side of the lockers.

Holly walked around to the other side of the room, schedule in hand. "What is wrong with him? He knows the place is going to be dead that night. It always is. I was going to take my daughter to the fair." She sighed again. "Goddammit."

"So was I," Carrie said. She nodded in Luciana's direction. "So was she. So was everyone."

"I'm still going," Luciana said. "My kids have been looking forward to this since school got out. I'm not gonna tell them they can't go because mommy has to work that night."

Holly drew her hand into a fist and, quite accidentally, crushed her schedule. She looked at it, at the two women with whom she shared the room, and laughed. Luciana and Carrie joined her.

"Take that, Lucky," Carrie said, and laughed again.

Holly sobered. "Dammit, I can't believe I have to be here that night. The whole fucking town will be at the fair. Who does he think I'll be serving drinks to, anyway?"

"At least you won't be on the stage flashing your tits to an imaginary audience," Luciana said. "And that's why I'm going to the fair. There is zero point to anyone being here on Saturday. I bet even the day shift will be dead."

"I agree," Carrie said, and lit a cigarette. "My daughter's old enough to be looking forward to the fair. I can't go home and tell her I can't take her. You know what that makes me look like?"

"A mother trying like hell to keep food on the table," Luciana offered.

"Yeah, but she won't see it that way," Carrie answered.

Holly blew a stray strand of blonde hair from her eyes. "Let me talk to Lucky. Maybe I can change his mind."

Luciana immediately turned to Carrie and both women mimicked fellatio. They lasted only a few moments before they burst into laughter.

Holly said, "Wiseasses," and smacked Luciana on the top of her head.

"Hey, hey, watch the hair!" Luciana said, but she could not sound angry so soon after the good burn she had gotten in on her boss.

"Is he here, yet?" Holly asked.

Carrie looked at the clock on the wall and said, "Should be soon. He had to bring the Caddy to the shop for something. Said he'd be back right after that."

Holly nodded. "He'll be in a mood. Oh, well. I'm going to ask him, anyway. Have a good show, girls."

"See ya out there," Luciana said.

'Thanks, honey," Carrie added.

A few moments later she was in her customary place behind the bar. She watched two of her regulars pay the five dollar cover to Vince and make their way inside. Their eyes went to the stage first, as happened with most people when they entered Lucky's. After a few moments of watching Gina they made their way to the bar.

Holly greeted them with her customary smile and got their beers ready.

Lucky arrived thirty minutes later. He entered through the front door, and Holly knew immediately whatever was wrong with his Cadillac remained wrong with his Cadillac. Lucky had his own parking spot in the lot right next to the side door. If he entered the club through the front entrance it was because he had been dropped off. She did not need to study his body language or see the look in his eyes to know his mood was somewhere south of happy.

Max, no stranger to Lucky's moods, beat a hasty retreat into the back room that served as office and sleeping quarters whenever his wife was, as Max put it, "having one of her episodes." While his stories relating the effects of his wife's episodes drew great guffaws of laughter from the mostly male patrons of the club, they were just as often ridiculed by the women who worked there. They could, after all, relate to the poor women who had chosen to be Mrs. Maxwell Luccino, even if they had to endure the little bastard's temper only for a few hours each day. None of the girls wanted to contemplate what marriage to such a man would be like.

Lucky walked behind the bar, scooped up a bottle from the top shelf and poured himself a tall one. He downed it with one prolonged gulp and slammed it on the bar hard enough Holly was surprised it did not shatter.

"Fucking Kyle Brothers," he said at last. He rooted around in his pants pocket until he found his cigar. He shoved it into its customary place between his teeth on the side of his mouth. He turned to Holly, although she got the distinct impression he was simply looking for the person closest to him. "That Caddy ran just fine until they got their fucking hands on it. Now it's in the shop every other week." He refilled his glass. "Goddamned thieves."

Holly opened her mouth to comment but closed it just as quickly. She herself had limited experience with Kyle Brothers Towing and Repair, but when she had dealt with them, they had been professional and courteous. She felt it might be the wrong time to point out her own positive experiences with them.

Unfortunately, it was also the wrong time to bring up the fact that Lucky would have a mutiny on his hands if he tried to open Saturday night. In the mood he was in he was likely to fire everyone. Instead, what she said was, "I'm sure they'll get it running again, Lucky."

He scoffed, removed the cigar from between his lips and downed his second drink. "Ah, that's a little better." He glanced at the stage as if seeing it for the first time. Luciana and Carrie continued to dance, and the crowd along the stage had grown to nine. He turned to Holly. "Who's on today? Isn't Gina supposed to be here?"

"She is," Holly said a bit too quickly. He had castigated her before for what he considered her rush to defend the girls. In fact, Holly thought of it that way, as well. It was Lucky's demeanor that made everything he said sound like a threat. She cursed herself for sounding defensive when she knew there was no need. "She's getting ready for a lap dance. The guy in the blue business suit. He paid already." She nodded her head in the direction of the customer.

Lucky took in the customer with a single glance and moved to the register. He opened it and started counting twenties. "Lunch crowd will be here any minute. At least tell me that worthless piece of shit Rincon is getting the grill ready."

"Got here about fifteen minutes ago," Holly said. "Should be ready."

Lucky grumbled but said no more.

Holly saw Gina emerge from behind the stage. She was trying out a new outfit and Holly could see it had the desired effect. Several heads turned in her direction, which produced irritated looks from Luciana and Carrie but had the opposite effect on the male patrons. Holly thought the red and black leather ensemble would be a big hit, especially with those able to afford to see it up close in the back room. Gina signaled to her customer, who got to his feet and followed her through the red velvet door. When it closed behind them, Holly activated the timer underneath the bar. She watched it tick down from ten minutes.

As predicted by Lucky and right on schedule, the lunch crowd began to trickle in a few moments later. She took lunch orders and brought them to Rincon. Most of the new arrivals took up places along the stage to watch the two young ladies do their thing. Lucky did not say much, simply sat at the bar and puffed on his cigar. She deflected a few looks from Luciana and Carrie; Lucky's mood was still far too foul to bring up Saturday.

The music was loud enough and the background chatter of the patrons was thick enough that for a moment, Holly did not recognize the scream for what it was. It could easily have been Axl Rose on the juke (God knew he hit some high notes on that first album) but several conversations ceased and more than one person turned their head in the direction of the red velvet door.

Holly took an involuntary step forward and tried to block out the music. At the same moment she convinced herself she had heard nothing, the scream repeated itself. Even Lucky turned on his barstool and looked.

Holly was in motion immediately. She ran around the bar and shouted, "Vince!" as she moved. Vince looked up from the magazine in his hands, saw the look of panic in her eyes, and moved quickly in her direction. Lucky was on the move, as well, although it took him some time to build momentum, given his size and lack of athletic ability.

Several patrons stood to the side of the velvet door but no one seemed eager to open it. Holly started to shoulder past them when Vince got there. The bouncer did not need to muscle anyone out of his way; the crowd parted like the Red Sea before Moses at his approach. He grabbed the door handle and yanked it open.

Holly could not see inside the room; Vince's bulk filled the doorway. But he remained there for only a moment. He charged into the room, cursing loudly. The first thing she saw was one of the mirrors which lined the walls had been shattered. Her own broken reflection stared back at her. There was blood, *a lot* of blood, in and around the center of the crack. The small mirrored ball still spun slowly from its mounting on the ceiling, and something soft and sexy from Alicia Keyes played on the room's sound system.

Vince had reached down and hauled someone from the floor. Holly thought it might be Gina, but a moment later she saw it was Mr. Blue Business Suit. He struggled to free himself from Vince's bear hug, but he would have had better luck trying to free himself from a real bear. The muscles in Vince's arms were corded and his face was red with the effort but he held the man tightly. Vince was shouting something, apparently to Blue Business Suit, but Holly could not make it out over the music. She thought she could guess at the nature of the conversation.

Vince hurled the man the length of the room. Blue Business Suit crashed onto and bounced off the black leather sectional that was the room's sole piece of furniture. He landed in a heap on the floor and Vince was on him again. When he moved from the center of the room, Holly got her first look at Gina.

Her face and neck were covered with blood. It flowed quite freely from a large gash on her forehead. It was in her hair and the floor around her head was slick with it. In the subdued lighting it appeared black. Her right arm twitched as if she were on the receiving end of an electric shock; the rest of her body was quite still.

Holly gasped and bolted for Gina. She dropped to her knees and reached for her but she pulled her hands back at the last moment. She knew next to nothing about first aid, but she knew enough not to touch or move someone with a possible neck injury. "God, no," she said weakly.

She turned her head quickly, saw the crowd massed in the doorway. Patrons jockeyed for position and behind them she could hear Luciana and Carrie calling for her. Lucky had joined Vince on the other side of the room. Blue Business Suit was no longer a threat; Vince had him down on his stomach and had planted his knee in the small of the unfortunate man's back. He held the man's wrists in one beefy hand. Blue Business Suit's face had contorted into a mask of fury and he snarled and squirmed and tried to throw Vince from his back. Holly took some comfort in knowing the asshole had no chance at success; Vince was fully in control and looked it. Lucky was shouting at the man, screaming, really, but Holly found she could not understand the obvious threats he spewed. Spittle flew from Lucky's lips and landed on Blue Business Suit's face.

Holly found her voice at last and shouted, "911! Call 911 right now!" She returned her attention to Gina without waiting to see if anyone bolted for the bar's phone or pulled out their cell.

She brushed the blood-soaked hair from Gina's eyes. Blood continued to pour from the wound on her forehead. It pooled in the recesses of her eyes and flowed slowly but continuously down her cheeks.   Tears clouded Holly's vision and she took one of Gina's hands in hers.

She looked about helplessly. Her eyes whipped past the crowd in the doorway, past Vince and Lucky and the man who had had the bad luck to pull this shit while they were here. Her eyes settled on the shattered mirror on the wall behind the sectional. She could see, quite clearly, the point of impact, and she could not stop herself from imagining how it looked as it happened. Gina's blood seemed to fill every crack and made them appear wider than they were.

"Please, someone help me," she said, as much to Gina as to those in the room.

Gina gasped and spat blood into the air. Holly managed to turn her head quickly enough to avoid getting it on her face or in her eyes. Gina's body convulsed with the next cough and Holly was certain she was having a seizure. But after a moment Gina lay still again. Her chest rose and fell, rose and fell, but rapidly and with shallow breaths. Holly felt the girl would die right there on the floor in the room reserved for lap dances.

Gina opened one eye, the one with the least amount of blood in it. Her hand traveled absently to her forehead, but Holly took it and held it against her chest. "Don't touch it, baby," she said through her tears. "Help is on the way. Just hang on."

Gina coughed again and more blood bubbled up from inside her. She wrapped her fingers around Holly's hand and squeezed. Holly laughed and cried and squeezed back. "That's it, honey, hang on to me. The ambulance is coming, they'll be here any minute."

Gina pulled her head off the floor. Not much, a few inches, but it alarmed Holly. She tried to gently force the young woman back down, but Gina's strength surprised her. She tried to talk, but the blood in her throat prevented much sound from making its way past her lips. She coughed again, spat more blood into the air. "She's still in there," Gina said weakly. "Find her, please, find her."

"What'd she say?" Lucky asked. He had left Vince with Blue Business Suit and loomed above and behind Holly.

Holly did not turn to look at him; her eyes remained fixed on Gina. "I don't know, I think she's delusional." She bent lower, grimaced, and put her ear in front of Gina's mouth.

Holly had to strain to hear her, despite their proximity.

"You have to find her, Holly," Gina said. "Don't leave her in there." Gina's breath felt very weak against Holly's ear and cheek. "Help her."

Gina's head fell back against the floor and she released her grip on Holly's hand. Holly squeezed her hand again but felt none of the warmth or strength from a moment before. "Gina?" she said, but she knew she would get no response. "Gina!"

The woman lay motionless on the floor. Holly watched her chest for some moments, hoping to see the rise and fall that would tell her Gina was at least alive. She saw nothing and was about to move back when Gina suddenly sucked in a long, slow breath.

Tears blurred her vision, but she held Gina's hand tightly. She heard someone from the doorway say, "Ambulance will be here in a few minutes." She did not reply, either to the man in the doorway or to Lucky, who continued to stand over both of them and ask stupid questions. Holly remained right where she was until the paramedics arrived and unclasped her hand so they could

take Gina from the room.

Chapter Three

The Customer in Cell One

Anderson stepped out of his Chevy and approached the precinct house's back entrance as he always did. Mr. Swain, the station's chief and sole custodian stood against the red brick façade and smoked his unfiltered Camels and waved to Anderson through a cloud of smoke. The late-afternoon sunlight made the smoke seem nearly cloudlike, the way old cinematographers shot Bette Davis or Rita Hayworth in the 1940s. The man's uniform greens were dirty, as they usually were this late into his shift. He ran a hand over his white hair which contrasted so forcefully with his dark skin and smiled at Anderson.

"How's it goin', Chief?"

Anderson smirked. "Goin' pretty good, Mr. Swain, goin' pretty good. And you know damned well I'm not the chief so stop calling me that. How about yourself?"

"It's Friday so I ain't complainin'," he said as he stamped out his cigarette and took another from his pack. "Got my brother-in-law comin' over tomorrow morning and we're gonna go out on Meriden Reservoir and do a little fishin'."

"You know that's illegal, right?"

Swain held up a finger to his lips. "Sshhh," he said, and smiled.

"Just don't get caught. The last thing I want to read in Monday's paper is how the department's custodian was under arrest for trespassing and unauthorized fishing."

"That's a real charge? Unauthorized fishing?"

Anderson nodded. "Better believe it. It's in the general statutes, but don't ask me which one."

Swain waved him off with another puff on his cigarette. "I'm too slick to get caught, anyway, Chief. Don't you worry."

"Slicker'n snot," Anderson said.

The old man laughed, a great, big guffaw that made Anderson smile. He walked past the custodian and opened the side door. He removed his sunglasses and made his way to the locker room. It was deserted and he was allowed to dress in peace, something of a rarity since the town had gone on its hiring spree a few months back and added four more officers to the department. He still did not know all the new hires by name, owing to the different shifts they worked. He would have to wait until the department's unofficial Christmas party to know them all. He took his time slipping into his uniform and when he was finished and presentable he made his way to the front desk.

The previous night had proved exhausting and Anderson knew it would not do to appear that way when he reported for duty. He was certain Captain Lange would be the duty officer; the man trusted no one else to man the front desk and oversee the department's change of duty shift.

The man involved in the traffic accident turned out to be one Jeffrey Newcombe, lifelong resident of Deacon's Landing and divorced father of two. The search for a second person from the wrecked Jeep had proved fruitless, and it was only a call to Newcombe's ex-wife that proved both his daughters were home and safe in their beds. They had managed to backtrack his whereabouts to his job at the tool and dye shop in Waterbury. He had apparently left work and was on his way to his apartment when the accident occurred. Anderson had chalked up the man's tortured pleading to find his daughter to delirium. Anderson's gut instinct was the man was not drunk at the time of the incident, despite the statement made by the kid in the Camaro that the Jeep was all over the road prior to the accident. There was no evidence alcohol was involved and the toxicology results would take a while. *Probably had a seizure*, he thought. By the time they knew for certain, Newcombe would be in the ground and his ex-wife would be awaiting whatever death benefits the man had secured for her.

A shitty situation from whichever angle it was viewed.

Anderson walked past the two cells that comprised the holding area of the Deacon's Landing Police Department. One was vacant, but the second cell contained a man in a rumpled and somewhat distressed business suit. The man lay on the single cot with one arm draped across his eyes. Anderson gave the man a cursory glance before he continued on to the front desk.

Captain Lange was on duty and Anderson took the roster and signed his name. "Captain," he said by way of greeting. He glanced at the clock on the wall and wrote down the time on the log sheet.

"Anderson." Lange did not look up from the paperwork in front of him.

"Who's the customer in cell one?"

Lange's impatience with all things Anderson was expressed as a long sigh. He did not look up from his paperwork, which Anderson could see was the crossword puzzle cut out of the day's newspaper and held against a blank police report. "A drunk who assaulted one of the strippers at Lucky's. They're patching her together at the hospital. Docs over there say it's fifty-fifty."

"Who's investigating?"

Lange continued to work his puzzle. "Bradley and Markowitz took the call."

Anderson picked up the top few papers in the Open Cases inbox and leafed through them. He stopped when he got to the report concerning the incident at Lucky's. The initial report was written in Markowitz's scrawl, only natural since Bradley's disdain for filling out such paperwork was well known. Anderson had no doubts the younger officer could look forward to filling our many reports so long as he remained Bradley's partner.

He looked at the time stamp on the report and saw that the assault happened while he himself had been sound asleep, mostly due to the events of the previous night. He saw the victim's information: Regina Saunders, age twenty-three, single with no dependents. It listed her approximate height and weight and other useless information. The names of the witnesses were included, and he paused when he got to Holly Wayne's statement.

He had not seen her in years, had not even thought much about her until last night's brief conversation with Murphy. While they had remained in the same town since their childhood, they did not cross paths often, if at all. Had it not been for their shared tenure at Deacon's Landing Elementary School, he might have lived his whole life with Holly as nothing more than a resident of his town.

It was her statement that caught his eye and made him pay attention. Markowitz's handwriting sucked, but he seemed to have taken extra care with Holly's statement: "She kept saying 'You have to find her' and 'Don't leave her in there'. But she couldn't tell me who she was talking about." He read the statement a second time, and then a third. The hair on his arms stood at attention.

He scanned through the rest of the report but none of the other witnesses had heard the wounded girl say anything. He was about to return it to its place in the inbox and track down Markowitz when he saw the name of the suspect. He froze for a moment and then held the paper closer to his face, as if proximity would change the name in Markowitz's handwriting.

"Benjamin Ford," he whispered.

"What's that?" Lange asked. He did not look up from his puzzle.

Anderson walked as calmly as he could back to the holding area. He looked again at the man on the cot, who had not moved from when he first saw him. His arm remained draped across his eyes and he appeared to be asleep. His breathing was slow and regular.

He wanted to wake the man, at least make him move his arm so Anderson could get a good look at him. He contemplated entering the cell and doing just that, but something held him in place and he simply stared at the sleeping man and tried to determine if he was indeed who Anderson believed him to be.

He cleared his throat. The prisoner did not stir. He did it again, loudly. The man on the cot snorted but otherwise remained motionless. Anderson reached for the keys in his pocket and nearly had them out when the prisoner dropped his arm and rolled onto his side, facing the cell door.

Anderson got his first real look at the prisoner. He froze with his keys partially out of his pocket. "Fuck me," he whispered.

****

Holly pulled into her driveway and put her Honda in park. She looked in the backseat and found Cassandra reading one of her many children's books. It was a pop-up book about a unicorn although the child was paying less attention to the title creature and its friends than the words on the page. Cassandra read quite well for a girl of seven. Her retelling of the little book's story was a close approximation of how Holly had read the book aloud to her; she even mimicked Holly's inflection. Holly herself was a voracious reader and she was pleased her daughter had discovered that particular joy for herself.

"We're home, honey," she said and removed her seatbelt. She opened the door and grabbed her pocketbook from the passenger seat. Cassandra mimicked her movements, substituting her backpack for the pocketbook. She sat and waited patiently for Holly to open her door. "C'mon, munchkin," Holly said as Cassandra stepped out of the car.

Cassandra especially liked her nickname. *The Wizard of Oz* had become her favorite movie since she had first seen it two years before. She was particularly fond of the munchkins and cheered when they made their first appearance. She was less enthused about the Wicked Witch, but as Holly's father had once told her, even he had been scared shitless by Margaret Hamilton's cackling alter-ego when he was a child. It seemed to be a generational thing, and Holly appreciated the sense of continuity it provided between parents and their children. They would not agree on music or fashion, but they could take comfort in their common fear of the green crone and her army of flying monkeys.

"Thanks, Mommy," Cassandra said as she exited the car. Her book remained opened, her eyes remained fixed on the page. "What's for dinner?"

Holly sighed. "Mommy hasn't decided yet. What do you want? Mac and cheese?"

Holly closed the car door and activated the alarm with her fob. She saw Cassandra's hand held up for her and she took it and they walked to the front door.

"Mac and cheese!" Cassandra shouted and laughed.

"As you wish."

A few moments later Cassandra was upstairs in her room and Holly was looking through the cupboards and hoping she had remembered to buy at least one box of mac and cheese. She was relieved when she found it behind the Fruit Roll-Ups and the canister of table salt. She removed it from the cupboard and started looking for an appropriately sized saucepan.

Despite her best efforts she flashed back to the scene in the private room at Lucky's. She had done her best to get the images out of her mind since leaving the club to pick up Cassandra from her mother's house. She had managed to hold it together as Cassandra gathered her things and said good-bye to Gramma. She had even kept a lid on it during the ride home, mostly because she took an alternate route that did not require her to drive past Lucky's. But with Cassandra upstairs and nothing more to occupy her mind but making dinner, she again saw the image of Gina lying in a widening pool of her own blood.

Tears spilled from her eyes and the breath caught in her throat. The part of her day spent at the club seemed like a dream. It was simply too bizarre to have actually happened. She choked back the tears and steadied herself. There would be time enough later to deal with this; at the moment she had Cassandra to look after.

She added the noodles to the boiling water. She could hear Cassandra in her room singing along to one of her DVDs. She walked to the base of the stairs and said, "Cassie, dinner in about five minutes. Start washing up, please."

"Okay, Mommy," came the musical reply. Cassandra ran from her room to the bathroom.

"And turn off your TV, honey."

"Sorry, forgot," she said, and ran back across the hall to her room. A moment later the music stopped and Cassandra once again made a break for the bathroom.

Holly returned to the kitchen and began setting the table. She was nearly finished when she was interrupted by the knock at the front door. She turned the burner on the stove to low and walked to the front door. She glanced out the front window as she did and saw the police car parked at the curb. Her brow furrowed. Her statement to the police regarding the assault on Gina had been pretty detailed despite her emotional state at the time. What, precisely, was the cop looking for? He could not be there for any other reason.

She opened the door and the police officer looked up and nodded at her. "Ms. Wayne? I'm Officer Anderson. Matt Anderson. Can I have a moment of your time, please?"

"Make it quick if you can, Officer. It's almost dinner time here."

Anderson nodded. "I will. I just have a question or two about what happened at Lucky's Club earlier today."

Holly folded her arms across her chest. "I gave a statement already."

"Yes, ma'am, I know, I read it."

"Then what's this about?" She was becoming aggravated, although she could not say why. Perhaps it had something to do with that image of Gina on the floor and the officer's neutral tone of voice. Something as violent and unexpected as the attack on Gina should have produced an emotional response from anyone, especially in a small town like Deacon's Landing. The cop, even if accustomed to such violence, should have felt something, at least as far as Holly was concerned. His casual tone and body language began to grate on her nerves.

"I'm interested in the suspect. Did you know him prior to this afternoon?"

Holly frowned and shook her head. "What are you talking about? What makes you think I'd know a piece of shit like that?"

Anderson swallowed. "Was he a regular at Lucky's? Do you remember seeing him there before?"

Holly shook her head again. "No, never. I mean, I don't think so. I don't remember thinking he seemed familiar as Vince was...what's the word? *Subduing* him?" She leaned a little closer to the screen door that separated her from the policeman. "I'm afraid I don't understand what it is you're after, Officer."

Before Anderson could elaborate Cassandra jogged up behind Holly and wrapped her arms around her mother's midsection. "Mommy!" she shouted. She giggled as Holly reached behind her and scooped her into the air.

"Hello, munchkin," Holly said warmly.

Cassandra threw her arms around Holly's neck and giggled again. She peeked out from beneath her blonde hair and said, "Who's that?"

"This is a policeman. His name is Officer Anderson. Can you say hello?"

"Hello," Cassandra said and buried her face in her mother's neck.

"Hi there," Anderson said, and his smile was warm.

Holly rocked back and forth for a moment before she put Cassandra down. "Are you all washed up and clean?"

"Yes I am!"

"Okay, dinner will be ready in a minute. Go sit at the table, please. I'll be right there."

"Okay," Cassandra said and sprinted away.

Holly watched her go before turning back to Anderson.

"She's very cute," Anderson said.

"Thank you," Holly replied. "Now where were we?"

Anderson cleared his throat. "Maybe this isn't the time. I didn't realize you'd be settling down to dinner." He reached into his shirt pocket and fished out a card. He held it out to Holly. "This is my number. Please give me a call at your earliest convenience."

Holly opened the screen door and took the offered card. She glanced at it before stuffing it into the back pocket of her jeans. "I'll do that."

Anderson took a step back. "Afternoon, ma'am."

"And to you," Holly said. She let go of the screen and it closed slowly. She closed the main door and walked back into the kitchen.

****

Anderson slid into the driver's seat and closed the door. He placed the key into the ignition but stopped short of starting the engine. He glanced again at the small white Cape Cod that Holly Wayne called home. It was unremarkable in every way, and almost indistinguishable from the rest of the houses on the street. The purple-pink shutters were the only standouts of which the house could boast. Even Holly's white Honda seemed to blend with the other vehicles that sat in the various driveways on either side of the street. The street itself was similar to many other streets in Deacon's Landing. It could be a nice neighborhood in which to raise your children, or it could be somebody's idea of suburban hell. Anderson thought perhaps it was a little from column A and a little from column B.

Holly had not recognized Ford during his assault on the dancer, that much was clear. He had watched her eyes carefully when he posed the question and he saw not a glint of recognition. *Well, why should she remember? It was almost thirty years ago,* Jen reminded him. *Not everyone is as anal as you are when it comes to the past.* True enough, but he felt certain she would make the connection. He believed it might come back to her when she heard the name of the suspect.

Then again, she did not seem to remember him, either, and they had shared one extraordinary experience together. *It's not like it was just the two of you, y'know,* Jen piped up again. And she had a point. What occurred on the final day of classes at Deacon's Landing Elementary School was hardly limited to him and Holly Wayne. Everyone inside the building that day shared the experience, and in a town the size of Deacon's Landing it was nearly impossible to find someone who was not connected to the tragedy in some way. Not to mention all the people who were not there but had retroactively placed themselves in the vicinity of the school.

He looked again at Holly's house, then turned the key and started the car. He buckled up and put the transmission into drive. He continued to watch Holly's house in the rearview until it was no longer distinguishable

from the others on the street.

Chapter Four

Door Number Three

Matty turned off the shower and reached for his towel. He ran it over his chest and arms quickly. Despite the hot water circling the drain and the steam still rising off the tiled floor he was cold. More than cold. His skin had broken out in gooseflesh even with the hot water pouring down on him. He could not allow himself to catch a cold; the lower level of DLES had been cold since school started, and seemed to be growing colder by the day. Or perhaps he was simply imaging it.

He had a lot on his mind lately, what with the fall little league season coming down to the playoffs. The last thing he wanted was to have his mother bench him because of a case of the sniffles or slipping grades. The game was too important, as were the bragging rights that would last them through the winter. He was not the best player on the team but his defense at third would be missed if the coach had to put Jaffe in the hot corner. He prayed it would not come to that.

He wrapped the towel around his waist and exited the shower room. The main section of the boys' locker room was deserted. Matty looked through the window into Mr. Mitchell's office. The small room was deserted although Matty could see and smell the cloud of cigar smoke that always seemed to hover near the ceiling. The silver Zippo lay on the desktop next to a pile of papers and the ever-present ceramic ashtray. He glanced at the clock on the wall above the office window. 11:26. He had four minutes to get dressed and up to Mr. Ford's classroom. Plenty of time.

He opened his locker and pulled on his jeans and a shirt. It was a few degrees colder in the locker room than it had been in the shower. His hair felt crusty when he ran his hand through it. Okay, so it definitely was not him. But why was it so damned cold? He shivered as he pulled on his sneakers.

The punch was a complete surprise and Matty backpedaled. His Nikes slipped on the water which made the tiled floor that much more slippery and down he went. He felt something warm run down his chin and his mouth was full of a coppery taste. It took him a moment to realize it was his own blood. He sat there on the floor of the boys' locker room and wiped a hand across his nose. It hurt like hell and his hand came away bloody. His eyes watered and he blinked away the tears. Steam rose slowly from the blood that coated his chin.

Kenny Atkins loomed over him like Dr. Doom. His ripped blue jeans and Aerosmith t-shirt made a poor substitute for Doom's famous body armor but it was close enough. Kenny's sidekicks, Danny Fisher and Timmy Williams, stood on either side of him. They sneered at him and laughed. Kenny's hands were balled into fists and Matty saw his blood drip from the knuckles on Kenny's right hand. Kenny's sneer put those of his sidekicks to shame.

"Get up, Anderson. Get up so I can knock you down again."

Matty grabbed onto the edge of the bench and hauled himself to his feet. "What's your problem, Atkins?" More blood dripped down his chin. The white-and-blue tiles beneath him were stained red and his sneakers were having a difficult time finding purchase. "And if you touch me again I'm gonna kick the living shit outta you. Fair warning."

Kenny laughed, his arms flew out from his sides like the wings of a giant bird-of-prey. This prompted intense laughter from both Danny and Timmy, and Matty knew his cheeks were as red as his chin; he could feel the heat radiating from them. After an exaggerated moment Atkins contained his laughter and again turned his eyes on Matty.

"You talked a lot of shit after the game on Sunday," Kenny said and jabbed a finger in Matty's direction. "You're talking more shit now. What am I gonna have to do to shut that stupid mouth of yours?"

In point of fact, it had been Ricky Grant who had rubbed the noses of Atkins and his teammates into the dirt after Sunday's game. Grant had put on a performance worthy of Doc Gooden himself and would have pitched a no-hitter if the umpire hadn't blown a close call at first. Matty had celebrated the win but no more boisterously than had anyone else on his team. Under normal circumstances he might have been inclined to tell Atkins he had the wrong man. But not after being sucker punched. His eyes burned with anger and for a moment he forgot about the temperature in the locker room.

Atkins turned to Manny, then to Timmy. "Ideas?"

"Maybe you should get some Crazy Glue and glue his lips together," Timmy said.

"I think we should break his teeth," Danny offered.

Kenny nodded slowly as if he were considering those options. He even stroked his chin for a moment. "What do you think, Anderson? Door number one or door number two?"

"I'll pick door number three," Matty said at last. "Kicking your ass and wiping the floor with Larry and Curly."

"Ooh," Kenny said and laughed again.

He threw another punch, a haymaker that would have put Matty right back down on the floor again. Matty blocked it and threw a punch of his own, but the tiled floor was slippery and his feet went out from under him. He grabbed onto Kenny's shirt with one hand and used the lockers to steady himself. He heard and felt the concert shirt tear in his grip. He would have maintained his balance had Timmy not gotten involved.

He shoved Matty sideways and Kenny recovered enough to cuff the back of his head. Matty was off-balance but realized they had shoved him in the direction of the door. He broke for it.

"That fucker ripped my shirt," Kenny said as if such a concept was utterly alien to him. He sounded both amazed and offended. "Get him!"

Matty made it to the door and flung it open. He could hear Kenny and his henchmen close the distance behind him. He hurled himself through the door, slid slightly on the linoleum and sprinted for the double doors at the end of the corridor. There was no one in sight ahead of him, which was just his luck. Mr. Mitchell almost never left his realm on the lower level, preferring to remain close to the gymnasium and swimming pool. So naturally he was nowhere to be found the one time Matty would not have minded seeing him.

Behind him he could hear the shouts and threats from Kenny; he heard nothing from Timmy and Danny except the sound of their footfalls and their labored breathing. Matty was at once thankful for their girth and overall poor eating habits. If he could outlast them and deal with Atkins one-on-one, he'd have a chance.

He never got to find out. Kenny launched himself at Matty and tackled him at the knees. Both boys went down in a tangle of arms and legs a few feet from the double doors. Matty got his hands under him and tried to rise but Danny and Timmy picked that moment to try to slow down and they fell on them. Matty's arms went out to his sides, a gesture of self-preservation; with that much weight on him he was certain his arms would snap like twigs. He collapsed onto his stomach and the breath was driven from his lungs.

Two things conspired to save him. The first was Kenny was just as trapped as Matty was. He could not shift the enormous weight off his back and his arms were entangled with Matty's legs. The second was one of the doors in front of them opened and Matty looked at two rather large feet in black sneakers take up residence inches from his head. He strained to look up and saw Mr. Mitchell standing in front of him. The man's half-smoked cigar poked out from the corner of his mouth. His coach's whistle hung from the cord around his neck, his hands were planted on his hips and he looked down on the boys with a scowl.

Kenny and his crew noticed Mitchell's presence at the same moment. They immediately went about freeing themselves from the pile, all three of them making excuses and pointing at Matty. Mitchell's scowl remained in place as he helped the boys up by hauling them to their feet in a ungentle manner.

"Shut your yaps, all of you," he thundered. He watched the three boys take a step back and regarded Matty. "What's this nonsense? And why is Anderson bleeding on my floor?"

Matty got to his knees and wiped at the blood on his chin. His breathing came in great gulps and he was thankful his lungs still worked. He watched from that vantage point as Kenny pointed an accusing finger in his direction. "He started it, Mr. Mitchell, I swear to God!"

"Yeah, yeah," Timmy agreed. "It was all Anderson's fault!"

"Is that so?" Mitchell helped Matty the rest of the way to his feet and stood him against the wall with the others. He started to walk slowly up and down the line, hands clasped behind his back, a drill sergeant inspecting a group of disappointing recruits. He chewed his cigar as he said, "And you boys expect me to believe Anderson started a fight with all three of you?"

"He did, Mr. Mitchell" Kenny pleaded. "We were in the locker room getting ready to go back to class and he jumped us."

"That's right, he did," Timmy said. He looked pathetically at Mitchell.

"We were minding our own business, Mr. Mitchell," Danny added.

Mitchell continued his pacing for another lap and finally came to a stop in front of Matty. He looked the boy over and his eyes returned to the blood on his lips and on his shirt. "That what happened, Anderson?"

Matty cast a sideways glance at the other boys. He was a firm believer in the theory that snitches got stitches, but Kenny and his crew seemed to have no problem pinning the whole thing on him. After a moment he said, "What do you think?"

Mitchell regarded the other three boys. He crooked his thumb toward the double doors. "You three get up to Mr. Gwiazdoski's office on the double. Anderson, go see the nurse."

Timmy and Danny whined, put their heads down and shuffled to the doors. Kenny lingered a moment and stared daggers at Matty. It was clear the boy wanted nothing more than to pummel him into the floor, even with a teacher present. Ultimately Kenny made no such move. He followed his posse through the doors and vanished from sight.

When they were gone Matty exhaled slowly. His mouth hurt, his nose hurt, and he would be surprised to learn he had not broken any ribs. He waited a few moments to give Kenny and his sidekicks enough time to vacate the stairwell and then he started for the nurse's office.

"You okay, Anderson?" Mitchell asked him when he was halfway through the doors.

Matty stopped for a moment and looked over his shoulder. "I'll live."

Mitchell nodded and Matty exited the corridor.

His time in the nurse's office was brief but painful. The good news was she found nothing broken. He would most likely have a black eye by morning but no lingering injuries. She iced down his nose for a few moments and when she was satisfied she gave him a lollipop and sent him back to class.

He opened the door to Mr. Ford's room and found his teacher speaking to the class about Hannibal's trek across the Alps. He quietly walked to the teacher's desk and placed the note from the nurse on top of the stack of tests Ford would hand out when he was finished with his lesson. He made his way quickly and quietly to his desk and sat and pretended to pay attention.

He was three questions into the test when the fire alarm sounded a short time later. Matty looked up, first at those around him, then at Mr. Ford. The teacher stood and waved one arm toward the door. "Okay, line up."

Matty stood and got in line and waited for Mr. Ford to lead them out of the room. When the students were ready Ford did just that. They took their rehearsed path from the building, but they had not even made it to the stairs when Matty smelled the smoke. It was not the cigarette smoke that permeated the hallway outside the teachers' lounge; it smelled more like the campfire he had built with his father in the backyard the previous summer.

Mr. Ford had picked up on it as well, for he quickened his pace considerably. Some of the other kids began to realize this was not a regular fire drill and they panicked. They began to push on the classmate in front of them and some of the girls screamed. Two kids went down behind Matty; he turned to help them but Mrs. Plaza was leading her class toward the stairs and she scooped up the kids and shouted for her class to keep moving.

There was a logjam at the bottom of the stairs as the second grade classes tried to squeeze through the bottleneck formerly known as the front entrance. Mr. Ford stopped and held up a hand to the children behind him. The smoke was thicker on the first floor; it swirled above their heads and obscured the ceiling tiles. Stopped on the landing, Matty could hear the sound of flames from somewhere in the vicinity of the second grade wing.

They had been told the most likely origin spot for a fire in the school would be the boiler room. It was located on the basement level and Matty mapped out its location in his head. It rested beneath the second grade wing, so perhaps the firemen who had visited the school and dropped that interesting piece of trivia on them were spot-on. He thought about Mr. Michaels, the school janitor, who spent an awful lot of time in the vicinity of the boiler room and hoped he was okay.

The smoke was growing thicker. Matty could smell it with every breath. It seemed to take an inordinate amount of time for the second grade to clear the front entrance and Matty knew he was not alone in his growing impatience. Behind him he could hear more cries and whimpering. Mrs. Plaza was trying to keep her students together but her shouts of "Remain calm!" were falling on deaf ears. Matty hoped there would not be a rush toward the doors. He had read about the circus fire in Hartford in the 1940s and he had no wish to reenact that particular tragedy.

The logjam cleared all at once and Mr. Ford once again waved to his class to follow him. Matty reached the bottom of the stairs and made the turn to exit through the doors when the explosion occurred.

The floor shook, dust and smoke choked the air, girls and boys screamed. Someone landed on top of him and for the second time in ninety minutes Matty was flat on his stomach. This time he was able to shrug off whoever was on top of him and get to his knees. He grabbed onto the kid in front of him and pulled him to his feet. His chest hurt a bit but he seemed otherwise unharmed. X-rays would reveal the cracked ribs later that night.

He looked down the corridor, past the front office where the secretary, Mrs. Lockwood, was abandoning her post. She emerged from the office with her coat half-on and her giant pocketbook dangling from one arm. He would remember this particular image for years afterward. Mrs.

Santos and Mrs. Cavanaugh's rooms, closer to the entrance, were already dark and empty.

The corridor stretched past the front office. Rows of lockers lined the walls. Posters with slogans on them such as "Believe, Achieve and Succeed At test Time!" and "I Want YOU To Do Your Best On Your Test!" (this one featured Uncle Sam pointing rather sternly at whomever stood in front of it) seemed to sway in the warm breeze that originated somewhere beyond the smoke that obscured the rest of the hallway. Matty paused there, waiting for those in front of him to move beyond the double doors.

Mrs. Plaza was behind him and she put her hands on his shoulders and urged him forward. He allowed himself to be guided through the double doors. He remained looking over his shoulder as he tasted fresh air. He could see the smoke billowing now from wherever it originated. The lockers reflected the orange-red of flames and Matty knew the fire department would not arrive in time.

And then he saw her. Although he was convinced of what he saw at the time, he allowed himself to be convinced by time and adults that what he had seen was swirling smoke and nothing more. The woman stood in the hallway amidst the smoke. Except Matty did not think she stood at all. He could not see her feet through the smoke, could not see anything below her knees, but he got the impression she was not in contact with the floor. She seemed to levitate, except that was not the word he was looking for. He searched through his vocabulary and came up with a word he felt was closer to what he saw: She seemed to *hover*. She was in distress, or perhaps she was angry at having been left behind when whichever classroom she was in had evacuated. Her long black dress seemed impervious to the flames; it undulated in the smoke but did not catch fire. She screamed, although Matty could not hear her above the chaos around him. He knew without knowing how that her scream was one of anger, even rage, and it had little to do with what was happening around her. She did not react to the smoke and the flames which now made the haze behind her glow red. Her arms were thrown out to either side and for a moment he thought of Christ on the cross.

Mrs. Plaza herded him past the entryway toward the parking lot and he lost sight of her. He looked back over his shoulder but he could no longer see far enough into the building. "Mrs. Plaza there's someone in there! We have to go back!" He struggled to free himself but found her hands were glued to his shoulders. He looked at her in disbelief. "What are you doing? There's someone still back there!"

"Don't panic, Matty," Mrs. Plaza told him and continued to move him toward the parking lot. "Keep it together!" The student body of Deacon's Landing Elementary School had abandoned all pretense of calm and they ran screaming and crying into the parking lot. Some did not stop until they reached home.

What Mrs. Plaza said next was drowned out by the sound of a second explosion. The ground shook and a cloud of smoke surged through the front doors with enough force to shatter the glass. It pelted teachers and students and poor Mrs. Lockwood. Many were knocked to the ground by the combination of the brief quake and the force of the expelled smoke. Most of the windows in the front of the building shattered and rained glass on anyone unfortunate enough to be within range.

Matty was able to keep his feet under him. He stopped running when Mrs. Plaza released her hold on his shoulders. He spun and looked back at the school. Smoke billowed up from two different places within the building. It rose into the October sky quickly, as if relishing its freedom. The flames were tall now, and likely visible to most of the town. Glass, papers and other school supplies lay scattered about the front entrance; some were still finding their way to ground level. The Uncle Sam poster, "I Want YOU To Do Your Best On Your Test!" had escaped the building and gotten caught in one of the rose-of-Sharon bushes near the front entrance. Its edges were singed. One of the double doors hung at an odd angle from its top hinge. The other door was blown wide open and it took Matty a moment to realize it was no longer attached to the building; luck or fate had brought it to rest against the building and to the left of its customary place.

The people still near the front entrance slowly regained their feet. Matty could see torn shirts and pants and a few bloody noses. Mrs. Lockwood had lost a shoe. Most of them looked as if they had just finished cleaning a chimney. Their clothes and faces were black. He saw Mr. Ruiz help another teacher to his feet. They looked dazed but they got it together quickly and retreated to the parking lot.

Matty kept his eyes on the opened front entrance. He wanted, *needed* to see the woman escape from the inferno that had claimed the school. He stood and waited and saw nothing. He swallowed when he realized he had most likely witnessed her final moments on earth. He hoped he was wrong but he did not believe anyone could have made it out alive after the second explosion.

He thought about Mr. Mitchell who was last seen on the basement level and walking in the direction of the boys' locker room, which happened to be very close to the boiler room. He scanned the faces he could see and came up empty. The guy was a notorious hardass but Matty wished him no ill. He hoped he made it out.

Kenny Atkins stood on the far side of the parking lot. Danny Fisher was at his side. Both boys seemed none the worse for wear, at least physically. They wore identical expressions of shock and looked genuinely scared. They were too far away for Matty to hear their conversation, but every few moments one or the other would gesticulate wildly at the school. After a moment he guessed they were talking about Timmy Williams. Matty did a quick scan of the area and did not see Timmy. Was he still inside the school? It seemed likely given his absence from Kenny's side. It would also explain why the boys appeared so frantic.

Matty swallowed and looked away.

Engine Forty-Two finally roared up the driveway and DLES's vice-principal, Miss Renna, ran to meet them. She shouted to the firemen and pointed at the building, but Matty could not hear her, either. Her blonde hair had escaped its customary ponytail and flopped this way and that with each gesture. It reminded Matty of the heavy metal videos he favored on MTV.

The firemen went to work.

Matty remained with his classmates until frightened parents began to arrive. Every police officer on duty had already found their way to the school and helped match the students to their parents. It was more than an hour after the fire alarm sounded before Matty's mother pulled up in her little yellow Omni. She surveyed the scene for only a moment before she threw her arms around her son and squeezed him until his injured ribs caused him to cry out.

Safely buckled into the passenger seat, Matty watched the school recede into the distance. He kept his eyes on the front entrance for as long as he was able. He saw no one emerge from there who was not dressed as a fireman. When the crest of Piedmont Street finally blocked his view of the school and there was nothing more to see but the smoke still rising into the air, Matty faced forward. He did not look back again for twenty-nine years.

Chapter Five

She's Still There

Anderson found the records room deserted and he was thankful for that. He knew what he was looking for and he knew where to look. He did not want to have to answer questions as to why he wanted to see those particular files. He had come down to the dungeon that was the records room directly from the locker room after his shift ended. While it was not uncommon to find an off-duty officer in his civvies poring over old records, there was the surprise of Captain Lange taking an overtime shift. If he happened to look at the hallway camera as Anderson entered the records room, he might be inclined to send for him and ask just why he wanted to browse through the reports of an incident from nearly three decades before.

Anderson was disappointed to find Benjamin Ford had been transferred to the jail in New Haven an hour before he returned to the station to go off-duty. He had wanted to speak to the man, a slight breach of protocol since he had not been assigned the case. He was certain the man he saw in the cell was formerly his social studies teacher. He was older and heavier and his trademark mustache was gone but that was him.

Holly did not recognize him at the strip club. It would not be important enough to include in her statement even if she did, but he saw no glint of recognition in her eyes when he asked her about the suspect. He did not know if Ford had been one of her teachers, anyway. It was one of the questions he wanted to ask her when she got around to calling him. But mostly he wanted to talk to her about her statement to the investigating officers. Specifically, he wanted to know more about what the victim said to her. It could not be coincidence that he heard the same thing from the accident victim the night before.

He took a seat and turned on the old Dell. It took a moment for the monitor to come to life and even longer for the startup to cycle. When the prompt finally showed up he entered his name and password and it was another few moments before the menu appeared. He navigated his way through the system until he reached his destination. The item button he wanted read *Official Reports 10/01/85-10/31/85.* He clicked it and forwarded past everything until he got to October 15, a Tuesday.

The report was filed by Officer D. Galullo, a name unfamiliar to Anderson. He scanned through the text and read the dry recounting of the destruction. He read the names of the five people killed in the tragedy, including Timothy Williams and gym teacher Bryan Mitchell. One of the victims was female, a Mrs. Burke whom Anderson did not know. The report said she had been a guidance counselor. He zeroed in on her and thought about the woman he saw in the smoke. It could not be her. Mrs. Burke's age was listed as sixty-two at the time of her death. Anderson had not gotten a clear look at the screaming woman but he was certain she had been much younger than that. Then again, after the passage of so many years he could not speak for his memory.

He scrolled through the rest of the report but nothing jumped out at him. He sat back and rubbed his eyes. There would be the fire marshal's report of the incident but he would have to go through official channels to see it, and that was not something he wanted to do quite yet. He thought of the library and the old editions of the *Sentinel* they kept in their database. He might have some luck there.

Without any intention of doing so he returned to the archive menu and scrolled up until he got to the reports dated 01/01/13-01/31/13. He clicked on it and scrolled down to the night of January 17.

Captain Lange had investigated this one himself. It was the one time Anderson was happy to see the prick. The report detailed the collision between the minivan and the Hummer. It had happened on Hamilton Road at 10:30PM. Both vehicles occupied one time. The driver of the

Hummer made it to Deacon's Landing Hospital but died on the operating table; the driver of the minivan was pronounced dead at the scene. The crude drawing on the report showed the much larger Hummer across the centerline and its point of impact with the minivan's driver's side front fender.

It listed the names of both victims but Anderson did not need to read that part. The names were burned into his memory and would remain there until he cashed in his chips. Michael John Tavares, aged forty-nine, divorced father of three, and an alcoholic of the first order. The report listed the number of empty gin bottles inside the Hummer.

And Jennifer Lynn Anderson. Aged thirty-three, married and three months from becoming a mother of one.

The report made mention of her pregnancy but not how far along she was; Anderson mentally filled in that information himself. The supplemental reports indicated Tavares' blood alcohol level as being four times over the limit, and noted the cocaine in his system at the time of his death. There were no such toxins in Jen's system, which surprised no one who knew her. The cause of death was blunt force trauma brought on by an asshole who never should have been behind the wheel. That was not what Lange had written, of course, but it was how Anderson thought of it when he pictured Jen's final moments.

All at once he no longer wanted to be inside the records room, nor even inside the station. He wanted to be back in the house he had shared with Jen. He quickly logged out of the system, stood and stretched his legs. He managed to make it out of the building without Lange seeing him and a few moments later he was driving his Chevy down the street.

He spent the rest of the night and early morning in his living room. He sat in his favorite chair with a bottle of vodka on the end table next to him. He did not bother with a glass.

****

Holly awoke with a start. The dream slipped away from her in an instant but it must have been pretty bad. Her chest heaved and sweat beaded on her forehead. She looked about her bedroom but the morning sunlight revealed nothing out of the ordinary. She put a hand on her chest and concentrated on slowing her breathing. After a few moments she succeeded. She tried to remember the dream but there was nothing. After a moment she thought perhaps that was for the best. She had experienced enough horror for one week, thank you very much.

She kicked off the covers and found her slippers. After a visit to the bathroom she made her way into the kitchen and started on Cassandra's breakfast. With the English muffins in the toaster and the cereal in the bowl she went to the front door and retrieved the morning *Sentinel.* She brought it back to the table and paged through it while she drank her coffee.

She found the article concerning Gina's assault on page three. It was accompanied by a mug shot of the assailant side by side with an older photo of Gina herself. The man looked the worse for wear after having his ass handed to him by Vince. It was obvious someone had tended to his wounds but there was no hiding the blemishes on his cheeks or the dark circle under his right eye that must look even darker today. *Good,* she thought. *And fuck you.*

It had been her intention to read through the article and see what the cops had to say, but she stopped when she happened to glance at the man's name. "Benjamin Ford," she said to the empty kitchen. She repeated the name and looked more closely at the photograph. The man did indeed look familiar but she had no idea why. His name was likewise familiar. She closed her eyes and tried to clear her mind. It yielded no results and after a few moments she gave up.

She looked again at the man's photo before her eyes moved up to the article itself. She skimmed through it, found nothing new or useful. She was quoted, as were

Lucky and Carrie. She smiled when she got to the part that said no charges were expected to be filed against Vince. And that was all.

She took another sip of her coffee and turned the paper back to the front page. The big black-and-white photo that took up nearly one quarter of the space was of a Jeep lying on its side in the middle of the street. The headline read: *One Killed in Single Car Accident.*

She skimmed through this article as well until she came to the victim's name. "Jeffrey Newcombe," she said aloud. There was no photo of the victim to accompany the article but it listed his age as forty-four. That sounded about right.

Holly reached for the phone but thought better of it. Her sister was likely still asleep and did not need to hear this sort of news first thing in the morning. If the story was considered newsworthy in Fairfield she would know. If Holly did not hear from her by eleven, she would make the call.

The police officer looking over the crashed SUV was named in the caption. "Mathew Anderson," Holly said. She stood and walked to the phone. Slid into the space between the phone and the wall was the business card the officer left with her yesterday. She took it down and read the name. She pursed her lips and glanced at the clock. She doubted he would still be on-duty so she would have to wait. She returned to the table and waited for Cassandra to come downstairs.

****

The one person who recognized Benjamin Ford immediately was Brian Murphy. He had arrived at the shop early, as he usually did, and went over the weekend's business. Only one tow job was listed, a Jeep involved in a single-car accident. It sat in the fenced area in the rear parking lot. He glanced out the window and saw it and whistled through his teeth. It was not the worst wreck he had ever seen but it made the top ten. He paid it little more mind.

He started the coffee and opened up the front door and retrieved the *Sentinel* which the paperboy so thoughtfully tossed into the bushes every morning. He lobbed it onto his desk and grabbed his clipboard. He sat and leafed through the work orders for the day. Business was not where he wanted it to be but they were doing better than most. It was enough to keep the guys busy and he was thankful for that.

He poured himself a hot mug and sat back down again. The front page contained a photo of the vehicle currently in the impound area behind him, and there was Matt standing next to it. He skimmed through the article quickly. One fatality, crash under investigation, yadda yadda yadda. He turned the page.

Page three contained the story of the incident at Lucky's and Murphy took notice. He did not know who Regina Saunders was, and the picture was obviously a few years old, but she bore a striking resemblance to Dakota. He read of the assault and how quickly the officers responded and of the girl's injuries. They sounded severe and the doctors at Deacon's Landing Hospital had yet to upgrade her condition from critical.

What caught and held his attention was the name of the suspect. "Ford," he whispered. "Mr. Ford?" He thought back to the first month and a half of his life as a sixth grader, when DLES was still in one piece. The man in the mug shot was older and looked a bit differently than Murphy remembered, but there was no mistaking him.

He read the entire article. His coffee sat forgotten on the desktop. He read what Holly had to say to the reporter, as well as the quotes from the other witnesses. He wondered if she recognized the former teacher. He glanced at the digital clock on his desk, then at the phone. He thought about calling Holly but he did not want to wake her. He would give her until noon, when the boys in the shop took their lunch and he could have the office to himself. She would certainly be awake by then and he could take the time to talk to her and make sure she was okay.   Maybe they could get together for drinks later assuming she could find a babysitter.

He made an addition to his mental to-do list and waited for the guys to come in.

****

Holly had indeed found a babysitter, but not for the purposes of meeting Murphy for drinks. After breakfast and with Cassandra watching cartoons in the living room she decided to go to the hospital to see Gina. She called her mother who was always willing to spend time with her youngest granddaughter and arranged the time. Cassandra was excited to visit Gramma anytime and she gleefully got washed and dressed. An hour later they were pulling into Sarah Wayne's driveway and it was all Holly could do to keep the child from bolting from the car before she'd had a chance to put it in park.

She assured her mother it would be for no more than an hour or two, which Sarah assured her was fine.

She took Cassandra by the hand and led her into the house with promises of lemonade and cookies. Holly watched them disappear into the old house and returned to her car.

It should have taken her no longer than ten minutes to get to the hospital from her mother's house, but Holly found herself taking an unplanned detour. It was a spur of the moment decision she would not be able to explain later.

The newspaper was rolled up and sat in the passenger seat. She unfolded it and looked again at the photo of the Jeep lying on its side. She slowed at the intersection even though she did not have a stop sign, thus incurring the beeping wrath of the car behind her. She pulled over and put the Honda in park. She looked at the photo and then at the quiet residential neighborhood she had invaded. It was farther down the street.

She drove until she could match the houses and the trees in the photo with the view outside her windshield. She pulled over again and turned the car off. She stepped out and looked at the street. It was unremarkable in every way, completely like every other street in town.

She took a few steps away from her car and examined the street. She saw the Jeep's tire marks and the shallow gouges in the asphalt left behind when the vehicle turned on its side and slid along the pavement. Whoever had cleaned up the scene afterward had done a remarkable job; Holly found a few bits of glass no bigger than pebbles but no other evidence the vehicle had been there.

She stood in the precise spot where her sister's high school boyfriend had died, although she did not realize it. She circled the spot slowly, and for no reason of which she was aware, she repeated what Gina had said to her as she lay bleeding in the private room at Lucky's: "She's still in there. Find her, please, find her."

The wind picked up, or perhaps it had been there all along and she had simply missed it. In any case Holly got the sudden urge to leave the area as fast as her Honda would take her. She trotted back to her car. She opened the door and paused and looked again at the spot where Jeffrey Newcombe gave up the ghost. She suppressed a chill and got back into her car.

The drive to the hospital was uneventful, although Holly spared a few glances into her rearview for no apparent reason. She pulled into the visitor's lot and found a parking spot. She climbed the concrete steps to the main entrance area of the hospital.

The building was large, six stories tall and taking up an entire city block. The red brick exterior was broken up by windows every few feet. Numerous cars and a couple ambulances sat in the parking area at the front entrance. She made for the doors.

As she got closer to the entrance she saw Carrie sitting on a bench to the left of the doors. She sat alone and smoked next to the sign that read: THIS IS A TOBACCO-FREE ZONE. She must have heard the *click-clack* of Holly's heels on the pavement because she looked up and waved. She did not smile and something in her body language raised the gooseflesh on Holly's arms.

"What's the matter, honey?" Holly asked as she closed the distance. Her pace began to quicken.

"They wouldn't let me in to see her, so I snuck in," Carrie said.

When Holly took the spot next to her on the bench, she could see Carrie's eyes were wet. Holly wrapped her arms around Carrie and smiled a little when the gesture was returned. She ended the embrace but kept her hands on Carrie's arms. "And?"

"Holly, she looked terrible!" The tears she had managed to hold back spilled from her eyes. "Her head is all wrapped up and she's breathing through a tube in her nose. I was going to go into the room but I didn't think I wanted to get a better look at her." She broke away from Holly and sniffled. "She's in bad shape. I think she's gonna die."

Holly draped an arm across Carrie's shoulders. After a moment she said, "We don't know that. Let's not get ahead of ourselves. She's young and strong and I'm sure she'll be okay." She was sure of no such thing but she saw no reason to say it aloud. "It'll be all right."

Carrie wiped her sleeve across her nose. "I hope so."

They remained in that position for a few more moments. Holly kept her arm on Carrie's shoulder and the younger girl sat and smoked.

After a few moments Holly put her hand under Carrie's chin and raised it a few inches. Carrie looked into her eyes, swallowed and nodded. "I'll be okay," she said, and Holly believed her.

"I'm gonna try my luck. Want to come with?"

Carrie shook her head. "No. No, I've seen enough for one day. You go ahead." She inclined her head toward the front doors. "She's on the fourth floor, D wing. I have to get back to the house. You know how pissy Josh gets if I'm out too long."

Holly half-smiled in sympathy. "Yeah, I know. Okay, you drive safe."

"I will."

As Holly got to her feet and started for the doors, Carrie added, "Good luck!"

"Thanks," Holly said and waved without looking over her shoulder.

****

Anderson awoke at noon. The afternoon sunlight streamed through the front window and stung his eyes, which he immediately closed. He held a hand over his eyes and sat up in the chair. His head swam and felt as if it had grown to twice its normal size. He groaned and lay back again. It was a few more moments before he tried again. This time he managed to get to his feet, but the room spun around him and he nearly went down on the carpet. He steadied himself on the arm of the chair and took his first tentative steps toward the bathroom. His feet kicked the empty vodka bottle that had wound up on the floor at some point during the night. It skidded across the floor and came to rest near the front door. He regarded the bottle for only a moment before he continued on his path to the bathroom.

A few moments later he was in the kitchen and boiling tea water. Coffee was wonderful first thing in the morning, but it did nothing to settle his stomach. Tea, he discovered after years of research, was much better suited for the job. He sat at the small dinette table and drank his tea and willed his head to return to its normal size.

You knew you were going to feel like this, Jen said from the chair next to him. *Vodka kicks your ass every time.*

"I wouldn't have had anything at all to drink last night if I hadn't gone over the goddamned accident report again," Anderson said. He looked at the empty chair in the empty kitchen. "This is all your fault." He did not mean it and he trusted Jen to know it.

Jen laughed. *Sure it is, Matt. Blame the dead woman. That's convenient.*

Matt finished the rest of the tea in one gulp and placed the mug on the table. "You know I was kidding."

Of course I do, Jen replied. *Being dead doesn't mean I've forgotten how to read you.*

"That's good to know."

He sat in silence for a few moments. He glanced out the kitchen window into the backyard. A few mourning doves strutted around on the lawn and pecked at random things they found in the grass. A squirrel had found its way to the birdbath and drank the water. It was the type of morning for which Jen lived, back when she did live. The birdbath had been her idea, as were the various feeders that dotted the backyard. She loved the animals, all of them, and was happiest when filling up the feeders or turning the garden hose on the birdbath. It had been her sanctuary, which explained why he rarely ventured into the backyard unless it was to mow the lawn and the occasional refilling of the animal feeders.

"I miss you, baby," Anderson said.

I know, Jen replied. *The feeling's mutual.*

"I'm sorry I wasn't there that night." It was the thousandth time he'd said it, and it was true.

She's still there, Matt. She's still there and you have to find her before it's too late.

Anderson's eyes went wide and he inhaled sharply, as if he had just placed his hand on a hot plate. His head snapped in the direction of the empty chair even as the chill worked its way down his spine.

"What did you say?"

But Jen was gone. He had the kitchen to himself, as he always did.

He looked at the empty chair, then around the kitchen as if his dead wife was really present and he had not simply been talking to himself. He had driven his fingernails into his palms with enough force to make him wince. He flexed his fingers and replayed Jen's words in his head.

Had she really said that? In the strictest sense, the answer was, of course, no. Jen had not said anything in quite some time. He felt alone, more alone than he had since he watched her casket lowered into the ground in Lichgate. And he thought of what she said.

That made him think of Holly Wayne and he suddenly hoped she would call soon. He also thought of the last words of Jeffrey Newcombe and the fruitless and unnecessary search of the crash site for the mysterious Danny. And, quite against his will, he thought of the woman in the smoke who hovered above the floor and screamed in rage while the school burned around her.

And all at once he knew what Newcombe had said. Perhaps it was the adrenaline surge that accompanied his arrival at the accident scene. Perhaps it was his desire to save the man's life, to save any life to make up for the one he could not save. Perhaps it was even that Newcombe was so far gone at that point that he was incapable of speaking clearly. Whatever the reason, he knew he misheard the dying man just as he now knew beyond doubt what Newcombe had actually said.

"My God," he said to the empty kitchen.

Chapter Six

The Legend of Dark Annie

Holly sat behind the wheel of her Honda. Her hands gripped the wheel with enough force her knuckles had long since turned white. She did not trust herself not to scream, so she reasoned it was safer to channel that anger and anxiety into a safer form. She had made it about as close to Gina as had Carrie. She caught a glimpse of her friend and froze in her tracks. After a moment she approached the glass slowly and peered into the room. She would not have recognized Gina had she not known her. The top of her head was bandaged as Carrie said. She had omitted from her account the blood stain in the center of the bandage. Although she had been warned about the tubes which disappeared into Gina's nose, it was still a shock to see them with her own eyes. She stood at the window looking into Gina's room for several moments before she summoned the courage to go inside.

Which was when the orderlies appeared from around the corner. They politely informed her that she was not allowed in this particular stretch of corridor and offered to escort her back to the public areas. She declined and went back on her own. In truth, she had not wanted to be any closer to Gina than the window allowed.

By the time she exited the building Carrie was gone and Holly made a bee line for her car. Her eyes swam with tears and her fists shook with rage. It took her three attempts to hit the right button on her key fob to unlock the door. She sat and choked back tears and tried to push the anger down into the pit of her stomach. She half-succeeded.

When she felt she could once again function she started the car. She fumbled through her pocketbook and found her cell phone. She had gone so far as to activate it before she realized she had left the police officer's business card in her kitchen. She called her mother instead.

Yes, Cassandra was fine; she was in front of the TV and playing a game with her princess dolls, the rules of which escaped Gramma. She had had lunch and was behaving herself. No, she would not mind watching her for a couple more hours if Holly had things to do. Yes, dinner together would be lovely. Holly hung up and drove home.

When she got through the door she went directly for the police officer's business card. Her hand stopped when she saw the message light flashed **1** at her. She hit the playback button.

"Hey Holly, it's Murph. Just calling to make sure you're okay. I heard about what went down at Lucky's yesterday. I'm at the shop til six or so. You can call me here or at home anytime after that. Gimme a ring so I know you're okay. Talk to ya later, darlin'." The message ended with the phone's automated voice telling her the date and time of the message.

Holly nodded. Murph was a decent guy. He clearly liked her. She wondered, and not for the first time, if her profession was what stopped him from asking her for a date. She suspected it was, although it was a rarity these days for her to take the stage. Until something better, and more permanent, came along, Murph would have to deal with her working at Lucky's. She would return his call, of course she would, but first she wanted to talk with Matthew Anderson.

She got his voicemail, which was perfect. She did not want to talk to a machine, she wanted *him*. She left a message anyway and hung up the phone. She started to dial Murphy at the shop but hung up before she got to the last digit. As much as she wanted to talk to him, she was suddenly tired and not in the mood for sympathy. She stood and walked into the living room. The sofa looked good and she felt she needed to lie down, anyway. *Just close my eyes for a few minutes*, she thought.

She was out cold almost the moment her head hit the pillow. She slept for an hour before the phone rang and it was Matthew Anderson's home number on the caller ID.

****

Anderson stopped his Chevy in front of Holly's house and saw her sitting on her front step. She squinted to get a better look at him and he stepped out of the car and waved to her. She nodded and waved back. "Hello, Ms. Wayne."

"I didn't recognize you without a police car around you."

"I have the day off," Anderson said as he made his way up the walk. *And thank God for that*, he added mentally. He was not drunk, not by any measure, but he still had something of a hangover going on. If history was any indication, he would not be back to full operating capacity until the next morning.

"Too bad it's so overcast," she replied. "I think days off should merit a little sunshine."

He stopped in front of her. "Can't argue with that." Actually, he could. His head felt big enough without the sun pounding down on him. He reached into the back pocket of his Levis and pulled out his notebook. "If it's okay with you I need to ask you a few questions about the assault at Lucky's. I also wanted to ask about the statement you made to the investigating officers, if you don't mind."

Holly shook her head. "Okay, shoot. Would you like to come inside? It looks like it might rain. And besides, I can offer you a drink."

"Sounds good," he said.

She stood and opened the screen door. He followed her inside.

"Please excuse the mess. The maid has the day off, too."

"No worries," he said, and wondered about her definition of "mess." Aside from a few scattered toys and children's books the living room was quite orderly. Picture frames were positioned strategically around the room. They adorned the entertainment center, the end tables, the walls. All were of Holly and/or her daughter. He picked up one such photograph and held it up to the light. This one was taken at a beach, and Holly knelt in the sand with her arms wrapped around her daughter. They were at the edge of the surf with the sun behind them. He guessed it was perhaps a year old, judging by the differences in the child in the picture and the one he met the day before. They both smiled widely into the camera. "Nice picture."

Holly looked over her shoulder and smiled. "Thanks. That was at Lighthouse Point last summer."

He heard the fridge open. "You have a very beautiful daughter," Anderson said, and he meant it. He returned the photo to its place on the entertainment center, took a moment to admire the size of the flat screen and entered the kitchen.

"I can offer you a beer, lemonade or coffee," Holly said from beside the refrigerator. "What's your pleasure?"

"Summer's more of a lemonade season, no?"

Holly reached into the fridge and pulled out a two gallon pitcher and brought it to the counter. "Absolutely." She removed two glasses from the cupboard and poured the drinks. "Please, have a seat. Make yourself comfortable."

"Thanks." Anderson pulled out a chair at the kitchen table. He placed his small notebook in front of him and sat and waited.

A moment later Holly placed a tall glass of lemonade in front of him and took the chair opposite him. Anderson picked up the glass and looked at the cartoon image of the Roadrunner with the customary dust cloud at his feet. He held up the glass and tilted his head slightly at Holly.

"When you have a child, pretty much everything in the house becomes child-oriented. The glasses came from Cassie's grandmother."

"Hey, I have no problem with the Roadrunner. I watched those cartoons all the time when I was a kid." He sipped the cold, pink liquid and it felt good going down.

Holly sipped her lemonade from a Marvin Martian glass. "Do you have any children, Officer?"

Anderson shook his head and swallowed his lemonade. "No. Almost once, but no." When he saw Holly's eyes widen slightly he held up a hand. "It was a long time ago don't worry about it. And please, call me Matt."

"Okay, sorry," she said. She put her glass down and folded her hands on the tabletop. "What would you like to know, Matt?"

They spoke at length. It took Holly a few moments to get through the emotions generated by the memories, but once she did, the words poured from her. She stopped only once, to dab at her eyes with a dishtowel; by the time she was finished she was nearly out of breath and her eyes were wet. Anderson made a few notes in his pad but much of what she told him he had read in the official report. When she reached the end of her account, he reached across the table and took her hands in his. It was a comforting gesture, nothing more, and Holly seemed to realize it and appreciate it as such.

She smiled sadly and said, "That's it."

"Ms. Wayne—"

"Holly," she said at once. "You've seen me cry, now. I don't think we need to get hung up on protocol."

He nodded and licked his lips. "Holly. You mentioned in your statement that Ms. Saunders said something to you before she lost consciousness."

Holly nodded perhaps a bit too vigorously. "Yeah. I can't remember her exact words. 'She's still in there, you have to find her.' Something like that. I'm sorry but it was a bad situation and I wasn't concerned with writing down a direct quote."

Anderson held up a hand. "No, no, it's okay. I wasn't looking for an exact quote. But you're sure that's in the ballpark, right? She said that or something similar?"

Holly nodded again. "Yes. It was that or something close to it." She sniffled and wiped her eyes. "But what does it matter? She was half-conscious by then. She didn't know what she was saying."

"Maybe, maybe not," Anderson said after a moment. "What if I told you the night before your friend was assaulted, I responded to an accident, a bad one. A man was killed."

"The one I saw in the paper? Newcombe?"

"Did you know him?"

"He dated my sister back in the day. I haven't seen him in years."

"I see. Yes, that's the one I'm talking about. As bad as it was, I've seen worse. But there was something else about it, something that didn't make the paper."

"And what was that?"

Anderson related the final words of Jeffrey Newcombe. He went into detail and watched her reaction. She was surprised and upset at the story, but the look in her eyes was more confusion than anything else. When he finished he sat back in the chair and watched her intently. He turned the lemonade glass around in short circles on the tabletop as Holly digested the story.

"I'm sorry," she said after a moment, "but that sounds incredible. Literally. What do you think it means?"

Anderson shook his head. "I don't know. But that's why I wanted to talk to you about this. When I read your statement it was like a punch in the gut."

Holly swallowed and said, "I know what you mean."

They sat in silence for a few more moments. Anderson and Holly took the time to drink their lemonade and look out the kitchen window into the backyard littered with toys. The swings on the swing set swayed slightly in the early-afternoon breeze. Anderson could hear the slight rattle of the chains.

It was not his intention to upset the woman but he felt what he had to say next would do just that. He hoped she would prove him wrong. He cleared his throat and said, "You went to DLES, right?"

Holly blinked a few times and nodded her head slowly. "Yeah, that was a long time ago. What brought that on?"

"I was there, too," Anderson replied. "Sixth grade, Mrs. St. Hilaire's class."

"Seventh, Mrs. Riggi." Her eyes narrowed. "You were there that day, too?"

Anderson nodded. "I was."

"That was one hell of a day," she said after a moment. She glanced out the window again. Her fingers tapped nervously on her Marvin Martian glass. "One hell of a day."

"That it was. But that's not why I brought it up. Do you remember Mr. Ford? He was a social studies teacher."

Holly's head snapped back in his direction suddenly and her eyes widened considerably. Her lips parted and she inhaled sharply. "The guy at Lucky's?" Her mouth hung open and Anderson could see recognition light up her eyes. "The one who attacked Gina? That was Mr. Ford?"

Anderson nodded calmly. "I saw him in the holding cell yesterday. I didn't recognize him at first. Christ, it's been so goddamned long. But that was him for sure."

"Son of a bitch," Holly whispered. "I read his name in the paper, saw the mug shot. I didn't put it together until you mentioned the school." She shook her head. "So he went from beating up teachers to beating up dancers."

Anderson tilted his head. "Teachers? What are you talking about?"

Holly took a deep breath and released it slowly. "Remember the story of Ann Carlson?"

Anderson felt suddenly cold. Of course he knew of Ann Carlson. He was positive everyone in Deacon's Landing over the age of ten knew the story, or, at least, some version of it. Accounts differed on the details but enough of the story remained constant regardless of the storyteller. And was it not Ann Carlson, in one form or another, that had brought him to Holly's kitchen on his day off? Yes, it certainly was. He said none of this; he simply nodded and replied, "Of course I do. Everyone does."

She shifted in her seat a few times before she stood and walked slowly toward the window. She stopped in front of it and stared outside. "I know there's a hundred different versions of it, but in one of those versions she was beaten up pretty good by another teacher. The rumor I heard was it was Mr. Ford."

"I never heard that one," Anderson said. "In fact, I don't remember hearing about anyone beating her up. Just that she disappeared under mysterious circumstances and hasn't turned up anywhere else. At least not under the same name."

"That's the part everyone agrees on." Holly continued to look out the window. "But I heard Ford did a number on her before she vanished." She shook her head slowly and rubbed her arms. The gesture would have looked appropriate if the temperature in the kitchen was twenty-five degrees cooler. "The legend of Dark Annie," she said softly.

Anderson sat back and stroked his chin. Even from across the room he could see the gooseflesh on her arms. He debated telling her what he came to tell her and there was Jen's voice again: *In for a penny...*

"In for a pound," he said softly.

Holly turned her head slightly in his direction. "What was that?"

He cleared his throat. "I know how this is going to sound, believe me. But this is mostly why I came to see you."

She turned and faced him, arms still folded across her chest. "What is it?"

"Newcombe had one more thing to say before we lost him. You have to understand he was pretty far gone by then, which is probably why I misheard him. I thought he said 'Danny.' But now I'm pretty sure what he said was 'Dark Annie.'"

Holly's brow furrowed. "So what? He was obviously delusional. He wasn't the clearest thinker even when I knew him. You said it yourself he was just about dead at that point. Who knows what was going through his head by then."

Anderson nodded. "I agree. But consider what he said before that. The same thing your friend said before she lost consciousness. That's too weird and specific to be a coincidence."

Holly shrugged. "I could have misheard her. It was a pretty fucking chaotic scene in that room. The music was going, Vince and Lucky were shouting at the guy, and he was screaming for his life. It's reasonable to assume I might have misunderstood her."

Anderson shook his head. "Reasonable, yes, but I don't think you did. I think you understood her perfectly." He stood and approached her. "And so do you."

She threw her arms up and released a long, slow sigh. "I don't know what I heard any more." She glanced at the digital clock on the stove. "Look, I'm sorry, but I have to go pick up my daughter now. It's getting a bit late."

Anderson frowned but nodded. It was a brush off and he recognized it as such. It was practiced, most likely on the drunks who populated Lucky's when one of them got a bit too frisky with her. It was polite and gentle, but there was strength beneath her tone that shut the door on any further discussion of the topic.

He picked up his Roadrunner glass and brought it to the sink.

"Just leave it there. I'll get it later."

He nodded and started for the door. "Thanks for your time, Holly. I appreciate it."

She nodded absently and looked out the window again. She shifted her weight from one foot to the other, her hands fidgeted and he thought he saw fresh tears welling up in her eyes. "You're welcome."

He reached the front door and placed his hand on the knob when she called from the kitchen, "Hey, will you be at the fair on Saturday?"

"I'll be on duty, so I assume so," he called over his shoulder. "Are you going?"

Holly appeared in the kitchen doorway. "Taking my daughter. Maybe I'll see you there." She seemed to have gotten her tears under control. Her voice trembled, but only slightly. She stood in the doorway with her arms once again folded across her chest.

"I'm sure you will," he said. He stepped through the door and closed the screen behind him. "Take care, Holly."

"You too, Matt," she called.

He allowed the door to close and walked slowly back to his car. The rain was holding off, but dark clouds to the west promised to open up before long. He sat behind the wheel for several moments before he started the engine. His thoughts lingered on Jeffrey Newcombe and Regina Saunders and the utter lack of connection they seemed to share. Perhaps Holly was correct and one or the other of them had misheard what was said. Or maybe he was correct, in which case some weird shit was going down.

He looked again at Holly's home and was not surprised to see the front door was closed. He put the Chevy in drive and made his way down the street. He thought about the fair and how nice it would be to see Holly there with her daughter. The fair always proved to be a fun time, even to a police officer on duty.

I wonder how much fun it'll be for Jeffrey Newcomb's kids, Jen said helpfully.

Anderson did not reply.

Chapter Seven

The Apocalypse

Five days after Anderson's visit with Holly Wayne and two days after Regina Saunders died in the ICU, the Deacon's Landing Fair opened its gates. It was mostly the same rides and attractions as the previous year, and every year before that. Anderson parked his unit just outside the south entrance to Misset Park and took a quick look around.

The crowds had already showed up and there were plenty more people on the way. He had passed through the intersection of Young Street and Wilkins Lane and seen Daniels, one of the rookies, directing traffic. He'd waved but Daniels was too preoccupied to notice him. The foul look on the officer's features told Anderson all he needed to know about the man's opinion of traffic duty. Daniels had waved through an old Firebird that belched thick, gray smoke and sounded like a lawnmower on its last legs. The old muscle car made him think of Murphy and the night at the soon-to-be-opened new school. He wondered if Murphy would show up and decided he would probably put in an appearance before the night was over. It was a rare thing indeed for a resident of Deacon's Landing to miss the fair, Murphy included.

He walked through the entrance and the kid with the long black hair and pierced eyebrows waved him through. Anderson's nose was assaulted with the smells that only seemed to permeate the park when the fair was in full swing. Popcorn, cotton candy, beer, soda, and the occasional faint whiff of weed combined to remind Anderson of the many years past when he attended the fair in a less official capacity.

It also reminded him of Jen. He saw the line for the Maze of Mirrors and could almost see her standing there with her friends. She was young, as she had been when they first met. She wore a denim jacket and off-white capri pants with a low-cut tank top. The small rose tattoo on her left wrist had appealed to him somehow. She looked up, saw him, and waved. Anderson blinked and she was gone, as gone from the line as she was the house they bought together. He swallowed hard and moved on.

The Ferris wheel was new. It stood in the center of the park's football field and towered above everything. The old one had always been a let-down; it was short and creaky and had eventually frightened off even the bravest of the town's residents. The new one was much taller and the paint was still new and mostly unblemished. Most of the cars he could see were occupied and the people who occupied the top-most cars waved down to the ants below.

There was music, as there always was. The small stage erected in front of the bleachers was lit up with pin spots of various colors and a drum kit sat covered with a large blanket. Two fairly large amps sat on either side of the stage. Of the musicians there was no sign. The DJ who was set up to the stage's right played his music and entertained the small group of teenagers who stood and danced in front of his system.

Anderson made his customary first orbit of the fair as he usually did. He looked over the games of skill and the rides and took mental notes of where many of the teens gathered. No one had ever been able to find the source of the weed smell at the fair, going back to when the source had been Anderson and his friends. There was a pool at the station house regarding who was most likely to make an arrest and at last find the guilty party. The money went unclaimed every year and the pot had grown to a few hundred dollars. It had become the Deacon's Landing PD's perpetual in-joke. Someone had even come up with a name for the scoundrel. Bob Stevens was the most wanted man in town who never existed. Anderson appreciated the sense of continuity. He could, of course, go to the Donald Duck rock and make arrests and claim the prize money, but he never did. Not that that would stop him from busting anyone he caught with the illegal substance should they be stupid enough to fire it up away from the confines of the party area in the woods behind the football field. This *was* a family environment, after all.

The sun had gone down behind the tall cedars that lined the western edge of the park. There was still plenty of daylight left but some of the concession stands and the rides had already turned on their fluorescents and flashing lights. He kept his sunglasses in place, if only to maintain the image most had of what a police officer should look like.

He waved to a few people he knew, including Murphy and two of the men who worked at his shop, nodded at others when they acknowledged him. The kid in charge of the ice cream stand offered him a free cone, which he declined politely. The kids, and a few adults, screamed as the small roller coaster went into what always appeared as a death dive before it leveled and slowed.

He spotted what he first took to be a group of parents huddled together on the side of one of the food stands. There were four of them, three men and a woman. They were older, perhaps in their late-sixties. He was too far away to hear their conversation but the woman gesticulated wildly and the body language of the others communicated stress to Anderson. He took a few steps closer to them and slid his glasses an inch down his nose.

He was still too far away to hear anything, especially with the sounds of the fair around him. He realized the woman was familiar to him. He saddled nonchalantly up to the food stand. *Burgers and Dogs!* read the sign above the rather large proprietor of the stand, and Anderson knelt down to tie his shoes.

He still could not hear much, and what he did hear sounded to him like a bad signal on his father's old ham radio. He peeked around the corner at the group; two of them had their back to him and the third was partially blocked by another. The fourth member, the short woman with the paisley bow in her hair who seemed familiar to him, listened intently as one of the men took his turn holding their particular court. When the man finished or perhaps just paused for breath, the woman shook her finger at him.

"All we have to do is nothing at all," she said quite loudly. Someone said something back to her and she replied, "No, I will not keep my voice down. No one knows what the hell we're talking about anyway. And even if they did, they'd think we're a bunch of crazy old fuckers who probably went senile a long time ago. No one would believe us, anyway, so don't worry."

Anderson returned to his first shoe and retied it.

"Dana," one of the men said, "whether or not anyone believes us is irrelevant. Bad things are going to happen and we can't just sit back and do nothing."

"Oh, yes we can," Dana replied. "And that's precisely what we're going to do."

"You can't be serious," one of the others said. "We're talking about *children*, for Christ's sake. Have you lost your mind?"

Dana's reply was drowned out by the mass squeal of the kids on the nearby waterslide. By the time the splashdown was past them and the kids recovered, the crowd noise made it nearly impossible for Anderson to make out any more of the conversation near him.

He straightened and stood and poked his head around the corner. The woman stopped in mid-sentence and froze when she saw him. It took her companions a moment to realize someone had joined their group. Their heads turned as one and they regarded Anderson. The men looked at him for only a moment before they found other things to look at; the woman recovered from her initial shock and regarded him with a cold stare. She folded her arms across her chest and tilted her head slightly in his direction.

"Something we can help you with, Mr. Anderson?" Her voice dripped contempt and authority.

Anderson knew immediately who she was. "You're Miss Verrastro, aren't you? You used to be a teacher at Deacon's Landing Elementary School."

"I see we remember each other," she said.

Anderson looked more closely at the men with her. Two of them looked familiar to him although he blanked on their names. "I remember you, as well," he said and indicated the men with a nod. "And I'm sorry, but I couldn't help but overhear some of your conversation."

The men looked uncomfortable and shuffled their feet. They looked down, up, anywhere but at Anderson and Verrastro. Anderson stood and waited for a response from one of the quartet. He was not surprised to see it was Verrastro who stepped forward.

She wagged a finger in his direction. "I did not know spying went with the job of the DLPD. That is what you were doing, isn't it? *Spying?*"

"Call it whatever you want. When I hear people talking about children being in danger, I pay attention. Now, would you like to explain to me what it is, exactly, you were talking about?"

"I would not," Verrastro said. She lifted her chin and looked down her nose at Anderson. It was a look she had likely honed in the classroom. Undoubtedly it served her well then; now all it did was grate on Anderson's nerves. It made him want to slap her, repeatedly.

"Miss Verrastro, I have the authority to hold you and question you if I believe you represent a danger to the public. Based on what I heard—"

"Based on your *spying*," she said.

Anderson swallowed. "You can explain it to me here, or we can have this discussion downtown. Your call."

Verrastro's lips disappeared and she lowered her head and glared at him. Her arms remained folded across her chest but her fingernails buried themselves in the sleeves of her shirt.

One of the men stepped closer to her and said in a voice loud enough for Anderson to hear, "What the hell are you doing, Dana? This is exactly what we need! Tell him."

Her head snapped in the man's direction so quickly he gasped and took a step away from her. "Keep your fucking mouth shut," she said through clenched teeth.

"No, don't keep your fucking mouth shut," Anderson said. His eyes travelled from Verrastro to the man who spoke. "If you know of something that's going to cause harm to someone, it would be in your best interests to talk. And sir, keep your hands out of your pockets, okay?"

The man reversed himself and dropped his hands to his side. He continued to shift uncomfortably. His eyes were wide, nervous, and they moved from Anderson to

Verrastro and back again. He opened his mouth, closed it. His eyes pleaded with both his companions and Anderson.

It was another of the men, the overweight one with the close-cropped white beard, who finally spoke. "Based on what Dana said, I assume you were a student at DLES, Officer?"

Anderson nodded. "That's right, yes."

"I can't say I remember you, but then again, it was a long time ago and I moved to Windsor after the...accident."

"You were a teacher," Anderson said.

The man nodded. "Grade eight, history. Scott Smith."

"I vaguely remember the name." Anderson looked again at Verrastro. Her hands were curled into fists and she shook with rage. Her eyes spat fire at both him and Smith, but she said nothing. "Go on."

"How much do you know about Ann Carlson?" Smith asked.

Anderson's brow furrowed. *Why is everyone asking about her lately? Two conversations about her in one week. What's the old saying? Once is happenstance, twice is coincidence...*

Three times is enemy action, Jen finished for him.

He thanked her silently. Aloud, he said, "Dark Annie. Just what everyone else knows."

Smith apparently shifted into teacher mode. He extended an inviting arm. "Go on."

"She was the teacher who disappeared just before the school year started back in eighty-five. She's become something of a local urban legend since."

"Most legends are based in fact," one of the other men said.

"Indeed," said the third.

Anderson looked at them both briefly before he returned his gaze to Smith. "I'm sorry, what does any of this have to do with what you were talking about?"

Smith opened his mouth but before he could get another word out Verrastro shoved him with both hands. He squealed and backpedaled and crashed into the side of the *Burgers and Dogs!* stand.

"You shut up *right now*, Smith! You hear me?" Verrastro's eyes were red and her fists quivered. She loomed over her former colleague as he slid down the side of the kiosk and ended up on his ass in the dirt. "We agreed!"

Anderson grabbed Verrastro from behind and pinned her arms to her sides. She shouted something and struggled against him but even her adrenaline rush could not overcome his strength. She kicked with both legs and twisted her body within his arms but she remained trapped.

"You did not just commit battery in front of a police officer," Anderson said. She continued to struggle but he held her fast. He freed one arm and reached for the handcuffs at his belt. "You are under arrest, Miss Verrastro. Don't make it worse by resisting."

Her struggles seemed to lessen but she renewed them when he got the first bracelet onto her wrist. She nearly wriggled free more than once and each time Anderson had to shift his grip on her. After a few more moments of struggle he got the second bracelet on her and secured them.

Her breathing was fast and heavy and her legs buckled at the knees. He wanted to allow her to drop to the ground but he maintained his grip on her and kept her on her feet. He concentrated on slowing his own breathing. He looked at the three men and was relieved to see they seemed in no hurry to cause him any more grief. One of them had helped Smith to his feet and they looked from Verrastro to Anderson. Anderson got the impression they were frightened, but not of him and no longer of Verrastro.

Then what?

Verrastro squirmed a bit in his grasp and he tugged on the chain connecting the bracelets. She squeaked and tried to pull away. He renewed his grip on the chain. It was clear he'd need to be rid of Verrastro before he could listen to what Smith and his buddies had to tell him. He reached for the mic clipped to his collar.

That was when the shit hit the fan.

****

Holly had arrived a few moments before Anderson and entered the park from the opposite entrance. Cassandra was in tow and she was already squealing with excitement. She gasped and giggled at nearly everything that entered her field of vision. Her excitement began when Holly pulled into the parking lot and the child caught her first glimpse of the large banner strung above the main entranceway: DEACON'S LANDING ANNIVERSARY

FAIR.   Beneath that, in smaller but distinct lettering: 1698-2014.   Cassandra remembered her excursion to the fair a year before; once Holly mentioned it over the morning's breakfast, Cassandra had talked about little else the rest of the day.

Holly was happy to see her daughter so excited, but she did not share Cassandra's enthusiasm. The news of Gina's death had brought her down quickly and dramatically. The call had come from Max. He'd sounded sad and more than a bit upset and Holly knew what he would say as soon as she recognized the unsteady tone in his voice. Had she not had Cassandra to look after Holly was certain she would have spent the past few nights curled up on her sofa and crying for her friend. As it was, she allowed herself to grieve only when the child was asleep.

Lucky apparently knew enough not to pressure her into working the night of the fair. She called him and said she was taking the night off and he had offered no argument. He even managed to sound comforting, a tone of voice not normally associated with Lucky Luccino. He even offered to pick her up and drive her to the funeral home but she hung up the phone and forgot about him.

She attended the wake, of course, and it had been brutal. Gina's parents, never fond of her choice of vocation, alternated their attention from their daughter's corpse in the casket to Lucky and Max, who did their best to look somber and conciliatory. She spent the hour and a half next to Luciana and some of the other girls from the club. Carrie was MIA, most likely a prisoner of the infamous Josh, who shared her home and her bed but whose contributions to the household consisted mostly of criticizing Carrie's job and their lack of money. When the wake ended Holly got out of there and cried most of the way to her mother's house. She regained control only when she pulled into her mother's driveway and saw Cassandra on the front porch, barely able to restrain her excitement for the fair.

She surveyed the fairgrounds and concluded most of the residents of Deacon's Landing were in attendance. It was not unusual, and in fact, she expected as much. The town's anniversary fair and the July Fourth parade were the two events that brought the people together. She would have been concerned had the crowd been less than she expected.

Cassandra dragged her toward the House of Bounce, the inflated castle with the open walls and the trampoline floor that had terrified her the previous year. Far from terrified, she giggled and said, "I wanna go in there, Mommy! I wanna go in there!"

Several children were currently inside and bouncing high into the air and laughing. There was a line leading to the castle's entrance. Holly surveyed the children waiting patiently and impatiently with their parents and concluded it would be safe for Cassandra. "Okay, munchkin, okay. We'll have to stand in line, though. See?"

Cassandra either did not hear her or did not care. She made her way to the end of the line, Holly in tow. The stood and waited. Cassandra started a conversation with the small boy in line in front of them. The boy's mother was familiar and it took Holly only a moment to remember her from the previous school year. They had spent some time chatting and waiting for the children to emerge from the grade two classrooms at the end of the school day. She could not remember the woman's name, but Cassandra called her buddy Nicky.

She turned back and looked up at Holly. "Mommy, I wanna go on the ride with Nicky! Please, Mommy! Please, please, please!"

Holly laughed and looked at Nicky's mother, who nodded and smiled. Holly turned back to Cassandra. "That's okay with me, sweetie."

"Yay!" Cassandra exclaimed. Nicky seemed just as excited and it made Holly smile.

She stood in the line and chatted with Nicky's mom while their children talked excitedly and squealed when someone reached an extraordinary height within the House of Bounce. When it was finally their turn the ride's attendant made them remove their shoes and ushered them into the rubber castle.

Their allotted time expired and they exited the castle. Holly assisted her daughter with her shoes. Cassandra was out of breath, but excited. She talked quickly and breathlessly with Nicky while they planned their next adventure. "Cassie, maybe Nicky and his mom want to do other things," Holly offered with a sympathetic look at the boy's mother.

"Mommy, I wanna play with Cassie!" Nicky exclaimed.

"And I wanna play with Nicky!" Cassandra agreed.

"Looks like they told us," Nicky's mother said with a grin.

"Apparently so," Holly agreed.

The children took off in tandem toward the center of the field. Holly and Nicky's mother, who had yet to volunteer her name, followed their children. They passed several game booths and stopped short at the cotton candy vendor. Their sweet treasure secured, they ran along together, holding hands.

The children got into line for the funhouse and the women were finally able to catch up to them. The children talked excitedly and Holly could not blame them. She herself had been a big fan of the funhouse as a child; she was also happy Cassandra had found a friend her own age to share in the fun.

While they moved up slowly to the front of the line Holly spotted Carrie and Luciana walking the grounds with their children in tow. She waved to them and they waved back and steered their entourage toward the fun house.

Holly had met Carrie's children a few times. Her son was eleven years-old and named Noah; the girl, Amanda, was a year older. She knew the names of Luciana's children, Jacob and Joshua, but she did not know which was which. They joined Holly and her nameless friend.

"Glad you guys got the night off," Holly said. "Hi, kids."

The children returned the greeting and Carrie said, "Yeah, Lucky's heart grew two sizes that day. He's still open but he gave all the girls the night off. Just drinks tonight."

Holly turned to Nicky's mother and said, "These are my friends, Carrie and Luciana."

The woman nodded, but her smile appeared forced. "I'm Joanne. Nice to meet you."

They shook hands and Holly knew the woman had pegged their profession at the mention of Lucky. She was polite, but her body language and her eyes told Holly she suddenly wished to be elsewhere. *So much for Nicky and Cassie spending much time together*, she thought. Carrie and Luciana's children were older and not likely to want to go on the same rides as Cassie; the boys already looked tortured at the thought of having to enter the funhouse.

"I'll take the kids inside," Joanne volunteered. Holly got the distinct impression she made the offer only to escape her present company. "I like the funhouse," she said quite unnecessarily.

"Thanks," Luciana said.

"Yes, thank you," Carrie added.

"It's not a problem."

She may as well have turned up her nose as she said that, Holly thought. The woman's distaste for her accidental companions was palpable. Holly was used to that type of reaction, but she saw no sign that Carrie and

Luciana had picked up on it. She let it go and pretended Joanne's generosity was genuine.

Carrie half-turned and opened her pocketbook to Holly. "Babe," she said.

Holly peeked inside and saw the freshly-rolled blunt that sat atop the clutter in Carrie's purse. It sat inside a plastic baggie the inside of which was sprinkled with some random residue. Holly's eyes went from the blunt to Carrie. Carrie raised her eyebrows and smiled conspiratorially. Holly smiled back and whispered, "I haven't done that shit in years."

"All the more reason to partake," Carrie replied with a laugh.

"Absolutely," Luciana agreed.

"C'mon, Holly, live a little." Carrie gave her a good-natured smack on the arm. "You have no idea what I had to go through to get out of the house tonight. I'm going to enjoy myself. And besides, we have to toast Gina."

"You mean we have to get toasted *for* Gina," Luciana offered.

"Exactly," Carrie said and laughed.

Joanne had apparently gotten the gist of the conversation. She looked away and frowned and held Nicky a bit more closely.

"I don't think so, guys, but thanks anyway," Holly said.

"Wuss!" Luciana said in mock-anger.

The line moved again and Joanne supervised the children making their way into the small cars that would take them inside the funhouse. She slipped into the last car and shot a sideways glance at the three women before turning her eyes forward. Holly caught the gesture; her friends were too busy waving to their children. The cars started with a jolt. The kids squealed and disappeared through the open doors and into the darkness of the funhouse.

"Let's go smoke this," Luciana said excitedly.

"You go ahead. I'll wait for the kids," Holly told them.

"You sure?" Carrie seemed genuinely disappointed. "We get the night off and you don't want to have a little fun?"

"It's tempting," Holly said, which was not altogether untrue. "But I'm good."

"Okay." Carrie shrugged her shoulders and led Luciana around the back of the funhouse. There was a wooded area that marked the boundary of the football field and Holly had spent some time back there herself in her younger years. She guessed their destination would be the Donald Duck rock. She watched them go and turned back to the funhouse and waited.

****

Murphy lucked out and found a parking spot somewhat close to the entrance. He took it and killed the

Chevelle's engine. Several kids who appeared to be of high school age cast admiring looks at the old muscle car. They took a few respectful steps away when the driver's door opened. Murphy rolled up the window and stepped out. He watched Thompson and McGrath exit from the passenger side and backseat, respectively.

They had wanted to ride with him to the fair, and although Murphy had nothing against them personally, he disliked fraternizing with the employees outside the shop. He made them go home and change clothes before he allowed them inside the Chevelle. The interior, like the exterior, was cherry, and no one was allowed into the car with anything resembling dirt on their person.

After the restoration was complete and he had it on the road, one of his buddies had pulled out a cigarette and was about to light up when Murphy set him straight. There was no smoking in the Chevelle, no eating, no drinking, no anything. Just riding. These rules applied to Murphy, as well, and he stuck to them. And woe be to anyone who broke those rules.

He was miffed when Thompson was a bit too zealous in closing the door. "Oh! What the fuck!" he exclaimed. When Thompson gave him a look of bewilderment, Murphy told him, "Watch the fucking door! This ain't your momma's Toyota." This elicited some guffaws from the group of teens who pointed and laughed at Thompson.

"Sorry, Murph," Thompson said immediately. "It got away from me."

Murphy let it go, mostly because there were children about and it would not do for him to become too angry. "Just watch it," was all he said.

"No problem," Thompson said, and he sounded sincere.

Murphy surveyed the crowds and found them to be precisely what he expected. It was the same thing every year going back to when he attended the fair with his mother and sisters. The games of chance were a bit flashier and more expensive, the Ferris wheel was new and bigger, but most of the rides and attractions were unchanged from his memories. The music, if you could call it that, was different and quite shitty, in Murphy's opinion. He would have preferred Poison or even Nirvana to the garbage kids listened to today. The smells that only came to Deacon's Landing in mid-August filled his nostrils and his head with nostalgia and for a moment, he was ten years-old again.

His father was already gone, God knew where. His mother, who would die a slow, painful death at the bottom of a bottle, was still young and alive. His sisters, Danielle and Desiree, were already trying to ditch him so they could hang with their older and cooler friends. Years later, they would reveal to him their destination and invite him into their group of older kids. They would disappear behind the field where a giant rock with Donald Duck painted on it pointed the way to the party spot. There was always a keg hidden there and plenty of joints to pass around. By the time he was seventeen, he was all but in charge of securing the alcohol and weed and he held that court until his twenty-second birthday when he passed the torch to the next generation.

It was inevitable he would see some of his teachers at some point; in a town the size of Deacon's Landing there was only so much to do and something of the magnitude of the anniversary fair drew everyone. The teachers would say something along the lines of, "Nice to see you, Brian. Are you excited for school to start?" He would nod or say, "Yes," even though it was far from the truth. And really, what kid wanted to see his teacher outside of school? Especially in the waning days of summer when vacation was nearing the end of its life. It always felt to him as if they were rubbing it in. They may as well have said, "Enjoy your free time while you can because in a few weeks you're *ours!*"

Murphy shook his head and the sounds and smells of the fair brought him back to the present. He took off his

Yankees cap, ran a hand through his hair and returned his headwear to its customary spot. He entered the fair with Thompson and McGrath in tow.

He headed for the first beer stand he saw. He allowed himself a single drink when he had the Chevelle out for a night. That was another of the Unbreakable Rules of Conduct. He paid for the beer, and for Thompson and McGrath's, and started his slow walkthrough of the fair.

He saw Anderson standing near the inflated water slide and speaking with a young couple and their small child. He nodded to Anderson and waved. Anderson waved back. A few moments later he came across Bradley. The officer stood in the center of a fairway, hands on his hips and standing almost ruler straight. His scowl was affixed to his face as it always was. He regarded Murphy and his companions with open contempt but said nothing. Murphy flipped him off and kept walking.

"Look at these geeks," McGrath said. "You'd think they never saw a carnival before. What's the big deal? They have the same shit here every year,"

"Hell yeah, they do," Thompson agreed.

"That didn't stop you guys from being here, did it?" Murphy asked.

"Aw, c'mon Murph," Thompson said, "what else is there to do in this burg? It's not like we have excitement waiting around every corner. We have to take what we can get."

"Fuckin' A," McGrath agreed.

"And now that we're out of the popemobile and we've had an adult beverage, I say we disappear for a few minutes and see if anyone's at the rock."

"There's always someone there," McGrath added. "Been that way since my dad was a kid. He told me so. He even says he knew the kid who painted Donald on that rock."

Murphy nodded. "And maybe if he hadn't smoked so much of that shit when he was a kid you wouldn't have turned out like you did." When McGrath gave him a wounded look, Murphy added, "No offense."

"C'mon, Murph, what do you say?" McGrath's voice contained just the correct amount of whining.

In truth, Murphy wouldn't have minded a hit or two. It had been a brutal week at the shop and he needed something more than a single beer to take off the edge. He found himself nodding but before he could voice his consent he spotted Kenny Atkins.

He recognized him immediately, although he had not seen him since eighth grade. Anderson's description of him a week before was accurate. Atkins' hair was long and greasy and looked as if it had last been washed during the Bush Administration, the *first* Bush Administration. It was white as snow beneath the grime. His eyes were set deep inside his skull and his cheeks were drawn. His 6'2" frame was emaciated; Murphy estimated his weight at no more than 120, tops. He looked like a heroin addict, which would not be the biggest surprise of the year. Before he left Deacon's Landing for parts unknown he had had a string of arrests for drug offenses. By the time Atkins dropped out of high school he was said to be living in a crack house and sleeping on a pile of old clothes. Murphy had no trouble envisioning that particular scene.

Atkins was alone, which also came as no surprise. He lingered near the beer stand and drank from the Styrofoam cup and watched the people and families pass in front of him. He wore a flannel shirt that might have been in style in 1993 and his jeans were ripped and dirty. His black biker's boots had likewise seen better days. Most of the passersby ignored him but a few parents held their children a bit more closely as they walked in front of him and more than a few went out of their way to give him a wide berth. *Some things don't change*, Murphy thought.

Thompson and McGrath had plotted their course to the rock and were already speaking excitedly about whom they might meet there and what they would do if the company included women. Murphy caught up to them, but he found himself looking over his shoulder at Atkins.

The man remained in place. Something had caught his attention. Murphy followed his gaze to the tilt-o-whirl. There was nothing out of the ordinary about the ride; kids, mostly teens, stood in line while their predecessors screamed and cried and laughed from within the spinning cars. Murphy found himself watching Atkins intently and he did not know why. It was something in his body language, perhaps, or something in his eyes. He could not put his finger on it but something was off.

He stopped and looked more closely at Atkins. Nothing abnormal presented itself, and no one else seemed to pay any attention to him. He appeared as nothing more than a scummy local checking out the major summer attraction in a small town where there was little else to do. Murphy swallowed and reluctantly looked away. He jogged to catch up to Thompson and McGrath.

They had made it to the edge of the field where the first wafts of illegal smoke reached their nostrils when the apocalypse arrived at Deacon's Landing.

Chapter Eight

The Woman in the Dark

The first explosion took the tilt-o-whirl. One moment the teenagers occupying the cars were shouting with excitement and perhaps a little queasiness. Their shouts were cut off, and for the span of a single heartbeat, those on the ride were silent. Then it dawned on them that something serious and potentially fatal had occurred and they screamed for a different reason altogether. The fireball was not large but it shot skyward with enough force and heat that several kiosks adjacent to the tilt-o-whirl were knocked over and scorched.

Anderson threw his prisoner to the ground and landed on top of her. Verrastro gave a short squeal and Anderson was certain he felt her left arm fracture even through his vest. He glanced up, saw the fireball and debris claw at the darkening sky. He lowered his head and tried to cover both it and Verrastro with his free arm. He looked away too late to avoid seeing two of the cars sail through the air.

There were screams from some of the townspeople nearby, but the cacophony was less than Anderson expected. The fairgrounds were vast and people on the other side had probably not yet realized the scope of the explosion. Debris rained down on Anderson and he hugged Verrastro all the more. It was small debris, pieces of support braces and personal articles of those unfortunate enough to have arrived early and beaten the line. There was a thunderous crash from somewhere to Anderson's left and he knew without looking one of the cars had returned to earth. He heard screams from behind him and guessed they came from Smith and his buddies. He did not look back.

He snaked his arm around his neck and grabbed at the mic. It was not in its customary place and he felt around blindly for it. He found its cord and followed it until he held the mic in his hand again. He shouted into it, "All available units to Misset Park! Ten-sixty-nine! Repeat, ten-sixty-nine at the park! Need fire and medical at the west entrance on the double!"

The sound of debris raining down lessened even as the shouts and screams intensified. Anderson lifted his head. Two of the tilt-o-whirl's cars remained in place. The occupants of one car were clearly dead; the bodies were burned, were still burning, and their embrace had become permanent. One boy in a tank top who looked to be of high school age struggled to free himself from the last car; the girl next to him hung limply halfway out of her seat. One of the cars, the one he had heard make its crash landing, lay on its side perhaps twenty feet from him. Part of the bracket that held it to the ride's platform had accompanied it on its journey. The car's underside faced Anderson and so he was blocked from a view of its interior. He saw a small arm dangling over the side from within the car.

He jumped to his feet and hauled Verrastro up with him. She gasped when she saw the scope of the devastation. She no longer struggled against the cuffs; she simply stood and gaped. A quick glance over his shoulder told him Smith and his companions were likewise unhurt. They had retreated a few steps and braced themselves against the kiosk. Anderson unlocked Verrastro's handcuffs and sprinted for the tilt-o-whirl.

That was when the second explosion occurred.

****

Murphy jumped when the ground shook beneath his boots. He ducked instinctively and threw his arms over his head. Thompson mimicked him but McGrath dove for the ground and stayed there. Murphy spun quickly and looked back the way they had come. He caught sight of the large but brief fireball and said, "Holy Christ."

"What the fuck was that?" Thompson shouted.

"Come on, we have to move," Murphy said. He dashed for the fairgrounds without looking to see if his friends were following. Behind him he heard shouts and questions from those who were already partying at the rock. He tuned them out and reentered the fairgrounds from behind the funhouse.

People were starting to react to the explosion as they began to realize something out of the ordinary had occurred. He sprinted past a few mothers who were clutching their children close; a group of teens stood excitedly to the side and pointed to the smoke rising into the sky. Some of the girls screamed or covered their mouth with their hands. Their boyfriends tried to appear brave or unfazed by the event but they failed at both. All appeared aghast.

He caught sight of a trio of women bolting up the ramp to the funhouse. They appeared quite frantic and Murphy could guess the reason. One of them, the shortest of the three, grabbed the double doors and flung them open. They disappeared through the opening.

The screams grew in both volume and number the closer he got to the smoke. He found himself pushing past small groups of parents and teens, all apparently rooted to the spot by the unexpected catastrophe. He gave up trying to squeeze through the crowds and began to actively shove his way through the immobile townspeople. He emerged from a rather large gathering of people and stopped in his tracks when he saw Atkins again.

He stood in the center of the fairground with his hands in his pockets. He watched the smoke ascend into the darkening sky with what Murphy could only think of as casual detachment. Unlike those around him, he seemed entirely at ease with what had occurred. His expression was blank, disinterested. After a few moments of watching the smoke Atkins turned and looked behind him. Murphy followed his gaze to the rotor.

It was the largest ride present in terms of the footprint it left. Entirely enclosed with the exception of its roof, the ride spun rapidly, much to the delight of both its patrons and the manufacturers of stomach relief tablets. It was never a particular favorite of Murphy's; being pinned to the inside of a spinning cylinder by centrifugal force was not his idea of a good time, especially with a few beers and carnival hot dogs in him.

Atkins was focused on the rotor. It was already slowing down; the operator inside had obviously realized something had happened. Murphy wanted to continue toward the site of the explosion but something about Atkins rooted him to the spot.

"What are you doing, Murph?" McGrath asked breathlessly from behind. Murphy realized for the first time his friends had kept up with him. "I thought we were gonna go see what happened."

"I'm fine right where we are," Thompson said. He was equally out of breath. He planted his hands on his knees and sucked in air. "I don't wanna have anything to do with what's going on over there."

Murphy ignored them. He took a hesitant step toward Atkins, who remained unmoved and unmoving.

The second explosion ripped the rotor apart. This time Murphy hit the ground and stayed that way. Above the noise of the explosion he heard people around him scream and gasp and swear. Someone collapsed to the ground next to him and he knew it was Thompson when he heard the man shout, "Jesus!"

They were close enough to the rotor that most of the debris flew over their heads. Some pieces of the canvas which had until recently covered the sides of the rotor landed around them. A small piece, no larger than a tablecloth, landed next to Murphy. It was on fire and the flame scorched his right arm. He pulled in his arm and tucked it beneath his chest. Something landed next to his head and he opened his eyes and saw a small pink tennis shoe with someone's foot and part of their ankle poking from it. He gasped and batted the thing away.

When he next looked up the rotor was blown apart. One section of its inner wall remained in place; its jagged edges were black. The rest of it, along with its occupants, had vanished. The sound of people running and screaming and weeping filled his ears. Someone hurdled him and Thompson and managed to clip the back of Murphy's head on the way by. Murphy caught a glimpse of the fat kid as he continued his full-speed retreat from the area.

Murphy jumped to his feet and looked about.

Any thought that the first explosion had been a tragic accident had apparently been driven from the crowd. People who had initially stood their ground or gathered in large groups to gawk at the tilt-o-whirl were now running in all directions. Smaller children were scooped up and held tightly by their parents as they ran as fast as they were able for the nearest exit. Screams and shouts filled the air and drowned out all else, even the crackling of flames from the two destroyed rides.

He grabbed Thompson's arm and hauled the man to his feet. Thompson stood beside Murphy and stared wide-eyed at the scene around them. McGrath likewise regained his feet. He brushed absently at the dirt on his shirt and jeans and looked dumbfounded.

"Let's get the fuck outta here," Thompson said.

Murphy ignored him and scanned the crowd for Atkins. He came up empty and after a few moments he gave up. There was simply too much chaos for him to find a specific person.

"C'mon, Murph," McGrath said. "Time to go."

Murphy took a single step in the direction of the parking lot when he saw Anderson cutting through the crowd. He was shouting, but Murphy could not hear him above the cacophony around them. He forgot about the two men at his side and made for Anderson.

****

Anderson tried to make it to the rotor, but there were simply too many people between him and it. They ran in different directions but they all seemed to be in his way. He pushed and shoved but made little in the way of progress. He heard sounds coming from his mic, many voices trying to outshout each other. He did not bother trying to make sense of them; the noise level in his vicinity was like that of a rock concert. He shouted, screamed, really, tried to make his voice heard above the chaos, but the people of Deacon's Landing were far too preoccupied with vacating the area to listen to his pleas to remain calm. He knew from his studies at the academy that most injuries in a situation like this were caused by panicked people stampeding over other panicked people. He could see no way to avoid that particular outcome.

In seemed like hours but was more likely minutes until he succeeded in reaching the rotor. There was not much left of the ride, and he turned away after he saw the large blood stain on what was left of the rotor's inside wall.

Screams of sheer terror came from all about him. Those unaffected by the explosions nevertheless wanted off their rides or out of the area. He ran past the House of Bounce and shouted for the kid in charge to clear the ride. It was somewhat unnecessary; several parents or older siblings had gone into the attraction and were actively pulling kids back out onto the fairgrounds. Several pairs of small shoes and sneakers were left behind as parents cradled their children in their arms and ran for the parking lots.

The lights at the northern end of the park blinked and then went dark. There were cries of surprise and fear from that direction, but Anderson had enough to occupy him in his immediate vicinity.

The kiosks he ran past were already evacuated and he turned his attention to the fair's newest and largest ride. The people on the Ferris wheel were screaming nonsense words and their arms flailed as if trying to get the operator's attention. From a distance Anderson could see the man doing his best to bring each car in safely. As soon as the car was within jumping distance of the ground the occupants vacated and bolted away. Parents jumped with their children in their arms. They were down to the last few occupied cars and Anderson was about to turn away when the explosion occurred.

It drowned out the cries of the few unfortunates who had had the rotten luck to be the last to board the ride. The fireball was not large, not compared to what had occurred at the tilt-o-whirl, but it was big enough and ugly against the darkening August sky. Girders emanating from the central hub bent, folded. The entirety of the Ferris wheel separated from its center with a scream of wounded metal. It stood for a few seconds, long enough for Anderson to believe it might stay in that position, before it leaned away from the main fairgrounds and began its fall.

Someone collided with Anderson from behind and he was knocked to the ground. The panicked man jumped back to his feet and disappeared into the retreating masses. Anderson looked up in time to see the Ferris wheel crash to earth. The sound of the impact was enough to override the screams of those still trapped within the cars. The ground shook with the impact.

A banner that was half-burned floated gently to the ground and landed directly in front of Anderson. Small flames consumed the edges of the banner but they were sputtering out. Its edges were gone and some of it was scorched but he found he could still read it: "Believe, Achieve and Succeed at Test time!" it proclaimed. He blinked and looked again but the banner remained. Anderson momentarily forgot about the Ferris wheel.

****

When the tilt-o-whirl died, Holly gasped and spun in that direction. She saw the fireball, heard the screams, and her hand rose of its own accord and covered her mouth.

Her first thought, which was shared by many, was that something had gone terribly wrong. She thought perhaps someone had accidentally ignited a propane tank belonging to one of the food kiosks, or an electrical short had occurred next to a generator. Her initial reaction was to hope everyone was okay.

Her second thought was of Cassie. She turned back toward the funhouse. Another group of kids who looked to be of high school age occupied the cars and were just entering the structure. The ride operator pulled back violently on the control lever and the cars shuddered to a halt. The kids shouted but some of the boys among the group grabbed at the safety bars and swung them up. The kids vacated the cars quickly; the ride's operator shouted for them to clear the area.

One of the women next to Holly took a few steps toward the kid operating the ride. "My son's in there, you have to turn the ride back on!"

The kid's head whipped back and forth between the funhouse entrance and the woman in front of him. He stammered, his eyes were wide with terror and indecision, his hands fidgeted.

Holly joined them, as did another woman who had been standing near them. The kid regarded all three of them with the same deer-in-the-headlights look. His mouth worked, but no sounds escaped him. He continued to alternate his gaze from the funhouse entrance to the women in front of him.

Holly grasped his shoulders and hoped he would find the gesture to be reassuring, or at least enough to focus him. It seemed to do neither. "Listen to me. Our children are inside the funhouse. Turn the ride back on and get them out of there." She leaned in closer and it was all she could do to keep her voice level and calm. "Do it now. Please."

The kid shook his head as if he had been in a daze and he said, "Okay, okay." He grabbed the control lever again and pushed it forward slowly. The cars so recently vacated by the high school kids jolted to life. The doors swung open and the cars disappeared into the darkness of the funhouse. "Your kids should be out in two minutes. The cars are timed that way."

"Thank you," Holly said and returned her attention to the structure in front of her. The women with her took a step back and nodded appreciatively to Holly. She shook her head slightly and folded her arms across her chest and waited.

The funhouse lost power a moment later. The flashing lights that outlined the structure winked out and the giant clown face above the entrance went dark. Other rides and kiosks adjacent to the funhouse went out at the same moment. Holly's jaw dropped and she looked at the kid again.

He stepped away from the control board, looked at Holly and the other women with naked fear in his eyes.

"I'm sorry," he said. He ran away from the funhouse as fast as he was able.

"No, you little shit, get back here," one of the women shouted.

The kid vanished into the crowd.

Holly did not watch him go. She swore and dashed for the funhouse entrance. It took the other women only a moment to realize what she meant to do and they joined her. Holly reached the doors and struggled to get her fingertips into the crack between them. She succeeded after a moment and flung the doors open. She dashed inside, the other women at her back.

It was pitch dark inside the funhouse and Holly could see nothing. She spun quickly and tried to shove the doors back open but she succeeded only in pushing one of her sudden companions backward. The woman squealed at the unexpected assault and swore and groped about blindly.

"Move, move," Holly said and finally felt the doors. She pushed against them but found them locked. She swore again.

One of the women said, "Hang on," and flicked a lighter. The light was meager but it enabled Holly to see a few feet in front of her.

"Cassie," Holly shouted. Her voice echoed back to her. She paused and listened but heard nothing more. "Come on."

Holly led the way. She kept one hand on the wall to her right and kept her feet between the two tracks on the floor. The woman with the lighter was a step behind her and to her left. Holly listened intently for any sound but she heard nothing but her own nervous breathing. They rounded several turns along the track but had yet to locate the cars with their children aboard.

The building shook suddenly and Holly nearly lost her balance. The woman with the lighter was unable to keep her feet under her and she went down. The light went out and once again they were in total darkness. Holly heard the heart-stopping sound of the lighter bouncing across the floor. There were shouts from outside the building and the sound of a second explosion. Holly coughed as she inhaled a lungful of dust which undoubtedly was shaken loose from the ceiling. "We need light," she said.

The woman with the lighter said from somewhere behind and beneath Holly, "I lost it, help me find it!"

Holly's hands shout about the grimy floor but she felt nothing resembling the woman's lighter. She swore loudly and climbed back to her feet. Holly shouted, "Cassandra!" and continued on as fast as she was able. She maintained her contact with the wall to her right and kept her other hand outstretched in front of her. The sounds from outside diminished somewhat. Holly did not know if it was due to her moving deeper inside the funhouse of if the park was being evacuated. She guessed it was both and that made her move a bit faster.

She heard echoes of voices and paused for a moment. She closed her eyes and listened intently. Her shoulders slumped when she realized the voices belonged to the two women who had accompanied her into the funhouse and were coming from behind her. Holly took all of three seconds to decide she did not want to wait for her companions before she continued on.

There was a sudden and pronounced drop in temperature. It had been warm inside the funhouse when she first entered. Now she felt as if she had entered an abandoned house in the dead of winter. She shivered and felt the gooseflesh rise on her arms.

Holly rounded another bend along the track when she bumped into something soft and cold in front of her. She gasped and felt blindly for the obstruction. It was not the last car in line in which she had placed her daughter; it was too soft and too tall for that. It felt like fabric. After another moment she came to the unlikely conclusion it was silk. *One of the dummies that springs out from the wall to frighten the customers*, she thought. She first tried to shove the object aside but it refused to move. She began to squeeze her way around it when something that felt like a hand settled on her arm.

Holly froze. The hand felt like it was made of ice. It was colder, if such a thing were possible, than the air around her. She quickly berated herself for the reaction. *I moved the thing and one of its hands fell on me. Big fucking deal.* She started to move forward again. The hand on her arm wrapped its icy fingers around her.

Something moved next to her in the darkness. Holly gasped. Every muscle in her body went rigid. She felt a slight, cool breeze on her neck and her ear and it made the hair on her arms stand up. No, not a breeze. A breath.

Where are my children? a woman's voice whispered. *You took them from me. I want them back.*

Holly shrieked and tugged her arm, trying to free it from the woman's hand. There was a moment of resistance, as if the woman in the dark did not wish their conversation to end. Then the hand was gone. Holly raced through the darkened funhouse on legs that felt suddenly like jelly.

She collided with the walls and more of the dummies that leaned halfway out of their respective alcoves, but she remained in motion. The faint voices from behind her now belonged to the two women who had accompanied her. She ignored them and shouted, "Cassandra!" Her voice echoed back to her, but after a moment she thought she heard something ahead of her in the darkness.

Stopping, Holly spread her arms beside her and felt the walls. She listened carefully for several moments and the sound repeated itself. A child's voice from somewhere ahead. She could not understand the words but she recognized her daughter's voice. "Cassandra! Mommy's coming! Where are you?"

The walls bounced her own voice back to her, but beneath that she heard Cassie shout a reply. A moment later, much louder, came Joanne's voice. Holly proceeded slowly, arms outstretched in front of her and she wished she had had the presence of mind to take the lighter from the woman when they first entered the funhouse. "Cassie, keep talking, baby. Mommy's almost there. Where are you?"

This time she could both hear and understand her daughter. "We're here, Mommy. The car's stuck."

"Something happened outside," Joanne said. "We felt a couple of tremors. Was it an earthquake?"

Holly did not answer her. She pushed ahead until she came to a large and hard plastic object in the center of the track in front of her. It took her only a moment to realize it was the last car in the chain that held her daughter. "I'm here, baby, I'm here," Holly said and felt her way along the car to the next one in line.

Cassie was crying from somewhere ahead of her and Holly quickened her pace as much as she dared. She could hear several other children near her and her hand came across a much smaller hand perched atop the car's safety rail. The child screamed and pulled his hand away and Holly whispered, "It's okay, it's okay, we're gonna get out of here."

"What happened to the power?" Joanne asked. "I thought these things had their own generators."

Holly ignored her. "Cassie, where are you, baby?'

"I'm here, Mommy," said the voice from the darkness.

Holly followed the cars with her hands until she came across another child's hand. This one was small and instantly recognizable. Holly reached down with both hands and found the safety bar. "I'm here, baby, I'm here.

Just hang on a minute so I can undo the safety bar." Holly pulled on it but it refused to budge. She tried again and received the same result. "Joanne, help me with this."

"On it," Joanne said.

Holly felt the bar move slightly and knew the woman in the next car had reached back and grabbed the bar. Holly pulled again and this time it lifted easily. Holly threw it up as far as it would go and found Cassandra and lifted the child into her arms.

"Mommy, I'm scared," Cassandra said.

"It's okay, baby. It's okay. We're getting out of here right now." She looked behind her at where she knew the boys to be. "Can you get the safety bar up? It'll move if you push really hard."

Jacob or Joshua said, "We'll try," and Holly heard much grunting from them. She also heard the safety bar hit its upper latch and knew the boys had succeeded. They exited the car quickly, nearly knocking Holly and Cassandra to the floor in their haste.

"Let's make sure we have everyone before we go," Holly said.

She heard several voices she did not recognize give their consent to leave, and she guessed they belonged to the children of the two women who had accompanied Holly into the funhouse. She heard from Carrie's children and Luciana's as well, and she guessed Joanne had Nicky with her. "Okay, let's go."

Holly supported Cassandra with one arm and kept the other am outstretched in front of her. She thought, *How fucking big can this place be?* and then she could see the outline of the exit doors ahead of them. She quickened her pace. The seam between the double exit doors spilled a sliver of light into the funhouse and Holly made straight for it. She reached the doors without incident and threw her shoulder into them. They parted obediently for her and she was through them in an instant.

Cassandra gasped and began to cry again. Joanne swore under her breath behind Holly and one of Luciana's kids said, "Fuck me."

Several areas of the park were in flames. There were fewer people running about than Holly would have thought, but those that were present ran in different directions and shouted and cried. The kid who was in charge of the funhouse was nowhere to be seen, nor were the women who had charged in there with Holly. Their children cried and stood close to Holly and Joanne.

At first Holly thought the Ferris wheel was gone, until she saw it lying on its side across part of the football field and the jogging track. It had crumpled to the topography of the slight hill which led from behind the home team's end zone to the curvature of the track. The center hub of the Ferris wheel and its base remained in place. The hub was blackened and several spokes jutted out and ended in jagged stumps.

There were no bodies near them, a fact for which Holly was grateful. She had no wish to expose Cassandra to that, and it left open the possibility the tragedy had claimed no lives. She knew it was fantasy, but it helped.

With the park nearly vacated Holly could hear sirens drawing closer. She led the way down the steps and back onto solid ground. She heard shouts from behind and turned and saw her two companions emerge from the funhouse. They screamed for their children and rushed to claim them. One of them glared at Holly as she hugged her son to her chest hard enough Holly thought the child might pass out. Holly shook her head and made for the parking lot.

They came across Luciana and Carrie and a group of people Holly knew had been at the rock when the explosions occurred. All of them looked at the fairgrounds with their mouths open and their eyes wide. The children ran to their mothers and hugged them and cried.

They continued on to the parking lot. Many questions were asked by those who had chosen to join the festivities at the rock. Holly kept her mouth shut except for the occasional comforting word to Cassandra. She continued to whisper those comforting words even as she pulled into her driveway.

Chapter Nine

Such a Thoughtful Young Man

Murphy groaned and rolled onto his side. His head pounded and protested any movement. He clenched his eyes and his jaw and coughed into the dirt. He groaned again and his hand moved and felt his head. *Still there*, he thought and opened his eyes.

At first, everything was a blur. He shook his head to clear it and immediately regretted the action. His head pounded as if it were about to explode. He stifled a groan that threatened to graduate to a scream and rolled onto his stomach. He did not know how long he remained that way. He could hear noise from all around him; voices, sobs, the crackling of flames and what sounded like the roar of a waterfall.

Then another sound. A single voice, close. It belonged to a woman and she whispered something Murphy could not make out. "What?" His mouth tasted like dirt and blood and he coughed again. And why was it so fucking cold all the sudden?

My children, said the woman. *Have you seen them?*

"Lady..." He stopped himself. Even speaking was painful. He got his hands under him and pushed himself to his knees. He cried out and clutched his left elbow. He did not know how he had injured it but it barked at him and made him curse. He waited for the pounding in his head to stop, or at least slow down, and he opened his eyes again. Several firefighters were perhaps thirty feet away. They manned a hose and directed its powerful stream at the remains of the tilt-o-whirl. Other first responders moved quickly in all directions, checking bodies, administering first aid to those they could help, ignoring those they could not. He looked about his immediate area. It was free of bodies, living or dead. There were no women, or men, for that matter, anywhere in his vicinity. The woman who had asked the question was gone. He was alone.

Murphy climbed to his feet and tried to remember how he had come to find himself flat on his stomach. He remembered the explosions, of course, and the chaos that followed. He remembered seeing Anderson and needing to speak with him, but he was not sure why. And that was when the fat bastard with the mustard-stained polo shirt plowed into him and knocked him down. Someone, McGrath or Thompson, had kicked him in the head in their mad dash to escape the park. And that was the last thing he remembered.

"Gonna kill those assholes," he said to no one. His head still pounded but his vision was clear again and he looked at the various firefighters and emergency personnel. They were not close to getting the fires under control, but they had managed to confine them to the areas of origin. The medical personnel fared better, and several townspeople were carried away on stretchers. There were far too many first responders present and Murphy knew without asking that some other towns in the area had sent help. It also meant many of the survivors would likely find their way to hospitals in Waterbury and perhaps Torrington. The hospital in Deacon's Landing would be unable to cope with so many patients at the same time.

And all at once he remembered Atkins. Atkins, who seemed to know the explosions were coming even before they happened. Atkins, who had stood and watched the tilt-o-whirl and then the rotor all but vaporize. There had been a third explosion, which Murphy had heard and felt just as he received that vicious kick to the head. He did not know what had exploded or where, but he was certain it had been preceded by Atkins standing and waiting for it to happen. Which was what he was going to tell Anderson before he was knocked down and out.

"Atkins," Murphy said, again to no one. He scanned the emergency responders, but came up empty. He walked slowly around the fairgrounds, pausing whenever the headache threatened to get worse. There was no sign of Anderson although he came across Bradley helping a paramedic lift a rather large and unconscious woman onto a stretcher. Several bodies lay where they had fallen and were covered with a sheet. Several burned limbs protruded from beneath those sheets and Murphy quickened his pace as much as his throbbing head and bruised knee would allow. He hoped Anderson was not under one of those sheets.

He spotted the policeman a few moments later. He was near the fallen Ferris wheel, helping a survivor from the crushed remains of the car she had boarded back when this had been a normal fair. A kid's body lay sprawled on the ground next to the car. Anderson did his best to shield it from the girl's eyes. Either he succeeded or she was too deep in shock to take note of it.

Murphy took a step in that direction when he stopped himself. Anderson, as well as the other emergency personnel, had their hands full and Murphy's suspicions about Kenny Atkins would not warrant much consideration at present. There were enough people at the park to help with the injured that Murphy knew he would be in the way. He walked slowly toward the parking lot.

The Chevelle was where he left it, the doors still locked. It was just far enough from the entrance not to be in the way of the fire trucks and ambulances which dominated the lot. He unlocked the door, slid behind the wheel and fired up the engine. He paused to look one more time at the fairgrounds before he put the Chevelle in gear and went home.

****

Dana Verrastro slept like shit the night before and it had little to do with being placed under temporary arrest by Anderson or his callous act of fracturing her arm. In truth, it also had little to do with the carnage at the fair. She had tossed and turned and replayed the incident with Anderson in her head. Smith and the others had ignored her and were about to spill their guts and that had *everything* to do with why sleep eluded her. *Since when did those weasels grow a spine?* When she refused to answer Anderson's questions she had assumed that would be the end of the matter. She had not counted on any of the men, least of all Smith, to offer information about what was clearly nobody's business, least of all a policeman's. The explosion at the tilt-o-whirl had undoubtedly kept her out of jail for the night, and it seemed to have had the added bonus of keeping Smith quiet. *At least for now.*

She had fled the park like everyone else and was already in her car and down the road before she heard the first siren. She did not look back to see if her former colleagues had recovered their wits enough to evacuate the area with her. If they were too stupid to see the obvious then they deserved whatever fate befell them. If she discovered they had all been killed she would shed no tears for them. Not after what they were going to say to the cop. Matters such as that were better handled in-house, as far as she was concerned.

Dana drove herself to the hospital and was admitted immediately. Word of what was going on at Misset Park had reached the doctors and they were busy prepping the ER but she complained loudly about her arm and one of them had finally gotten around to examining her. They would have no time for a cast so she had been fitted with a sling and told not to use that arm for a few days. She scoffed at them and complained some more, but it got her nowhere. She was forced, reluctantly, to leave. The first ambulance was screaming into the parking lot as she made her way down the street. She watched some of the scene on television before she tired of it and went to bed.

She made it down to her kitchen and started the coffeemaker. She turned on the small television that sat atop the counter and turned the channel to the morning news as she always did. She caught the weather and traffic reports (high-eighties by noon and a major clusterfuck on 84 East past exit 23) and then it cut to commercial. She made her coffee and by the time she sat down again the news had returned.

As expected, the lead story was about the trouble at the fair. Manny Soto stood with his microphone somewhere on the outskirts of the football field while behind him emergency crews moved across the frame. There was still a bit of smoke rising into the morning air but it seemed the fires had been put out. She could see two ambulances and a fire truck in the background and the remains of what she assumed was the Ferris wheel.

"The death toll currently stands at twenty-four but that is expected to go up as more victims are found," Soto informed her with what looked like barely-concealed excitement. "Doctors at DLH have informed us that several people taken there last night are in critical condition. Other area hospitals have yet to release any news on the patients they received."

Soto's image was replaced by that of the burning remains of the rotor. The flames were bright against the smoke which poured upward into the twilight. Panicked people ran in every direction. Soto was still talking, but Verrastro tuned him out and watched the video intently. The footage looked to be recorded on an epileptic's cellphone; it rarely stayed still or level long enough for Verrastro to recognize the images. She thought she saw Anderson run across the frame but she could not be certain. She cursed the would-be videographer's incompetence and wished someone with a backbone had recorded the event. The same ten or twelve seconds of footage repeated itself and she scooped up the remote. There were other local stations and maybe one of them had more information.

Before she could change the channel she heard the knock at her front door. She glanced at the clock on her stove. 6:18. *Who the fuck is this?* She answered herself immediately. *Anderson.* Who else could be at her door at such an early hour? *He wants to resume our discussion from last night, maybe even take me into custody. Well, fuck him.* All she had to do was not answer the door. He'd go away eventually; she couldn't imagine he'd be brash enough to kick in her door and enter the house.

He knocked again, louder this time. She placed the remote on the counter and walked into the living room. She could see out her picture window without being seen by the bastard on her front porch. She expected to see his police car parked in front of the house. What she saw instead was a white panel truck with **Baribeau Bros. Industrial Construction** stenciled on the side sitting in her driveway.

"What the fuck?" Her brow furrowed. She ran through her mental rolodex for anyone she knew who worked there and she came up empty. A sales call? This early on a Sunday? And what could they sell her? She was not in the market for anything they were peddling. She pulled her robe more tightly around her midsection and walked to the front door as quietly as she was able. The man knocked again and her front door rattled in its frame.

Her first instinct was to pause, then to run to the phone and call the police. Something about the brashness of the man at her door scared her. She took a step back before she stopped herself.

Four decades in the classroom had left her little patience for such insolence.   Whoever was out there was about to give her a damned good reason why they were pounding on her door at such an hour. And if that reason was not to her liking... She strode purposefully to the door, unlocked it and threw it open.

The man standing on her front porch was tall and painfully thin, nearly anorexic. His white hair was long and greasy and dirty. His clothes were filthy and far too big for his frame. One of his ancient brown work boots had no laces. His hands were nearly black with grime as were his arms, face and neck. He looked at her and smiled and his teeth were nearly as black as the rest of him.

Verrastro's jaw dropped a few inches and her eyes went wide. Her mouth worked but she could produce no sound other than a weak stammer. In the moment before the dirty man crossed the threshold and entered her home, she wished it had been Anderson at her door after all.

She backed up as the man entered the foyer and closed the front door behind him. His smile remained in place as he reached behind him and pulled a large knife from his back pocket. He held up the knife as if he wanted her to inspect it. It caught the light coming through her picture window and Verrastro regained the ability to move.

Turning, she bolted for the kitchen. She grabbed the phone off the wall and turned it on, but her fingers felt numb and she dropped it. It landed on the floor and bounced once. She spun quickly and the man was standing behind her, still holding up the knife and still smiling.

"She's waiting for you, Miss Verrastro," he said.

He swung the knife in an elegant arc in front of his body. This time Verrastro followed her instincts and raised her hand to protect herself. She felt the knife slide across her fingers and she blinked and stared dumbfounded at the four stumps that remained. Blood spurted from them and pattered on her robe and on the floor. There was no pain, simply the shock of seeing her hand's suddenly unfamiliar appearance. She held it up in front of her eyes and then she looked at the floor. Her fingers lay where they fell and absently, she thought, *I'm making a mess of my kitchen.*

Her eyes moved back up and the man held up the knife again. This time the blood on the blade stopped any reflection of light; it made the weapon appear as dirty and dangerous as the man who held it. He took a step forward.

"You can't do this," Verrastro whispered. She looked at her hand again, at the blood spurting from the stumps of her fingers. She turned her hand over and held it in front of her, a crossing guard directing motorists to stop so the children could cross the street. "Please." This, too, she whispered.

"Turn around, Miss Verrastro," the man said politely. His smile seemed pleasant enough despite his blackened teeth. He put his hands on her shoulders and gently turned her until she faced away from him. "That's a good girl."

She looked at the television and saw Manny Soto was still at the high school. He remained in place while emergency crews worked behind him. In a part of her mind that was still functional, she looked for Officer Anderson. *He can help me*, she thought. *That* is *what he gets paid for, after all.* But she did not see him. A state trooper walked past the camera accompanied by two firemen. She reached out with her unwounded hand but she had little mobility with her arm still wrapped in the sling. "Help me," she whispered.

She felt something cold and sharp glide across her throat and something red splashed across her counter and covered part of the television screen. She gasped, or tried to, even as her knees buckled. She was suddenly on her back with no recollection of how she got there. She hoped absently she was not lying on her severed fingers; it would be inconvenient if they were broken when the doctors reattached them.

She looked at the dirty young man who stood over her with the knife in his hand and the smile on his lips. "Close your eyes, Miss Verrastro," he said. "You look tired."

Such a thoughtful young man, she thought. She did as he asked.

****

Atkins watched her go. He stood over Verrastro's body for a few moments before he wiped the blade on her gown and slid it into his belt. His attention was caught by the TV and he walked to the counter and sat in the chair. The image was partially obscured by the red haze that dripped down the screen slowly. He watched the reporter at the high school and listened to him read a statement from a state trooper. He paid it little mind; most of his attention was focused on the images behind the reporter.

He could see the remains of the Ferris wheel in the distance and what looked to be two bodies lying under a tarp. Medical personnel moved back and forth and continued to administer to those they thought they could save. He wished the talking head would get the fuck out of the way so he could see more of last night's aftermath but the man seemed to love his screen time. Atkins resigned himself to glimpses of wreckage over the reporter's shoulders.

He noticed the cup of coffee sitting on the counter. It was far enough away to have escaped the jet of blood that resulted when Verrastro's jugular went. He picked it up and sipped it and watched the news.

When he had seen enough he picked up the remote and turned off the TV. He walked upstairs and found Verrastro's bedroom. Her bed was made neatly with the pillows on top of the comforter. The comforter itself was dark brown. Not perfect , perfect would have been black, but close enough to get the job done. He removed the comforter from the bed and went back downstairs.

He set the comforter on the kitchen floor and hesitated. She had made no mention of him leaving a message like he had before, but he felt she would want him to do so. He knelt and slid his fingertips through the pool of blood on the linoleum and went to work. When he was finished he rolled Verrastro's body into the comforter gently and wrapped it up.

He carried her into the living room and he looked out the picture window. It was still early enough for a Sunday morning that he saw no one on the street. He opened the front door and took a tentative step outside. His eyes moved from house to house but he saw no sign of activity. The screen door closed behind him slowly. He moved quickly to the truck. He had to lay the body on the ground while he opened the back panel. It rolled up loudly and he wished he had thought to steal a quieter means of transportation. He picked up the body and tossed it into the back of the truck. It landed on another body and the comforter loosened a little and Verrastro's wounded hand fell out. It no longer bled.

He closed the panel and walked back to the cab. He felt he had a few more hours left before the truck became conspicuous and he'd have to use something else. It would not be reported stolen until the following morning when one or the other of the Baribeau brothers got to the yard and noticed it was missing. By then, of course, it would be well hidden. Until then, well, he had a few more stops to make.

****

Like Verrastro, Anderson did not get much in the way of sleep. In fact, he had not slept at all. He was released from the scene at the high school when the state troopers began to show up. He had protested, as had Bradley and the other local officers but Captain Lange had given them little choice. He had stuck around long enough to hear the state bomb squad pronounce the area secure and then he'd made his way slowly to his unit. The parking lot was full of emergency vehicles and more were arriving. He caught sight of a few vehicles from as far away as Torrington. There were also a few civilian vehicles and he hoped the owners were still able to claim them. Most he knew would wind up in the impound lot until a probate judge got around to hearing the cases.

He removed the folded banner from beneath his shirt and placed it in the trunk of his unit. No need to take precautions to avoid being seen; the emergency crews had other things to occupy their attention. He resisted the urge to unfold the thing and look at it again.

There was little else to do after he left the high school. Most of the town had been there and it seemed everyone went straight home. A few cars were on the road and more than a few gatherings of neighbors discussing what they had witnessed. One such group waved him over and asked if he knew any further details of what had happened. He told them no, but that the state police were on the scene and they would all be hearing about it shortly, he was sure.

Anderson returned to the station and spent two hours typing his official report of the incident. He stopped several times while he tried to come up with the proper phrasing to describe what he had seen. There was no mention of the banner which had floated to the ground in front of him, or its present location inside his trunk. No one would believe him, anyway, and it might cause Lange to schedule him an appointment with the department shrink, Dr. Cantoni. There was a distinct possibility everyone who was at the scene would be forced to speak with her about their experiences and feelings, anyway. Anderson wished to avoid that scenario if at all possible. Cantoni had an unnerving habit of getting her subjects to reveal everything to her, whether they wished to or not. Best to steer clear of her couch until he could sort out what exactly he had seen. He finished his shift and went home.

Anderson parked his police unit in his driveway as the sky was beginning to brighten. A breach of department policy, but he was too tired and emotionally drained to give a shit. He got as far as removing his shoes and belt before he collapsed onto his bed. He lay there and stared at the ceiling and willed himself to fall asleep. It did not work.

He got up, poured himself a glass of vodka, then another. He sat in the living room and tried reading a book. He got three pages in before he realized he could not remember anything he had just read. He put it down and wandered aimlessly around the house. He wound up in the empty garage. His Chevy was still at the station; the second bay was empty as it had been for the past year and a half.

"I miss you, baby," he said.

He waited for Jen to reply, but she did not. Perhaps she had taken the day off.

He wandered back inside the house and returned to the bedroom and laid down again. He turned on the ceiling fan and hoped the cool breeze would lull him to sleep. That did not work, either. He watched the sun crest over the trees outside his window.

He got up again, showered and went down to the kitchen and made himself some toast. The newspaper retrieved from the front lawn and he read it with his coffee andtoast.

Twenty minutes later he exited through his garage and opened the trunk of the police unit. He took the banner and walked back inside the garage. He needed to see it again, but the idea of having the thing inside his home made him uneasy. The garage made him feel slightly less so and he unfolded one of the lawn chairs stacked against the wall and sat down.

Anderson unfolded the banner and spread it out on the garage floor. He had half-expected it to have changed back to whatever it had read before the fair turned into a

Michael Bay movie but it had not. "Believe, Achieve and Succeed at Test Time!" it encouraged. Anderson stared at the banner and rubbed his temples. He lost track of time until he heard the clock in the kitchen play its musical tone. He rolled up the banner again and placed it standing in a corner. He was halfway to the door before he decided he did not want to leave the thing under his roof. He walked it back to the cruiser and tossed it into the trunk.

Anderson washed up again, taking particular care with his hands before he dressed in a fresh uniform and drove down to the station.

Mr. Swain had the day off and so was not present at the back door to greet him. Anderson made his way to the locker room, mostly to see if anyone was down there. The room was deserted, but there was a note taped to his locker. He opened it and read Lange's scrawl: *Come see me.* Anderson frowned and made his way upstairs. It seemed his decision to take his unit home after his shift was going to cause him some trouble after all.

Lange was in his customary place behind the front desk. The newspaper was on the counter beside him, but he seemed busy with genuine police work, if filling out reports could be called such. Anderson saw the paper had yet to be cracked open; the Sunday circulars which always went into the trash immediately still jutted from inside its bulk.

Anderson cleared his throat and said. "You wanted to see me, Captain?" He steeled himself for a reaming.

Lange looked up from his paperwork and nodded. "Yes, Anderson, I do. Take a seat." He extended a hand and indicated the stool next to his.

Anderson took it and folded his hands on the counter. "Sir?"

Lange removed his glasses and said, "A couple things. The state forensic team thinks the explosions last night were caused by good ol' TNT. It's very preliminary, but Lt. Norkus relayed the info to me. Assuming it wasn't someone making this shit in their basement there's only one place in town it could have come from."

Anderson nodded. "Baribeau Brothers."

"Correct. We're trying to get hold of them now. I want you to take a ride up there and see if they're missing any. They should have surveillance cameras so if someone did break in there we might get lucky with the video recording."

"Got it."

Lange cleared his throat and said, "There's something else, unrelated. That guy we had here last week who killed the stripper. You remember him?"

"Ford," Anderson answered perhaps too quickly. He had, of course, talked to Markowitz about the man's identity, but he had said nothing to Lange. The last thing he wanted was the captain to order him to stay away from anything resembling the case when he had needed to speak with Holly. Having once known the suspect would have disqualified him from assisting the investigating officers. He hoped Lange did not pick up on his momentary lapse.

The captain did not. He continued with a nod. "Yes, Benjamin Ford. I received a call this morning from New Haven Correctional. He escaped sometime last night. He was there for the night count and gone this morning. They're still trying to figure out how. It's unlikely he'll show up here, but I want you to keep your eyes open out there just in case. Copy?"

"Roger," Anderson answered.

Lange reached beneath the counter and pulled out a laser print of Benjamin Ford and handed it to Anderson. The younger officer took it without bothering to mention he would not need it to identify the suspect. Anderson was quite familiar with the man's appearance.

"The funeral for the girl he murdered is this morning. Given what happened last night I doubt it will be well-attended, but you never know. When you're finished at Baribeau Bros. I want you at Lichgate just to be on the safe side."

Anderson thought of Jen and wished Lange had given the assignment to someone else, but all he said was, "Yes, sir."

"All right, then. Dismissed." Lange turned back to his paperwork and paid no more attention to Anderson.

Anderson beat a retreat out of the station and returned to his unit. The printout of Ford's mugshot went above his visor and Anderson swore under his breath. He had intended to pay a visit to Verrastro and resume their discussion from the night before. He had also planned to track down Smith and see what else the man had to say. All that would have to wait at least until after Gina Saunders' funeral.

His watch informed him it was 8:45 AM. He would need to boogie if he wanted to make the funeral. He put the car in gear and left the stationhouse at a higher rate of

speed than he had intended.

237

Chapter Ten

Funeral Parlor Vibe

It had been a long and miserable night in the Wayne household. Cassandra had been utterly unable to sleep and Holly had stayed up with her. The poor girl cried for hours after they arrived home. It came in stages; she would cry for ten or fifteen minutes, stop, then start again. Holly sat on the sofa with Cassandra in her arms and rocked slowly back and forth. She wiped her daughter's nose and dried her eyes and awaited the next round.

Sarah Wayne had called her daughter and was relieved to find them at home. She asked about the incident at the park and Holly told her everything she knew. She left out the part about the woman in the funhouse; she simply did not know how to describe what had occurred. Her mother offered to come over and Holly politely refused. She would see her in the morning when she came over to watch Cassie while Holly went to the funeral. She hung up the phone and returned her attention to her daughter.

Cassandra finally succeeded in nodding off about thirty minutes before the morning sunlight crept through the front window and invaded the living room. Holly herself drifted off shortly thereafter.

In the dream the hand stabbed out of the darkness and wrapped fingers of steel around her forearm. Holly struggled to free herself, but the hand felt as if it were welded to her skin. It pulled her toward the darkness and away from Cassandra and Holly was powerless against it. The voice was female and came from inches in front of her nose but Holly could see no one. *Where are my children?* the woman asked. Holly continued to struggle and she felt her feet skid slowly across the floor. She could not see into the darkness in front of her but she knew she did not want to be in there. Her free hand pulled at the fingers wrapped around her arm but they remained in place. *You took them from me. Bring them back. I want my children.* Holly leaned back and threw all her weight behind her. Her feet disappeared into the darkness. She shrieked and woke up.

She did not know if her scream was real or part of the dream, but she was relieved to find Cassandra still asleep in her arms. She settled back into the sofa and tried to ignore the cold sweat which coated her body. It made her shirt and shorts cling to her skin. She wiped her forehead with her free hand.

She remained on the sofa with Cassandra in her arms until she heard her mother's car pull into the driveway. As gently as she was able she moved Cassandra to the side and stood and stretched her legs and arms. She walked to the door and opened it and watched her mother walk up the driveway.

Moments later she was in the shower. It was already warm within the house and the day threatened to be a scorcher. She resisted the urge to crank up the hot water and instead left the dial in the middle. When the soap stung her arm she looked at it and gasped. She did not know how she had managed to miss the handprint on her forearm but now it caught her attention and held it. It looked like bad sunburn which had already begun to peel. Flakes of skin sloughed off under the lukewarm water. The fingers of the handprint were long and thin and too prominent not to be noticed. She felt around the edges gingerly and winced at the pain caused by her probing. The wound was red and becoming more so. Despite the warmth of the morning and the warm water beating down upon her she shivered.

She washed up and took care to avoid the patch of dead skin on her arm. After her shower she toweled off and walked into her bedroom. She had taken her black sleeveless dress and hung it on the molding abov her closet before she left for the fair. She looked at it and knew she would need something different. It took her a few moments to put together an outfit that would look appropriate at a funeral and hide the handprint on her arm.

She sat at her computer and Googled the appearance of the wound. After several explanations that seemed ridiculous she settled on frost-nip. It, too, was ridiculous, at least on the surface, but it described the condition of her arm precisely. Low-level frostbite. In late-August. *Good luck explaining to a doctor how that happened.* She finished getting dressed and went downstairs.

Cassandra was still asleep on the sofa. Her mother sat next to the child and sipped a cup of coffee she had made herself. Holly told her mother she would not be gone long and thank you again for watching Cassie and she left the house. Lichgate was three miles away. Holly resisted the urge to scratch at the suddenly itchy and tender area on her arm.

****

Anderson pulled into Lichgate and followed the main road until he came upon the funeral scene. As Lange had predicted the turnout was somewhat meager. Anderson did not take a headcount, but estimated the number of mourners to be somewhere south of twenty. A shitty deal, especially for the murdered girl's family, but the events of the previous night made it not altogether unexpected. There would be quite a few funerals in the coming days, everyone knew, and the staff at Lichgate would be kept busy indeed.

There was no sign of Benjamin Ford, also as Lange had predicted. Anderson scanned the area around the mourners and the freshly dug grave and saw no one suspicious. In fact, he saw no one at all. The cemetery was deserted aside from the family and friends of Regina Saunders.

He put his unit in park and opened his notebook. He had taken a few pages of notes during his interview with Ed Baribeau. The man was upset; no, more than upset. He was livid. He seemed less angered by what his dynamite had done than with the fact that someone had dared to break into his place of business. Three full cases of dynamite had walked away either Friday night or Saturday morning. More likely, it had driven away, since he was quick to tell Anderson one of their panel trucks was missing as well. What troubled Anderson more than anything was Ed Baribeau's insistence that the explosions at the fair could not account for all the missing dynamite. "There's more than enough left to knock down a good-sized building," he said with what sounded like pride.

The surveillance tapes were gone, removed from the machine in the office. The burglar was nothing if not thorough. The man paced about his office stomping his feet and letting loose every expletive Anderson had ever heard and a few he had not. They walked out to the garage and stood in the empty spot where the panel truck should have been and Baribeau continued to pace and swear. The reaction was not entirely unexpected. The Baribeau brothers had a reputation for hostility and aggressiveness and many in Deacon's Landing wondered how anyone could work for such people. That they were very good at what they did and paid their employees fairly seemed to be the only reasons they remained in business.

The man's mood was not improved when Anderson told him the state police would likely come to interview him as well. He told Anderson he hoped to catch the perpetrator himself before the police caught him. *Be the sorriest day in that cocksucker's life,* was the exact quote. Anderson knew because he had written it down verbatim. He cautioned Baribeau against taking the law into his own hands, but that was mostly because it was expected. He doubted either brother would spend much time searching for the burglar. Not when there were jobs to do and employees to abuse and alcohol to drink. He thanked Ed Baribeau for his time and he called in and requested a full forensic investigation since he himself did not have the time. Then he left for the funeral.

Anderson looked up from his notepad when he heard a woman's broken sobs coming from the gravesite. An older woman dressed in black was nearly screeching into her husband's chest and Anderson guessed it was the girl's mother. He looked about again and saw the cemetery remained otherwise empty.

Several mourners made the sign of the cross and the priest at the head of the proceedings said a final prayer for Regina Saunders. The mourners began to drift away slowly from the gravesite. The murdered girl's family remained and accepted the condolences from those in attendance. Anderson saw Holly in the company of another woman he did not know. They walked toward Lichgate's main road slowly, supporting one another and dabbing at their eyes with tissues.

One of the mourners separated himself from the others and walked slowly to Anderson's car. He almost did not recognize Murphy in the suit and tie until the man stood no more than fifteen feet from Anderson's unit. He waved and took a position next to the driver's door.

"Murph," Anderson said with a nod.

"Anderson," Murphy replied. He watched Holly and the other woman step inside Holly's car and then returned his gaze to the family of the dead girl. They continued to stand and look down into the rectangular hole in the ground which had become their daughter's permanent residence. The mother wept openly.

"Bad shit last night," Murphy said after a moment.

"That's an understatement. Glad to see you made it out okay."

"You, too. You guys know what caused it yet?"

"We're working on some leads," Anderson replied. "I'm afraid I can't say any more than that."

Murphy nodded. "A lot of people got fucked up. I saw it firsthand. I imagine DLH is really busy about now."

"Not just them," Anderson said. "All the area hospitals took patients. This is gonna get worse before it gets better."

Murphy nodded and stood against the car with his arms folded across his chest. He continued to watch the dead girl's family beside the grave. "Did you know her?"

Anderson shook his head although Murphy did not see the gesture. "No. I'm here on semi-official business. You?"

Murphy shrugged. "A little. Just from the club. I came mostly for Holly. She was close to the girl." He stopped and watched Holly's car pull away from the curb and disappear behind the mausoleum. "I'm not sure she knew I was here. She didn't look up much during the ceremony."

"Well, if she was friends with the victim that's understandable."

Murphy nodded again. He turned away from the remains of the funeral and pushed his sunglasses down to the bridge of his nose. "Listen, I saw something last night you might want to know about. It's not concrete evidence but I think it's pretty fucking suspicious."

Anderson had been watching the people at the open grave but he turned his eyes to Murphy. It had more to do with the man's tone of voice than with what he said. "Shoot."

Murphy licked his lips. "The first explosion was at the tilt-o-whirl, right?" When Anderson nodded Murphy continued. "Now, I missed that one. But the second one, the rotor, that one I saw as it happened. And something fucked up happened just before it blew." He related his observation of Atkins prior to the demise of the rotor and the Ferris wheel. He paused for breath only once and when he finished Anderson was already turning the key in the ignition.

Murphy stepped away from the car. "You know where Atkins is?"

"I'm gonna start at his father's house," Anderson replied. He slipped the transmission into drive and reached for the radio.

"Want me to come with?"

Anderson shook his head. "Hell, no. I'll have backup meet me at the residence. But I'll need you to stop by the station later to make a statement about what you just told me."

"Call me," Murphy said.

"No doubt." Anderson eased away from the curb and waited until he exited Lichgate before he hit both the flashers and the gas pedal.

****

Holly nearly pulled into her driveway before she thought better of it and continued down her street. She stopped at the intersection, made a U-turn and pulled next to the curb. She put the car in park and sat and stared down the street at the white cape she called home. She wondered if Cassandra was awake yet. She hoped not and her reason for doing so was selfish.

Gina's funeral sucked, as all funerals did. If Holly had to attend alone it would have sucked even more, perhaps to the point she would have had to make a discreet exit. She was determined to hold back the tears, but one look at the hole in the ground and Gina's parents and she lost all semblance of self-control. Thank God Luciana had been there. Even so it had been difficult to contain herself.

When it was over and they were making their way out of Lichgate Luciana took the small marijuana pipe from her pocketbook and fired it up. Before she knew what she was doing Holly grabbed the pipe from her and took a big hit. They spent the rest of the ride back to Luciana's apartment silently passing the pipe back and forth. It was the first time Holly smoked since she learned she was pregnant with Cassandra. It felt good, fucking *great*, actually, but it kicked in full force a few moments after she watched Luciana disappear into her apartment building. Holly did not know how she made it home. She also did not know if she would be able to handle Cassandra in her present state. Best to spend a few minutes and ride out the worst of it before she walked through the front door.

She pulled up her sleeve and looked at her discolored arm. The marks remained, but enough skin had peeled off that the wound no longer resembled a handprint. She looked as if she had had a close call in the kitchen...or at the fair. "Frost-nip," she said aloud. She touched the edges of the wound tenderly and winced at the pain. She coughed and rolled her sleeve back down. Somehow her mother had missed it this morning and Holly did not want her to notice now. She could not explain the origins of the wound to herself, let alone to anyone else. Best to keep it hidden for the present.

She turned on the radio and sat back and felt the effects of the green smoke Luciana provided. It felt good and it soothed her nerves but she still regretted it. She gave herself another ten minutes before she went home.

****

Anderson stopped his unit half a block from the Atkins residence and killed the flashers. There was no other police unit on the street so he sat back in the seat and waited. He could see the front of the house clearly from his vantage point. There was no panel truck either in front of the house or in the driveway and the thing was too big to be in the single car garage. The driveway was likewise empty, which meant the elder Atkins' car was inside the garage or nobody was home. Anderson did not know which option he would prefer.

The exterior of the house had seen better days. The wooden slats that made up the façade appeared rotted and several were missing. What little paint clung to them was the color of green vomit. The few remaining shudders were dark blue, almost black. Two large pine trees dominated the front yard and did a magnificent job of screening the house from sunlight. On the brightest days the house remained sheathed in shadow. It was said most towns had a house or two the children avoided walking past; in Deacon's Landing, this was the one.

It was not a new development. Even in Anderson's childhood the Atkins residence had served to scare the shit out of most kids. Being dared to enter the yard was a popular pastime with bullies and their hapless victims. On Halloween night the light on the front porch remained dark and no one dared toilet paper the house or write "cheap" on the windows with soap. The house had been in better shape back then, but only just. The years since Mrs. Atkins had run away and left Mr. Atkins to raise their son by himself had been less than kind to the residence.

Or to those within, Anderson thought.

He glanced at his watch. It had been seventeen minutes since he called for backup and still he had the street to himself. No dogs barked, no children ran though the sprinklers or rode their bicycles around the street. Even the adults were not in evidence. He thought about what that would mean if he went to the house by himself and came across Kenny Atkins. As much as he wanted to question the asshole there was no reason to rush in there.

Almost against his will he watched his hand move the gear lever into drive and his foot eased off the brake. His unit rolled slowly across the pavement until it came to a stop in front of the house. He looked through the side window even as he put the unit in park and turned off the motor.

The house was no prettier up close and for a moment Anderson was nine years-old again and racing past the house in order to spend as little time in its crosshairs as possible. He suppressed a shudder despite the eighty-two degrees and wished his backup would arrive. With more than a little surprise he watched himself open the car door and step out onto the pavement. He closed the door and looked up at the old Colonial.

The windows on the second story were black with dirt and pine needles and the glass looked ancient. *No tax credit for energy saver windows for you*, he thought. He walked slowly around his unit and peered down the short driveway. The one-car garage stood (*leaned* would have been a better term) at the driveway's end with its door closed. The windows in the garage door looked to be as old and dirty as those on the house. He watched himself walk down the driveway and he became aware his hand rested on the butt of the police issue in his holster. There was no sign of a threat, no sign of anything, but his hand remained there nonetheless.

He reached the garage and peered through the windows. There was just enough light filtering through the grime that he was able to see the garage was empty. A large and ancient oil stain covered most of the garage floor. Several wood cabinets that might have been manufactured around the time Gehrig made his farewell address at Yankee Stadium lined one wall. A large toolbox stood to one side; several drawers were open and numerous tools poked out from within the box like ribs protruding from a badly decomposed corpse.

Anderson peeled his eyes from the garage and looked about the backyard. It was in no better shape than the rest of the property. There was little in the way of grass and what there was grew in isolated patches. More pine trees were in evidence and the fallen needles felt like carpet beneath his shoes. He kicked a pine cone near him; it skidded and bounced across the yard and disappeared into what at one time was most likely a garden.

He approached that area of the yard, his hand still on the butt of his issue. Several gardening stakes jutted from the ground and leaned this way and that. A few sunflowers taller than Anderson bent toward the ground. The garden itself was overcome with weeds that strangled anything closer to ground level. If Atkins Sr. had any lettuce or squash plants down there they were doomed. He started to turn away from the garden when something at its center caught his eye. Anderson beheld the marijuana plants for only a moment before he smirked and made his way around the other side of the house. It was good to have a bargaining chip when dealing with an Atkins.

A sun porch that had been added onto the house back in the eighties poked out from the side. It seemed ridiculous with the pines from both the front and backyards providing an effective shield against any sunlight reaching the room. Both the screens and windows were closed and filthy. It was raised off the ground just enough that Anderson could not look inside. He caught sight of a ceiling fan spinning at full speed inside the porch and it bothered him for reasons he could not explain.

He made his way around to the front of the house and saw a second police unit pull up behind his. He walked to it and saw Daniels step out. The rookie greeted

Anderson with a half-assed salute and shut the door to his unit.

"Wassup, Anderson?" He slid his baton into his belt and regarded the house.

"Maybe nothing but keep your eyes open. Follow me."

"Right behind you." Daniels sounded eager.

Anderson had hoped it would not be one of the new hires that responded to his call, but he would take what he could get. Daniels seemed like an okay guy but he had not worked extensively with him since he came on board. Something that worked in his favor, however, at least as far as Anderson was concerned, was that Daniels had only just moved to Deacon's Landing when he was hired. That meant he knew nothing about the town's resident haunted house or the family who dwelled within. To him, it was simply another house, albeit one whose owners could not be bothered with anything resembling routine maintenance. That was fine with Anderson.

They moved up the front walk and reached the door. Anderson tried the doorbell and was utterly unsurprised to hear nothing from within the house. He glanced sideways at Daniels before he knocked on the screen door. They waited a few moments before Anderson repeated the knock.

Daniels reached past him and opened the screen. "DLPD," he said too loudly and wrapped his knuckles against the front door.

It swung open a few inches with a loud protest from its hinges. Daniels took a step back and looked at his partner. Anderson glanced at the kid in the policeman's uniform, but only for a moment. He leaned in closer to the open door. "Anyone home? This is the police department. Mr. Atkins?"

He heard nothing from within the house. He pushed the door open and peered inside. The small foyer led directly into the living room. Two ancient sofas, their stuffing hanging out of various tears in the fabric, took up most of the space in the large room. Two end tables and a coffee table that would not fit in Anderson's truck made up the balance of the furniture.

To their left was the dining room. The table looked to be large enough to accommodate twenty people although Anderson counted only a dozen chairs. One of them was clearly for show; one of its legs was broken six inches from the floor and supported by a short stack of books. One of the books appeared to be a bible.

Anderson could see no more from the front porch. He looked again at Daniels, nodded, and for the first time in his life he entered the Atkins house.

It was warm inside. More than warm. Anderson began to sweat almost immediately. *I wonder how much of that is due to the heat.* "Mr. Atkins? DLPD, sir. We need to speak with you." He received no reply. He moved forward and allowed Daniels enough room to come in behind him.

Old picture frames with equally old pictures inside them graced the walls of the dining room. It was dark and Anderson started to look for a light switch when Daniels beat him to it. An old chandelier which hung from the ceiling above the dining room table blazed to life. Far from making the room appear inviting, it instead reminded Anderson of a funeral parlor. The wallpaper was sickly green and its faded generic pattern reinforced the funeral parlor vibe. Anderson eyed each framed photograph as he passed. Most appeared to be very old, certainly old enough to predate Kenny Atkins' first appearance on earth. The children staring out from the photographs were more likely Kenny's parents judging by the style of their clothes. One was of Atkins Sr. during his days in the Navy. His uniform was crisp and faded and the look of pride that might once have been in those eyes had likewise dimmed with the passage of time.

It took him until the last photograph before he found one of Kenny. This, too, was faded with time. He appeared to be three or four years-old. He stared out from behind the glass with a wide smile that was minus one of his front teeth. Anderson thought of the punk kid in school and had a difficult time reconciling that with the young child in the photo. He appeared happy, an emotional state not normally associated with the kid unless he was tormenting someone at school. They moved away from the photograph.

There was an open doorway at the end of the dining room and to his right a narrow staircase ascended into the darkness of the second floor. "Mr. Atkins, this is the DLPD. Are you home?" Still nothing. He turned and motioned Daniels to the stairs. The rookie nodded and moved in that direction.

Anderson passed through the doorway and entered the kitchen. The small table was as old as everything else he had seen thus far. Its four rickety chairs stood covered with dust. There was some type of food in several bowls and plates on the tabletop but Anderson could not begin to guess what he was looking at. The food had turned long ago. Flies and gnats buzzed excitedly from bowl to dish and back again. He counted three ashtrays on the table, all of them filled to overflowing. A few half-smoked joints were visible among their legal cousins. The smell assaulted Anderson the closer he moved to the table.

He looked about the room, saw several cabinet doors and drawers half-open. The sink was piled high with more dishes and bowls. The ancient gas stove was covered with congealed grease and other substances Anderson could not identify. There was another open doorway at the other side of the kitchen and a closed door to his left. He did some quick calculations and guessed the closed door led to the sun porch. He shined his flashlight through the open doorway and saw it was a small den. An old black-and-white sat atop what looked to be a child's dresser. More old and neglected furniture adorned the room. He turned in the direction of the sun porch.

He heard Daniels ascend the stairs at a normal pace. The kid was not cautious. Anderson assumed Daniels' attitude was the product of his new-hire status and his unfamiliarity with Deacon's Landing's resident haunted house. He wanted to make a name for himself, that much was clear by his eagerness. Anderson hoped the rookie at least remembered his training and slowed things down a bit when he started to check the rooms on the second story.

Anderson approached the door to the sun porch. There was a window, but a curtain on the other side obscured the view of the room. The curtain might have been made of white fabric, but it was as grimy as everything else within the house. Anderson squinted through it anyway. He could see the silhouette of the ceiling fan spinning and he saw what looked to be another television. This one was larger than its companion in the den. It was also in color. The set was on and appeared to be tuned to a cooking show. He moved his eyes to the left and saw the outline of the man in the recliner.

Anderson knocked on the door. "Mr. Atkins? This is Officer Anderson of the DLPD. I need to ask you some questions, sir." He watched the man on the other side of the door not move a muscle in response. Anderson swallowed. "This doesn't look good," he said to the empty kitchen. He grasped the doorknob and turned it and opened the door.

If he had choked at the smell in the kitchen he nearly vomited when the stench within the sun porch assaulted him. It was almost a physical presence. He took a step back and instinctively covered his nose and mouth. His eyes squinted and began to tear. He waved at it and retreated another step and coughed. He fumbled around in his back pocket and retrieved the kerchief he kept there and held it to his nose. "Christ Almighty." The ceiling fan spun and scattered the smell into the kitchen. The odor seemed eager to spread itself throughout the house. He coughed into the kerchief.

Anderson forced himself to reenter the room and moved slowly to its center. His eyes never left the corpse in the recliner. Atkins Sr. sat as if he were engrossed with what was on the TV, but his viewing days were over. His t-shirt had probably been white at one time but was now the color of rust. The blood had come from his throat, which appeared to have been cut with something very sharp and serrated. The flesh around the wound was more torn than sliced. Anderson looked about the area around the recliner and saw the old hacksaw on the floor. Its teeth were stained with dried blood.

Anderson coughed again and turned away and dabbed at his eyes with the kerchief. The two words on the wall above the television set were written large in the victim's blood: **DARK ANNIE.** He did not know how long he stood and stared at the words, but apparently he held his breath as he did so. His lungs protested the lack of oxygen and even the stench within the room was preferable if not welcomed. It took more willpower than he thought himself capable of marshaling, but he turned his eyes from the wall.

Despite his strong desire to be anywhere else he leaned in closer to the corpse. The man had been dead a long time, a week or more, perhaps, although it was impossible to know. The process of decay had already turned the skin gray and mottled. His eyes were wide and expressionless; his mouth hung open and dried blood had caked at the corners and stained the stubble on his chin.

"Daniels!" he shouted. "Daniels, get down here now!"

It took only a moment before he heard Daniels pounding down the stairs. He charged into the kitchen and stopped short and covered his mouth with his hand. "What the fuck is that?" He sounded both surprised and offended. He advanced at a much slower pace and reached the doorway to the sun porch. "Jesus jumped-up Christ, that's bad!"

Anderson did not take his eyes from the corpse. "Get on the radio to dispatch. Call this in. Tell them we need detectives at this location and a forensics team." When the rookie did not move from the doorway, Anderson said, "*Now*, Daniels."

The older officer's tone of voice must have snapped Daniels back to his senses. He mumbled a "Yes, sir," and ran from the kitchen.

Anderson took a step back from the corpse. He glanced at the saw on the floor and the blood on its teeth and tried to image what that had felt like. He shuddered and walked slowly from the room. He did so backwards; he could not bring himself to turn his back on the corpse or the weapon.

Or of what had been written on the wall.

Chapter Eleven

Too many Eyes and Ears

Murphy arrived at the shop bright and early on Monday and started the coffee. He retrieved the newspaper and poured himself a cup and sat at his desk. The front page of the *Sentinel* contained a large photograph of the Atkins house with numerous police cars parked in front of it. An ambulance was there as well and two paramedics were wheeling a stretcher into the house. The headline was large and predictably sensationalist and in bold type: **1 FOUND MURDERED IN DL**. He skimmed through the article, but the police refused to identify the victim pending notification of next of kin. It would be obvious to anyone in town the victim had been either Atkins Sr. or Jr.; the house was too recognizable and infamous to be mistaken for any other residence.

He returned again to the photo and looked for Anderson but there were too many men in uniform on the scene and none faced the camera. Nonetheless Murphy knew he was there and he felt somewhat proud of himself for pointing the cops in the right direction. *As long as they don't mention my involvement,* he thought. *I've worked too fucking hard at this reputation to have it ruined now.*

All of page two concerned the incident at the fair. Several witnesses were interviewed as well as a lieutenant with the Connecticut State Police. The death toll had climbed to twenty-nine since Sunday morning. That number sounded low to Murphy and he thought, sadly, it would increase in the weeks ahead.

The articles and interviews were full of the bullshit he had come to expect whenever something unexpected and tragic occurred. He wondered how long it would be before the political and religious nut-jobs blamed their latest whipping boy, the gays, for what had happened. If what had occurred the other night made the national news (he had yet to see a CNN or Fox News truck in town) it was only a matter of time before some talking head or other blamed the whole thing on homosexuals and abortionists. He shook his head and turned the page.

He paused on page four and skimmed through the article about the stolen school bus. The photo which accompanied the article showed the buses lined up at the depot and a rather stern-looking man standing in an empty spot with his arms folded across his chest. "Yeah, good luck with that," Murphy said. "The cops are gonna be a little too busy the next few days to chase down some kids on a joyride." He put the paper on his desk facedown.

He went over the work orders but stopped after the first few. Was he really going to go back to the normal routine after what had happened Saturday night? Could fixing a starter solenoid or replacing a brake line really be considered that important after the incident at the park? He thought not. Then again, it might do some good to have the boys concentrate on something other than chaos and carnage. He had even softened his attitude concerning McGrath and Thompson and their leaving him behind when the excrement collided with the rotating oscillator. Maybe that solenoid and the rest of the repairs scheduled for the day were a blessing.

Murphy went through the rest of the work orders and sipped his coffee and waited for his employees to show up.

****

Atkins huddled in the dark. He pulled his knees to his chest and felt the cold cinder blocks at his back. He let one hand fall and land palm-up on the ice covering the concrete upon which he sat. The impact stung his knuckles but the pain registered only in a small corner of his mind. He was more aware of his breathing, which came in quick, shallow breaths. Sweat beaded on his forehead and his arms despite the frigid temperature inside the room. His hair hung in front of his eyes and he blew at it absently.

This was home now. He had tried to return to his father's house the night before but the street had been cordoned off by the cops. He had watched several cars turned back by the blockade, and the few that were allowed to pass had turned into driveways farther up the street. He had sat in his father's old Chrysler and contemplated his chances of being allowed past the roadblock. There was only one reason to see such a thing on that quiet road and that meant he could not return to his father's house. Ever.

So he had asked for a new home and she had invited him into hers. It was certainly large enough but it fell short when it came to creature comforts. His eyes fell again on the benches just a few feet in front of him. They would be marginally more comfortable than the concrete floor, but he had not been invited to make use of them and the last thing he wanted was to anger his new hostess. Best not to take chances.

Atkins thought about the ones he had already assembled and then of those he would be asked to gather.

It was a lot of work, but that did not bother him. His father's one saving grace had been instilling a sense of responsibility in his son. Or trying to. Kenneth Atkins took many years to learn that particular lesson.

It was not learned in high school; what little time he actually spent there consisted mainly of selling weed and cocaine to as many customers as he could create. When crack hit the big time he switched to that and watched in amazement as his customer base grew by leaps and bounds. He left high school in his third year and began to Ping-Pong between jail and living on the street. He broke the first rule of dealing and started to get high on his own supply. His father threw him out for good soon after that.

Atkins wandered around the state for some time, working odd jobs and never staying in one place for very long. He made it all the way to Miami once but the dealers there were big time and he learned very quickly what happened when you fucked with them. He peered through the darkness and fancied he could see the scars on his arms where the torches had touched his skin.

The reopening of Deacon's Landing Elementary School, now dubbed Deacon's Landing Magnet School, had made the national news and he watched the story on CNN while staying in a crack house that had working cable and electricity. And she had come to him in his stoned stupor and called him back home. He left the crack house and Miami that same night and hitchhiked his way north.

The highway sign read **ATLANTA 30 mi**. by the time a trucker took pity on him and let him in the trailer. Atkins spent the next day and a half bouncing around the inside of the trailer and stealing a bite from the pallets of groceries being shipped to New England. He wondered, although not often and never for long, when the withdrawal symptoms would hit him and they never did. Could it be possible he was one of the lucky ones who would never be represented on *Celebrity Rehab* or on anti-drug posters? It seemed so. He had kicked the habit without even trying. It was certainly because of *her*, and Atkins silently thanked her for her help even as he wished to God she had left him to whatever fate he had earned.

He had to walk from Fairfield and that part sucked. The rich cocksuckers gave no thought to picking him up and so he wandered up I95 and then Route 8. The rain washed the grime from his skin and clothes and provided a source of water. He ate road-kill a couple times just to put something in his stomach. He was never hungry or thirsty at any time during his trek back home, but some part of his brain insisted he take in sustenance.

When he crested a hill in Waterbury and looked down on the town of Deacon's Landing he sat down and masturbated until he vomited. He stayed on the hill, sitting with his legs crossed as if he were practicing yoga, and waited until the darkness came. Then he returned home.

She put him to work right away. After his father was gone she sent him to Baribeau Bros. with a specific mission. It was her idea to remove the surveillance tapes from the manager's office. Atkins was grateful for that; his mind no longer seemed to work properly and the thought never occurred to him. She told him how to rig the timers but left it up to him as to where to place the explosives. She seemed pleased with his choices.

She directed him to certain people in and around Deacon's Landing, but allowed him the freedom to execute his tasks as he saw fit. Some of the others were gone, out of state or out of this life. Those who still drew breath he would deal with eventually, but for now, he had enough targets to keep him in the vicinity of Deacon's Landing.

"There are so many," he said to the empty room. "The cops are stupid but they'll connect the dots sooner or later." He disliked what he was about to say and he hoped it would not anger her. "I won't be able to get them all."

She did not sound angry when she replied. If anything she sounded somewhat pleased with him, as if she were proud of a pupil who was finally showing signs of learning something. Her response was a single word and it filled him with light and satisfaction. Of course. He should have thought of it himself. His smile widened the cracks in his scabrous lips.

"Fisher," he repeated.

His voice would have echoed had he spoke loudly enough. Something as significant as this deserved to be heralded by something more than him pissing himself. Atkins slid slowly down the wall until he lay on the floor. He remained curled in the fetal position and rocked himself slowly back and forth. "Fisher," he said and smiled again.

Atkins fell asleep and dreamed of his old friend.

****

Holly's shift at Lucky's ended at seven and she said good-bye to Vince (who insisted on another hug) and walked out to the parking lot. She removed her keys from her pocketbook and unlocked her door. Two cars pulled into the lot and Holly recognized one of the drivers as a regular. She waved to him and smiled and slid behind the wheel.

It had been a light shift, which she expected given what had occurred at the fair. She was thankful for the few customers who showed up. She hadn't made much in the way of tips, but the summer was almost over and Cassandra would be back in school and she would have fewer expenses. As long as there were no unexpected car repair bills or other such expenditures they would be fine.

She pulled out of the lot and headed home. She stopped at the light and reached down and turned on the radio. Katrina and the Waves filled the car and Holly looked dubiously at the radio. "Really?" she asked. WERD usually stuck to what was now considered classic rock and roll; she was used to hearing Cinderella and Queensryche and maybe a little Bon Jovi. *How did this shit make it on the air?* Someone must have requested it.

She was about to change the station when she glanced in her rearview and was greeted by the man in her backseat. Holly gasped and her heart nearly stopped. Her first instinct was to scream but she found she could not utter a sound. The man who was formerly a social studies teacher at Deacon's Landing Elementary School reached forward and pressed something cold and metallic against her throat. Holly froze.

"Drive," Ford said. "And don't break the speed limit or try anything stupid. Understand?"

She stammered but managed to get out, "Please. I have a daughter."

"Then you should do as I ask, should you not?"

Holly nodded as much as the steel against her throat allowed. When the light turned green she eased onto the accelerator and turned onto Saugus Ave. She stopped at the next light and looked sideways into the next lane. A young girl in a blue Prius pulled up to the light next to them. Holly willed the girl to look over, but she was too busy gabbing animatedly on her cell. When the light turned green again Holly hit the gas and wished the girl dead.

Ford told her which turns to make and Holly made them. She did not like the area into which she was driving. It was isolated with woods on both sides of the road. *A perfect place for a body to be found later.* She pushed the thought from her mind. Nothing mattered but doing what Ford told her and surviving to see her daughter again. Her palms were covered with sweat and it forced her to tighten her grip on the steering wheel. She felt a drop of it slide down her cheek.

They came to the bridge which spanned the Naugatuck River and Ford ordered her to stop at the midway point. Holly pulled off to the side and put the Honda in park. "Please," she said. "Please don't hurt me."

"Shut up," Ford hissed. He turned and looked back the way they had come. He seemed satisfied with the lack of traffic and returned his attention to Holly. "You were there, I know you were. DLES, right?"

Holly nodded perhaps a bit too vigorously. "Yes."

"I thought I recognized your name in the newspaper. Who was your teacher, Riggi or Levine?"

"Riggi. Are you going to kill me?" The question was out before she knew she was going to ask. Tears streamed from the corner of her eyes.

"Riggi," Ford repeated. His voice dripped contempt. "She completely coked out after the fire. Did you know that? Lost her job, started walking the streets for a living, if you know what I mean." He licked his lips. "Oh, of course you know. You work at a strip club. I bet you know all about that kinda thing."

Holly's breath hitched in her throat. She managed to get out a single word. "Please."

"I tried to stay with it," Ford continued as if Holly had not spoken. "Got a job teaching at a private school in

Hartford. It didn't work out. Wound up in the insurance business. But I was never built for that bullshit. I was a *teacher*. Do you understand?"

She did not but she nodded nonetheless. She cast a quick glance at the rearview but saw no cars headed in their direction. The sky was growing dark and several streetlights had come on since they left Lucky's. Was Ford stalling for time? Waiting for the sky to get dark enough so he could kill her with no chance of being spotted if someone happened to drive past? Holly thought that was precisely his plan.

He looked over his shoulder again, saw the same absence of cars coming in their direction. "And now it's all over. I'll never teach again." He leaned over and opened his door. He stepped out slowly and managed to keep the cold metal pressed against Holly's throat. "Get out," he said.

Holly reached for the door handle slowly. Her door was open no more than an inch or two when Ford grabbed it and yanked it open all the way. She gasped and more tears spilled down her cheeks. He pulled the knife around the door frame and reapplied it before Holly could take a breath. He grabbed her arm and pulled her from the car. He spun her around and pressed her against the rear passenger door.

"Please don't kill me."

"Shut up," he said almost matter-of-factly. "This isn't going to end well."

Holly thought of Cassandra and what this was likely to do to her. She would not be alone in the world; the girl's grandmother would take her in and love her and care for her. But she would live her life knowing her mother had been murdered. Holly hated the image of Cassandra crying herself to sleep at night and her mother aging and trying to provide for the girl. It made her angry, something she had not anticipated since she saw Ford's bruised face in her rearview. She gritted her teeth.

"I'm sorry it has to be like this," Ford said.

"Mr. Ford, you don't have to do this." Her voice was calmer than before but it still quivered. "Put the knife down and we'll talk about it. I won't go to the police, I promise."

"I had no intention of attacking that stripper. I was sitting there enjoying the lap dance and the next thing I knew I was beating her with both fists. I didn't even realize something had happened until that gorilla pinned me to the floor." He took a shuddering breath. "It was all her fault, not mine."

Holly's eyes flashed anger and her hands curled into fists. Knife at her throat or not, she could not allow the murdering bastard to justify his actions by blaming Gina. "That's a lie," she hissed. "Gina was a sweet girl. She didn't deserve what you did to her."

With a roar that was more bestial than human Ford yanked her off her feet and dragged her toward the other side of the bridge. Holly gulped and struggled to maintain her balance. There was more strength in him than she would have guessed and it took several moments before she got her feet under her again. She grasped the top of the safety rail and looked down into the semidarkness. She could see the river flowing perhaps thirty feet below. It was wide at this juncture and the water did not flow rapidly. She could barely make out the rocks that jutted from various points and she calculated the odds of avoiding those rocks when Ford pitched her over the side. *Assuming he doesn't cut my throat first.* She decided Cassandra would be an orphan either way.

Ford was pressed against her back again and the blade returned to her throat. "Not your friend," he hissed. "I wasn't talking about the stripper. I meant *her.*"

At first Holly looked about to see if there was a third person who had somehow joined them when she wasn't looking. The bridge and, unfortunately, her entire field of vision, were devoid of people. Her confusion lasted only a moment before the anger returned. She did not or care who this "her" was any more than she cared to listen to Ford's insane rambling. She placed both hands on the safety rail and braced herself. She had no choice but to go on the offensive. If she surprised him enough she might be able to get back to her car before he could recover. She felt she had to take the chance.

"She made it up to me, though, I guess," Ford said with a snort. "Got me out of jail." He held his left arm out in front of Holly. "Even if she did get a little rough with me."

Holly looked at his arm. There was a patch of dead flesh that looked precisely like the mark on her own arm. Her breath caught in her throat.

"She told me I could walk right past the guards. And you know what? I did just that. It was fucking weird, let me tell you. It was like I was the invisible man. Claude Rains, move the fuck over." His snort became a laugh but it lasted only a moment.

When he spoke again, his voice had once again become calm. "She wanted me out of there so she could take care of me like she's doing with the others. Considering what we did to her, what *I* did to her..." He shook his head. "Not gonna happen. Not to me, sweetheart." He looked at her solemnly, as if he was about to impart something very profound and important. "We're all dead."

The hitch in his voice made her forget momentarily about the blade. She turned and saw the tears brimming in his eyes. He stepped away from her and the blade vanished over the side of the bridge. He pulled himself onto the top of the rail and locked eyes with Holly. He leaned back slowly, gently, his arms outstretched like the wings of a bird of prey. "She'll see to that, you mark my words." He leaned further back until gravity grabbed hold and he disappeared over the side.

Holly gasped and looked over the rail. She watched Ford land on several small rocks. There was a spray of blood darker than the water around it. His arms and legs smashed into the water with enough force they bounced out. The sound of the impact caused Holly's stomach to constrict and for a moment she thought she would vomit.

Ford remained pinned to the rocks for only another moment. The river pulled eagerly at his limbs and it rolled him onto his side and enveloped him. He surfaced again perhaps ten or twelve feet farther downstream. He was facedown and his arms remained outstretched as if he were trying to fly. Somehow she could still see the mark on his arm.

Holly watched until she could no longer see the body. Then she bolted for her car.

****

Fisher sat in his living room and cursed the television. His beloved Sox were down to their last out and trailed 7-2. It would not be so bad if they were playing anybody other than the fucking Yankees. Pedroia stepped to the plate and took a few practice swings, but Fisher had no illusions about how the game would end. He picked up the beer can on the end table next to him and found it empty. He cursed this, too, and got up and walked to the refrigerator.

He returned to the sofa and cracked it open and upended the can as Pedroia flied out to shallow right. If there was one saving grace about this it was that he was not listening to the game on the radio; John Sterling's usual cry of, "Yankees win! *Theeeee* Yankees *win!*" grated on his nerves like little else. Even his job did not annoy him as much as that call.

It had been a shitty shift but that was hardly outside the norm these days. He had no one to blame but himself, of course, and that angered him even more. He knew the job was shit when he agreed to accept it. He took it because being a security guard at one of the larger telecommunications corporations in the country had seemed ridiculously easy. The pay could be better but really, how could he refuse a job when it consisted mostly of walking around an empty building and stealing a little jerk-off time in the ladies' room when the mood struck? But it had quickly become boring and he took to popping caffeine pills just to make it to the end of his shift. Then to come home and watch his team get crushed...It was insult added to injury and it seemed to be happening more frequently with each passing day.

He changed the channel and caught the local news. They were still talking about the murder of Atkins Sr. and Fisher wished the story would just go away. The man had been a douchebag as long as he had known him. He still remembered how he had tanned Kenny's ass and threatened to do the same to Fisher when he caught them smoking cigarettes behind the house. Normally Fisher would have dared the man to hit him but that strategy would not have worked on the elder Atkins any more than it would have worked on his son. Either would gladly take him up on his offer and so Fisher had kept his mouth shut and watched his friend beaten nearly unconscious. The lesson was not lost on Kenny; to Fisher's knowledge the kid never touched another cigarette again, although he found other vices later. Fisher chose simply not to smoke around Mr. Atkins and that was that.

And now someone had taken him out of the game of life like Lester should have been taken out before Cano hit the grand salami. Fisher watched the images of the Atkins house on the screen and smiled. *Good. Fuck him. However it went down I hope it hurt. Serve the prick right.* He smiled again and polished off his beer.

He was on his way to the fridge to get another when he heard the knock at his front door. He stopped and glanced at the clock on the microwave. It read, 11:14 PM. "Who the fuck is this?" He opened the refrigerator and pulled out a fresh soldier and returned to the living room.

The knock repeated itself just as he was about to sit down. He swore and stomped to the door. He removed the chain and threw the door open and the angry words he had prepared died in his throat.

He had not seen Kenny Atkins in years, not since he fled Deacon's Landing for parts unknown in the mid-90s. But there was no mistaking the identity of the badly-disheveled and dirty man who stood in the hallway outside his door. "Atkins," Fisher said.

Atkins' lips pulled back from blackened teeth and he said, "Danny. How's it going?"

"What do you want?"

The smile remained in place. "I want to come in. Aren't you going to invite me?"

"What are you, a fucking vampire?" He stepped to the side and motioned for his uninvited guest to enter the apartment. Atkins' smile widened and revealed more teeth in desperate need of dental work and he stepped across the threshold. He took a few steps inside and Fisher closed the door behind him. He did not reattach the chain.

Atkins looked about the apartment with his hands on his hips. "Not a bad place you got here. Reminds me of an apartment I had in Miami."

"Is that where you got off to?" Fisher walked around him and resumed his place on the sofa. He cracked open the beer and lit a cigarette. His eyes fell on the television and a reporter was still standing in front of the Atkins house. Fisher picked up the remote and went back to the previous channel. The NESN announcers on the post-game show were trying to put a positive spin on the disaster at Fenway but Fisher wasn't listening.

"Among other places," Atkins said. "Mind if I sit down?"

Fisher waved at the recliner next to the sofa. "Knock yourself out."

Atkins took the offered seat and glanced at the television. "Sox got their asses kicked again, I see. Oh well, what are you gonna do? And you could have left it on the news. I don't care. It's not like I don't know about it."

Fisher took a sip of beer. "I'm sorry about your dad, bro." It was an outright lie, but he assumed it was expected of him to express sympathy. "He was great guy."

"He was an asshole."

Fisher paused in mid-sip. He suppressed a cough and put the beer back on the end table. He puffed on his cigarette. "Do the cops know who did it?"

"They probably have a good idea, yeah. But listen, I'm not here to talk about that. I need you for something. Are you in?"

Fisher tilted his head slightly and picked up his beer again. "What is it? You know I'm working full time now? So if you want my help on some kind of pick-up or deal you have going down I'm not interested."

Atkins leaned forward and rested his elbows on his knees. He laced his fingers and said, "That's not the Danny

Fisher I know. That motherfucker was always down for some shit."

"I have bills to pay," Fisher replied. "The bitch really fucked me in the divorce. I have child support payments to make and rent and alimony and all that other shit. I don't do things like that anymore."

"I disagree." He reached into his back pocket and produced a large knife. He held it up to the light and seemed to admire it. He turned it slowly in his hand.

Fisher's breath caught in his throat. He leaned back on the sofa and held up one hand. "Whoa, man, don't do anything stupid."

"And what would that be?" He continued to turn the knife slowly. "We're friends, right? We go back a long way. And I'm telling you I need your help."

Fisher swallowed and clasped his hands together to stop them from shaking. His heart hammered in his chest and he felt the color drain from his face. "With—with what, exactly?"

Atkins smiled but it never quite reached his eyes. The blade caught the light from the lamp and reflected onto his gaunt features. "All those cocksuckers who got away from us back then, the ones who did us wrong and lived to talk about it." He brought the knife down with enough force it drove itself into the end table. The beer can and the ashtray tumbled off and landed on the carpet. Fisher made no move to recover either. "That's what I need your help with."

Fisher stared at the knife for several moments. He thought about throwing himself at Atkins before he could free the knife. He outweighed the man by at least one hundred pounds but he did not like his chances. Atkins was a crazy son of a bitch, always had been, but he seemed to have taken his insanity to a whole new level. He had always been slightly nervous around him, but this was something altogether different. This was not nervousness; this was terror.

"Um, okay, sure. Why not, right?" He licked his lips and his hands fidgeted. All he had to do was get some distance between himself and the crazy fucker and he would run faster than Jesse Owens to the first cop he saw. But that was for later. "Who's first on the list?"

Atkins told him. At first the name was unfamiliar to him. Then it dawned on him and his eyes went wide and his mouth hung open. Fisher tried to stop his hands from shaking long enough to light another cigarette.

****

Anderson wended his way through the reporters and bystanders and reached the riverbank. Despite the late hour there were numerous people present. Not for the first time he cursed the asshole who invented police scanners. Lyons and Ferguson were in the process of lifting the large and mangled body of Benjamin Ford onto a stretcher.

Markowitz and Daniels pitched in and between the four of them they managed to get the body secured. Ferguson covered the corpse with a sheet but Ford had not been a small man and Anderson felt a second sheet would be needed. The paramedics either disagreed or did not have another sheet because they pushed the gurney up the hill and toward the ambulance with the man's arms sticking out from either side. Several gasps escaped from the crowd. Anderson watched them load the body into the ambulance and close the rear doors.

He had arrived at the station in time to watch Holly leave in her Honda. He read her statement and joined the search for Ford's body. He was farther upriver when the call from Markowitz came over the radio. He did not expect a crowd beyond a few reporters and he was surprised to see how many people had come to watch the escaped murderer's body taken from the riverbank. He moved them back to allow the ambulance to leave and he spoke with Markowitz about the discovery.

He was on his way back to his unit when he spotted Smith in the crowd. The man waved him over. Anderson moved through the crowd and he and Smith separated themselves from everyone else. Anderson noted how frightened the former teacher seemed.

"Mr. Smith," Anderson said.

"I'm surprised I had to come looking for you, Mr. Anderson. I expected you to pay me a visit after what happened at the fair."

"I've been kinda busy," Anderson replied. For no obvious reason he flashed back to the banner in the trunk of his police unit. He swallowed hard.

"So I've heard." He looked at the body on the stretcher and shook his head. "Poor Ben. Can't say as I'm surprised, though. Not after what he did to that dancer."

"You knew him."

Smith cocked an eyebrow in Anderson's direction. "Of course. We worked at the same school for six years."

He leaned in close but it was unnecessary; no one was near them and the crowd's attention was still focused on the riverbank. "Are you on-duty tomorrow?"

Anderson shook his head. "As a matter of fact, no. It's my day off."

"Good. Come to my house." He lowered his voice and Anderson had to strain to hear him. "We need to talk."

"Why can't we talk here?"

It was Smith's turn to shake his head. "Too many eyes and ears around here. Come by tomorrow, say, eight o'clock."

"In the morning?" Anderson looked at his watch. He would be off-duty in thirty minutes. That would not allow for much sleep. He looked at Smith skeptically.

"Yes, in the morning." He sounded annoyed. As annoyed as Anderson felt. "What, too early for you?"

"If you're going to make a statement about what you and the others were talking about at the fair you should come down to the station."

Smith shook his head. "Not a chance. My house or nothing. What's it gonna be?"

Anderson frowned. "Okay, but this better be worth it."

"It will be."

He walked away from Anderson and got in his car and drove away. Anderson watched him go.

Chapter Twelve

Wait 'til This Song is Over

Their first order of business was to ditch Atkins' 89 Lebaron. When Fisher saw the car sitting in the parking lot of his apartment building he knew beyond doubt Atkins had murdered his father. If he allowed himself to be completely honest he had suspected as much when he first heard about the elder Atkins. What little doubt he still entertained went by the boards when he saw the car. It followed the cops would be searching for the rust bucket so they would need alternative means of transportation. Fisher did not bother to act surprised when Atkins announced they would be using his Explorer.

The old Foy factory on Route 6 was ideal. It had been closed for years and the property was an eyesore which the state wanted gone. Without funds for demolition and no buyers the old factory lingered and slowly surrendered itself to the elements. It was not patrolled, nor was it alarmed, Atkins assured him. They set off for it.

Fisher was unsurprised that Atkins had him take the lead. Had he been so obvious in his desire to ditch him and head for the nearest cop? He did not believe so, but Atkins must have sensed something. He had not threatened him, at least not directly, but he felt Atkins' eyes on him since they walked out of the apartment.

Each side road they passed, each intersection they came to, Fisher thought of just gunning the Explorer and making a break for it. Atkins' old Lebaron would have had little chance of keeping pace with the powerful V8 under the Explorer's hood, but each time the opportunity came and went and Fisher remained on course for the factory. At the last intersection before the turnoff he looked longingly at the darkened road to his right. All it would take was a sharp turn of the wheel and a heavy foot on the accelerator and he would leave Kenny Atkins behind. He managed to turn the wheel an inch or two in that direction but he stopped himself. He slammed his open palm on the steering wheel several times and turned up the factory driveway. He wiped at the tears in his eyes and made deals with God he honestly intended to keep.

And yet he found himself in the parking lot of the long-dead factory.

He stopped the Explorer twenty feet from the factory wall. Atkins pulled up next to him and indicated the partially collapsed wall to their right. "I'll be parking in there. Get out of your truck."

Fisher did as he was told. He walked around to the front of the Explorer and leaned against the bumper. He watched the Chrysler disappear slowly into the shadows that enveloped the building's interior until all he could see were its brake lights. A moment later they winked out and Fisher heard the engine die. He heard the door open and then close and thought, *This is it. My last chance. Get in the truck and go, asshole.* He did not. Atkins emerged from the darkened interior of the building and walked slowly to Fisher. He opened the Explorer's passenger door and stepped into the vehicle.

Fisher looked longingly at the darkness within the factory and wished he'd had the balls to move while Atkins was still inside. He turned and saw him sitting in the SUV and waiting patiently for Fisher to join him. Fisher swallowed hard and opened the door. The Explorer fired right up and they pulled away from the old factory.

"I'm gonna need directions," he said. "I have no idea where he lives."

"I'll get you there, don't worry."

In point of fact Fisher was not worried at all. If he believed in anything it was in Atkins' ability to do exactly what he planned to do. He did not know how his old friend came by the information, but he trusted its accuracy. They turned onto the main road and Atkins directed him to make a left. Fisher did as ordered.

Atkins said, "Walking on Sunshine." He leaned forward and turned on the radio and Katrina and the Waves filled the Explorer's interior.

Fisher did not bother to ask how he managed that.

****

Anderson pulled up in front of Smith's house and was not surprised to see the older man sitting on his front porch. He was reading the morning paper and sipping at his coffee, but he took a moment to wave. Anderson waved back and turned off the Chevy. He yawned, but the cold morning air that greeted him when he opened the door kept him awake and alert and he was thankful for it. It made him remember to pull the small notepad from above his visor before he closed the door.

Smith had a small patio set on his front porch and he sat facing the street. The cup in his hand released coffee-scented steam into the gray sky. An unlit cigar and a single wooden match sat in the ashtray on the table. "Good morning, Mr. Anderson," he said with a nod and a smile.

"Good morning," Anderson replied as he mounted the steps to the front porch. "Kinda cold to be sitting out here, no? Overcast and damp." He glanced at the front page of the paper and saw a photograph of the scene at the riverbank.

Smith had returned to his newspaper. He spoke without looking up. "Yeah, it's gonna rain like a son of a bitch."

Anderson waited a moment, then two, but the older man seemed content to read his newspaper and sip his coffee. Anderson cleared his throat and reached for the notepad in his back pocket. "Mr. Smith, if you have something to tell me shouldn't we get on with it? I'd rather not spend my entire day off standing on your front porch. Nothing personal."

Smith waved a dismissive hand in the air. "If you're so inclined. But we'll go inside. What I have to tell you is dark enough without storm clouds hanging over our heads." He scooped up his coffee and left the newspaper on the table. He opened his screen door and motioned Anderson inside.

"I'm getting myself another cup of coffee. Do you want one?"

"Sure, if it's no trouble," Anderson replied and looked about the living room. Smith's house was of the same style as Holly Wayne's and it was most likely built around the same time. It was of identical layout and he even had a similar dry sink in the same place Holly chose for hers. There were no photographs on Smith's walls but there were a number of small paintings that looked like they came from Sears or Penny's. The furniture was nondescript but looked comfortable.

Anderson entered the kitchen in time for Smith to hand him a cup. He nodded in the direction of the small, round kitchen table and Anderson took a chair. He waited patiently for Smith to join him. The old man turned on a small transistor radio on the counter and reduced the volume to a background buzz. When he sat down he placed a cup of sugar and a quart of milk on the table. Anderson took out his pad and opened it and pulled the pen from his shirt pocket.

Smith gripped his cup with both hands and stared into the dark, swirling liquid for several moments. He cleared his throat more than once before he spoke. "I asked you about Ann Carlson, remember? That was her name before she became known as Dark Annie. She came to DLES in January of eighty-five, just after the Christmas break. She replaced Maureen Petrillo, who had taken a more lucrative position at a private school in Manhattan." Smith paused to sip his coffee. "You have to understand the pay back then was miserable, even more than it is today, at least in the public sector. We were sorry to see her go. She was a damned good teacher. Kids loved her."

"I don't remember her," Anderson said. "But I was still in St. Mark's School then. I went to DLES the following fall." He took a sip of his coffee and tried to hide his reaction to the unpleasant, bitter taste. He reached for the sugar.

Smith continued as if Anderson had not spoken. "The male teachers liked Ann immediately. She was gorgeous. Long black hair, hourglass figure, big tits. And she took care of her appearance, you know? She cared what others thought of her. She didn't overdo it on the makeup, her hair was always just right. She taught eighth grade science and math, and her male students were old enough to appreciate her, too. I imagine she caused more than a few of them to pleasure themselves at night when they were alone with their thoughts." He took another sip from his cup. "Some of us, too." He let out a short bark of a laugh.

"There was some remodeling going on in the lower level of the school. Ben Ford's brother was head of the contractors' union and he ran the whole thing. Big job, would take all summer. That's why they started it while school was still in session. The boys' and girls' locker rooms were being renovated and believe me when I tell you the guys working down there always loved it when Ann had to take her class to and from.

"The female teachers weren't crazy about her, though." He smiled and the smile quickly turned into a laugh. "Riggi, Verrastro, Boutote, they didn't like her at all. It didn't take them long to start whispering behind her back. That she fucked her way into the school, about how she dressed, you name it. I'm sure Ann heard some of it but if she did she didn't seem to care. She went about her business in a professional manner."

Anderson stopped writing and held up a hand. "Mr. Smith, what does any of this have to do with what you and your friends were talking about when I saw you at the fair? Both you and Verrastro implied children were in danger. Can we get to that part?"

Smith eyed him with obvious impatience. He had apparently slipped back into teacher mode and he regarded Anderson as a student who had just interrupted a lesson. But they were not in school and Anderson did not much care if the man was offended. He was not in the business of being polite.

"All of this is relevant, Officer Anderson. I wish it wasn't. I wish we did not need to have this conversation. But we do. So sit there and take your notes. Understood?"

Anderson bit his tongue, but said nothing. His pen hovered above the page.

"By the time the school year ended in June, Ann had become my favorite colleague. It wasn't just that she was pretty—the men of my generation called a pretty woman a 'dish,' if you can believe that—it was her personality, as well. She was always happy, always smiling. She referred to her students as her children, as if she had given birth to each and every one of them. You know, she didn't hand out a single detention for the six months she was there. Not a one. That you don't have to write down, I guess. Sorry. Got a little off-track there."

He finished off his coffee with the next sip. "It was at the end-of-year party that things started to go downhill. Y'see, several of the female teachers did a little digging and found out Ann had had an affair with the father of one of the students. Wasn't even her student, they probably just saw each other at a parent-teacher night and things happened, as they sometimes do. You might know who I'm talking about. You found the guy's body a couple of days ago, right?"

Anderson stopped writing and blinked at Smith. "Atkins?"

Smith nodded. "That's the one. No idea what she saw in an asshole like that but I guess the rumor was believable enough. The story stayed out of the papers, but Atkins' wife knew and she left him not long after that. Left her kid behind, too."

Anderson flashed back to the Atkins residence and the sight of Atkins Sr. sitting in his recliner and watching a cooking show with eyes that no longer saw.

"No accounting for taste," Anderson mumbled.

"Excuse me?"

Anderson shook his head. "Nothing. Forget it. You were saying?"

"Apparently these teachers went to Miss Renna, who was the VP, but she didn't think it warranted her involvement. Neither did Mr. Gwiazdoski, the principal, because nothing ever came of it. Until later, of course."

"What do you mean by that?"

Smith sat back in his chair and folded his hands behind his head. "Well, that affair she had with Atkins started Verrastro going. She did some more digging and found out Ann had had affairs with a few other fathers at some other schools. According to her, Ann had been sleeping with these men left and right. I don't know how much of it was true, but does it really matter? The stories were out there. The damage was done.

"That summer Ben Ford was getting married. This was big news. You wouldn't know it to look at him, but Ben was loaded." He paused and looked into his empty cup. "Or, more accurately, his family was. His father was the richest man in town back then. The old man didn't sit on the town council, but believe me, he had every single one of them in his pocket. Police department, too. It was assumed the old man even ran the contractors' union for his eldest son. The union wasn't corrupt, not exactly, but they were very amenable to what the Fords had to say. Know what I mean?

"Anyway, Ben had a stag party and I was there. We started at the Elks Club before the party moved to Lucky's. We walked in, a bunch of us already drunk and more than a little horny from watching the porn movies Ben's brother-in-law provided at the Elks. And who do you think we saw dancing on the stage?"

For an instant Anderson did not know. Then he said, "It had to be Ann Carlson."

Smith nodded. "You're right. It took me a second to recognize her. You have to understand, when you know someone only in a certain context and then you see them like that, it takes the brain a minute to process the information. I think those of us who knew her from the school recognized her all at the same time. I stood there with my jaw on the floor and my eyes bugging out of my skull. And she was *hot*. That was another thing about it. She was at that moment the most gorgeous woman I had ever seen."

Anderson tapped the ball of his pen slowly onto his notebook. "Okay, so she was working as a stripper during the summer."

"Right. Most of us worked another job during July and August. If you wanted to keep food on the table and the air conditioners running you didn't have much choice. This was how Ann earned her money."

Anderson flipped the page and continued writing.

"She wasn't ashamed when she saw us. She waved and kept dancing to that 'Walking on Sunshine' song and when we sat next to the stage she came over and danced for us. Ben, especially, was interested in keeping her attention. And since he was the groom-to-be, the rest of us just kept handing him dollar bills so she would hang out on our side of the stage." He paused for breath. "The nickname Dark Annie was created that night. It was mostly because of her black hair, but there was another reason. One of Jack the Ripper's earlier victims was a prostitute named Annie Chapman. She was known as Dark Annie, too, also because of her hair color." He leaned across the table. "See, it all fit, at least in our highly inebriated minds. One was a hooker, one was a stripper. What's the difference?" His voice became a whisper. "Add to that all the alleged lovers Ann had in her life..." His voice trailed off for a moment before he said, "Things went south after that."

Anderson swallowed and tried to ignore the chill he suddenly felt on his arms. "How so?"

"We closed down the bar that night." His voice was still a whisper and Anderson had to strain to hear him. "Well, a few of us did. Most of Ben's buddies had split by then, but I was still there. We waited in the parking lot for Ann and when she came out Ben started talking her up. She had changed into this long, black evening dress that wouldn't have been out of place at a high society shindig. Ben wanted to take her home that night and he made no secret of it. Ann was hesitant, but she must have had a few drinks in her, too, because she eventually agreed. They got in his car and off they went." He stopped and looked at Anderson. "That was the last time I saw Ann Carlson. She was reported missing a few days later when the strip club's owner got tired of seeing her car in the parking lot."

"You think Ford had something to do with her disappearance." It was not a question.

Smith threw his arms in the air and then rubbed his eyes. "I don't know. I'd like to think not. The guy was a friend of mine, you know? But he was also a bit of a bull-shitter. Ben said nothing happened between them and that she left his place later that night. But it was always in the back of my mind that the last time I saw her she was getting into his car. It's easy enough to imagine things getting out of control once they got back to Ben's place. Maybe she changed her mind or maybe Ben was so wasted he couldn't perform. He did have a temper, I can tell you that."

Anderson placed his notepad and his pen on the tabletop. "Mr. Smith, what does any of this have to do with children being in danger? I'm sorry, but I don't see the connection."

"Don't you?" He stood and walked to the counter again. He turned on the coffee maker and tapped his cup gently on the countertop while he waited.

Anderson thought back to the day Deacon's Landing Elementary School belched smoke into the autumn sky. He thought of the woman in the smoke and flames who screamed but not, apparently, in pain. He remembered being pushed through the door by Mrs. Plaza and the look on Mr. Ruiz's face as he whispered to another teacher, "Dark Annie." He tried to swallow but his throat was bone dry. He finished the putrid coffee with one pull. It tasted even worse cold but it did the job.

"You think she's still there." And all at once it hit him. The final words of Jeffrey Newcombe and Regina Saunders. "Holy Jesus."

"I think it's *possible*. I don't know for sure. But if anyone in Deacon's Landing had the resources to make someone disappear it was old man Ford. Oh, there were search parties and fliers all over town. We looked everywhere but she never turned up. And Ben's father had enough clout to make the police department launch a half-assed investigation, too." The coffee maker dinged and

Smith reached for it. "I think if any of the cops got too close to the truth they would suddenly be given a higher priority case."

Anderson held up both hands. "Hang on. You're saying the DLPD *intentionally* screwed up the investigation?"

"You really have no idea how powerful Ben Ford's family was back then. All someone had to do was suggest Ann left town. There was no evidence she didn't. Eventually, people simply stopped asking questions about Ann Carl—"

Smith stopped suddenly, frozen in place. His eyes were wide, his mouth open as if he were lip-synching a heavy metal scream. The coffee continued to pour from the pot and it overflowed the cup and ran all over the counter and his hand. He did not react to the scalding liquid.

Anderson leaped to his feet and ran the few steps to Smith's side. He upended the coffee pot and grabbed it from the old man's stiff hand. "What are you doing?" Anderson placed the coffee pot in the sink. He tried to take the cup from Smith's hand but the older man's fingers were vice-like in their grip. "Mr. Smith, Mr. Smith, what's wrong?" He instinctively reached for the mic clipped to his collar before he remembered he was off-duty and out of uniform. He took a single step toward the phone on the wall next to the table when he heard something that stopped him in his tracks.

He turned and approached Smith again slowly. His eyes moved past the former teacher and settled on the radio. Anderson reached out a hand that suddenly shook and turned up the volume. A woman's voice proclaimed quite excitedly she was walking on sunshine and asked if it felt good.

Anderson looked from the radio to Smith. Then there was a sharp pain that stabbed into the back of his head and the world went dark.

****

Fisher bolted into the kitchen in time to see someone collapse to the floor. Atkins placed the tire iron back in his belt and regarded the man at his feet. Then he turned his full attention to the older man with the overflowing coffee cup who stood next to the counter. The old man turned, saw the two new arrivals in his kitchen. The coffee cup fell from his hand. It shattered on the floor and the hot, black liquid splashed on the walls, the cabinets and the younger man who lay face-down on the linoleum. Fisher leaned against the open doorframe and folded his arms across his chest. He was not particularly fond of what was going to happen next.

The first one had shocked him. He barely remembered Mr. Ruiz and had not recognized him when they saw him on his morning jog. But Atkins had made him screech to a halt in front of the man and he'd jumped out and went to work on him. Fisher watched from behind the wheel until he threw open his door and purged his stomach of the fast food burgers they had picked up before the drive-thru closed for the night. He continued to wretch until Atkins opened the lift gate in the back of the Explorer and loaded the body inside.

Two more former members of the Deacon's Landing Elementary School faculty had joined Ruiz in the back of the SUV. Fisher recognized Mrs. St. Hilaire but he had no idea who the man was. He was still trying to figure out how Atkins was finding them. He directed Fisher on which turns to take and in front of which houses to stop. He seemed to know where Mr. Ruiz would be even before they found him. It troubled him nearly as much as what Atkins did at each stop.

Smith had not moved since their arrival. He simply stood in place and looked at Atkins with tears streaming down his cheeks. His lips quivered and he licked them repeatedly. His eyes never left Atkins. Even when the tall, gaunt figure reached past him and selected a large knife from the butcher's block on the counter behind him, Smith remained a statue.

"It's all over now, Mr. Smith," Atkins said. His voice was calm, as calm as it had been with the others they had visited since leaving the Foy factory. "No more living in fear for you."

Smith remained motionless. "She sent you." It was a statement, not a question. He had not once looked in Fisher's direction. Fisher thought the man was unaware of his presence, unaware of anything that was not Kenny Atkins.

"She did." Atkins brought the blade up slowly and drew it across Smith's throat. He sidestepped the spray of blood that erupted from the wound. Smith made no move to stem the blood flow. He stood and stared into Atkins' eyes until his knees buckled and his eyelids fluttered closed. He collapsed to the floor and gasped a few times and then lay still.

Fisher was stunned to see the man go without any fight whatsoever. Even St. Hilaire, as old and infirm as she was, had struggled, however weakly, with Atkins. It made no difference in the end, but she had at least tried to save herself. Had Smith been so overcome with terror he was incapable of putting up a fight? *Weak asshole probably got what he deserved, then.*

He looked up and saw Atkins wiping the blade on Smith's trousers. He did not do a particularly good job; even from the doorway Fisher could see there was still blood on the blade where it met the handle. Atkins either did not notice or did not care. He returned the blade to its home and turned and regarded Fisher.

"Pull the truck around back, put him with the others."

Fisher swallowed nervously but he walked out the front door and to his Explorer. He looked at the Chevy parked in front of him at the curb but only for a moment. He started the engine and looked down the street and thought about gunning it and getting the fuck out of Dodge. It's not like Atkins could catch him on foot. And even if he commandeered the Chevy out front or whatever the old man had in his garage he was certain he could get away with a large enough head start. Instead he pulled into the driveway and around the back of the house as he was told.

Atkins opened the back door for him and Fisher walked into the kitchen. His hand was covered with blood. It dripped slowly from his fingers. Fisher paused in the doorway when he noticed what Atkins had written on the wall with the dead man's blood. It was the same message that adorned the wall in Mrs. St. Hilaire's living room. He picked up the old man's body and grimaced when some of the blood smeared on his shirt sleeve. He said nothing and carried his burden out to the Explorer. When the body joined its new traveling companions beneath the tarp he went back inside.

Atkins was seated at the kitchen table. An old transistor radio had joined him there. Fisher was unsurprised by the song coming from the single small speaker. "We're all set, Kenny." He kept his eyes on the floor, unwilling to look at the name Atkins had written on the wall next to the small table.

Atkins seemed not to hear him. His lips moved along silently with the song on the dead man's radio.

Fisher's eyes went to the unconscious man on the floor. Smith's blood had sprayed onto his back and into his hair. There was a pool of it where the old man fell and it slowly spread across the linoleum and seeped between the unconscious man's fingers. Fisher looked more closely at him and gasped. "Hey, isn't this Matty Anderson?"

"Mm hmm."

"He's a cop, Kenny. Did you know that? We have to take him with us. Blindfold him or something and take him with us. Or kill him. Either or."

Atkins continued to lip synch until the song ended. When it started again he looked at Anderson and then at Fisher. "No. She didn't say anything about him. There's no extra credit for taking him out so we leave him as is."

Fisher blinked. "Extra credit? What the fuck are you talking about?"

Atkins shot him a look and Fisher felt the blood drain from his cheeks. He took an involuntary step back. He held up his hands in surrender. "Okay, okay. But shouldn't we get the fuck out of here?"

"Wait til this song is over," Atkins replied. "I kinda like it."

Fisher started to protest but just as quickly closed his mouth. He stood and waited for the fucking song to end and hoped Anderson would not wake in the meantime.

Chapter Thirteen

Breaking News

It is the jostling and jolting that wakes him up. Anderson opens his eyes slowly, painfully. His head hurts and he feels the back of it. There is a large lump under his damp hair. He pulls his hand away and sees the blood which coats his fingers. "What the fuck?" he says weakly.

The little girl next to him giggles and covers her mouth. "That's a bad word, mister. My mommy says it sometimes, but she told me I can't say it."

Anderson turns his head slowly to regard the child in the seat next to him. She is young, very young. She wears a blue dress with white flowers on it. A matching bow is in her blonde hair. She has a pink Hello Kitty book bag in her lap. He can see a few brightly-colored books poking out of it. She laces her fingers together and puts *them on top of her book bag and looks forward. She leans in close to him and whispers conspiratorially, "Now we should be quiet. The bus driver doesn't like it when we talk."*

Anderson regards the girl with open confusion. He looks about. He is indeed inside a school bus. All the seats are occupied by small children. They sit quietly in their seats and look straight ahead. He glances out the window and does not recognize the street. "Where are we?"

The little girl places one finger to her lips but does not otherwise react to him. She returns her hand to its companion in her lap.

He looks to the front of the bus and sees a woman behind the wheel. Her hair is dirty blonde and she looks to be of slightly below average build. He suspects he knows who she is and when he sees the rose tattoo on her wrist his suspicions are confirmed.

He stands from his seat and the little blonde girl turns her head at him and shakes it vigorously. A look of terror crosses her eyes. "No, mister, no. Sit down before she sees you. She'll get really mad!"

Anderson places a hand on the little girl's shoulder and says, gently, "It's okay, honey. I know her."

The girl shakes her head again. "I don't think so."

Anderson's brow furrows. He leaves his seat and walks slowly up the aisle. Several children try to grab his hands as he passes them. Several gasp in terror but none speak. The few at whom he glances shake their heads as vigorously as had the little girl. He ignores them and continues forward.

He comes up behind the driver and peeks over her shoulder. "Jen?"

She tilts her head slightly, but her eyes never leave the road. "Hello, Matthew."

The tension leaves his shoulders and he smiles broadly and hugs her. She takes one hand off the wheel long enough to wrap it around his arm and then she returns it to the wheel.

"Careful, honey, I'm driving."

Anderson does not want to end the embrace, but Jen has a point. He pulls back and takes the unoccupied seat directly behind her. "It's good to see you, baby."

"Good to see you, too. How am I doing so far? I think pretty good, especially considering I've never driven anything this size before."

"You're doing just fine, baby, just fine. I can't believe you're here."

"I can say the same thing about you," Jen replies. "I wasn't expecting you this trip."

Anderson reluctantly pulls his eyes away from his wife and looks out the windows again. "Is this Piedmont Street? Why does it look so different?"

Jen makes a sweeping gesture with one arm as the bus stops at an intersection. "Because most of these stores are gone now." The bus comes to a complete stop and she points at the gold brick building to their left. "Marcelina's closed up shop in ninety. Barnes' Arts and Crafts in ninety-two. And a few of those restaurants are gone as well. Ain't progress a bitch?"

Anderson smiles sadly. "I remember Marcelina's. My grandfather took me there as a kid. They had baseball cards and a whole rack of comic books and enough candy to sink a ship." He looks at the old storefront as the bus shudders back into motion. It takes only a moment for Marcelina's to escape his field of vision. Anderson is amazed to find his eyes are wet.

"Happy memories," Jen says.

"Yeah."

He notices his hand on the safety rail. He sees the blood that is starting to dry on his palm, his fingers. He holds it in front of his eyes. "What happened to me? Babe, am I dead?"

Jen shakes her head. "No, my love. You're unconscious on Smith's floor. This is all in your head." She casts a sideways glance at him over her shoulder. "I'm sorry."

He feels the back of his head again. His hair is becoming stiff and the lump hurts like a son of a bitch when he touches it. "What happened?"

The bus stops at another intersection. Jen activates the right blinker and after a moment she makes the turn. The bus hits a pothole that was repaired in 2009 when the street was torn up and repaved. Anderson remembers because he took the extra duty to play traffic cop during the excavation. The bus rocks on its suspension and it makes Anderson's head throb. He grimaces and closes his eyes until the pain subsides.

When he opens them again the bus is pulling into the driveway of Deacon's Landing Elementary School. Anderson recognizes the old façade even at a distance. What bothers him more than seeing the school in its original state is seeing the smoke billow into the sky. He can see no flames, nor are there teachers and students fleeing the building. From the driveway it appears the school is deserted.

Except the teachers' parking lot is full of cars. There are vintage Oldsmobiles and Hondas and Pontiacs, all from the seventies and eighties. Mr. Gwiazdoski's ancient Ford Falcon sits in the first space closest to the building.

Anderson shakes his head slowly. "Babe, turn around. We shouldn't be here."

Jen does not reply. The bus completes the journey up the driveway and stops in front of the school. The old double doors that always made him think of eyes watching him stand dark and closed. He tries to see inside the building, but they are too far away for him to see any detail. He does not see flames or smoke at the front of the school and that makes him feel marginally better.

The doors to his right open and Anderson looks first at them and then at the woman behind the wheel. It is no longer his dead wife. He has never seen Ann Carlson but he knows it is her. Her jet-black hair is long and her breasts are indeed quite large. She is younger than he expected and quite beautiful. She favors him with a smile.

She sits back in the seat and peeks into the rearview mirror. "Okay, children, here you are."

The children begin to stand obediently and shuffle single file to the front of the bus. Anderson jumps to his feet and blocks the exit with his body. "No, no, kids, go back to your seats. You don't want to get off the bus here."

The first child in line, a young boy no older than five or six, says, "Mister, please let us go. This is our school."

"No it isn't," Anderson replies. He looks above the boy's head to the rest of the children. "I'm a police officer. Please go back to your seats at once."

Dark Annie wraps her fingers around his arm and squeezes until Anderson winces in pain. She pulls him slowly closer to her until their noses nearly touch. Her lips pull back from her teeth and her eyes narrow. "Kindly do not interfere, Mr. Anderson. These children need to go to school so they can learn."

Anderson pulls his arm back, but her strength surprises him and he succeeds only in making her tighten her grip. Blood wells up between her fingers. Anderson gasps in pain. She pulls with more strength and Anderson loses his balance and tumbles into the seat he had taken when the bus driver was his wife.

The obstruction removed, the children begin to file off the bus. Anderson tries to grab for each one as they pass him but they are just out of his reach. When the little girl with the Hello Kitty *book bag approaches Anderson redoubles his effort to grab her. His fingertips glance off her shoulder before Dark Annie pulls him back again.*

The little girl, who Anderson now recognizes as Cassie Wayne, pauses for a moment and turns her head in Anderson's direction. "It's okay, mister. Miss Carlson loves us. She'll take good care of us."

She files out the door slowly. She pauses when she steps onto the curb, turns and waves to him. She joins the procession filing toward the double doors of Deacon's Landing Elementary School. The last few children behind her in line exit the bus quietly and orderly and follow her to the school.

Anderson tries to scream at them but no sound escapes his lips. He pounds on the seat with his free hand and still he remains silent, still the children approach the double doors. They open seemingly on their own and the children disappear through them without breaking stride.

Dark Annie releases her hold on his arm and pulls the lever that closes the bus's door. She places both hands on the steering wheel and looks over her shoulder and smiles at him again.

****

Anderson awoke on the cold linoleum of Smith's kitchen floor. His head throbbed more than it had in the dream and he moaned and clenched his eyes shut. He felt something cool and wet on his face. When he opened his eyes at first all he saw was red. He blinked and some of the red disappeared and he knew it was blood. He lifted his head from the floor and saw the puddle around him. He got his hands under him and struggled to his knees.

There was a fair amount of blood on the kitchen floor. It was on the walls and the small table as well. The name drawn in red on the wall made Anderson think of the sun porch at the Atkins residence; the scrawl was exactly the same, as was the name. A broken coffee cup lay next to him. Its contents had mixed with the blood and created a color Anderson had never before seen.

He reached for the counter and used it to pull himself to his feet. He shook his head to clear it and instantly regretted the action. He felt the back of his head, as he had in the dream, and received the same result. The lump was large and his hair was wet with blood. *Not my blood*, he thought. *Smith's.*

He became aware of another voice in the kitchen. His eyes were drawn to Smith's radio. It sat in the center of the table and a male monotone voice was reciting the day's headlines. *I've got some breaking news for you*, Anderson thought.

He reached into his back pocket before he realized he left his cell in the car. He eyed Smith's cordless in its cradle on the wall. He staggered to it and managed to keep his feet beneath him on the slippery floor. He reached for the phone and stopped. He saw the bruise on his arm that looked suspiciously like a woman's handprint. He felt around the edges of the bruise and winced and pulled his hand back.

He reached for the phone with his other hand and picked it up and dialed 911.

****

While Anderson lay unconscious on Smith's floor, Atkins directed Fisher to three more houses. The first belonged to a woman Fisher did not know, but he recognized Mr. Wallace and Mr. Brault. He felt a pang of guilt when Brault went; he had been the only teacher Fisher could stand in his whole academic career. He did not exactly like the guy, but he loathed him less than the rest of his teachers. Not that it mattered. Atkins had decreed Brault had to go, and so he did. The back of his Explorer was full and Fisher hoped they would not have to resort to using the backseat. They did not. Brault was the last one and Atkins gave Fisher their destination.

He pulled into the driveway of Deacon's Landing Magnet School. Atkins told him to drive around back and Fisher did as he was instructed. The loading dock area was heavily wooded and he could not see the road or any houses. Even the sounds of the town's traffic were muted.

Atkins told him to back in between the panel truck and the school bus. Fisher did not question the presence of either vehicle. He knew from the local news that the panel truck was reported stolen and had some connection to what had happened at the fair. He glanced sideways at Atkins and wondered if his old friend was capable of mass murder. Then he glanced in his rearview at the tarp in the back of the SUV and he answered his own question.

When Fisher killed the engine Atkins turned and said to him, "Help me get them inside. It'll go quicker with two people."

Fisher nodded wordlessly and stepped onto the new pavement. He walked around and opened the lift gate. The loading dock doors were located next to the glass face of the cafeteria windows. Atkins walked to the door next to the loading bays and swung it open. He kicked a wedge of wood under the door and it remained open. When Atkins joined him at the back of the SUV, Fisher asked, "Why didn't the alarm go off?"

"That's been taken care of," Atkins said. He grabbed hold of the first body, Brault's, and hauled it from the vehicle. He motioned for Fisher to help him.

They entered through the open door and Fisher shivered. There was a forty degree difference inside the loading dock that he somehow knew had nothing to do with the absence of sunlight. Atkins led them across the dock, past the boxes of canned vegetables and fruits. Fisher's eyes widened and remained glued to the wooden box labeled TNT. It sat on the floor next to a case of construction paper. Fisher continued to stare at the box until they passed through the doors and into the corridor on the other side.

"The auditorium," Atkins said when they reached the base of a wide staircase. He led the way up the stairs and onto the main level. He took a left and guided Fisher and their burden past rows of lockers and closed classroom doors. Several motivational banners and posters greeted them on their way to the auditorium. The main level was only slightly warmer than the basement. Fisher's breath frosted the air and he tried to ignore the goose bumps on his arms.

They reached the wide double doors to the auditorium and Atkins pulled them open while he braced the body against the wall. The smell hit Fisher all at once and he gagged and nearly dropped the body. The auditorium was dark, but he could make out the rows of seats to either side of the wide center aisle. The stage at the far end of the room was wide and the heavy red curtain was pulled to the side.

What caught and held his attention, however, was the last row of seats. The occupants of those seats were older people; most appeared to be in their sixties or seventies. They sat with their hands in their lap and faced the stage. He looked at the nearest person and saw her throat had been cut. Blood had run from the corners of her mouth and her neck and most of her housecoat was the color of rust. He had no desire to see the rest of them and so he focused his attention on Atkins.

Atkins led him to the far left of the auditorium. He squeezed himself between the last two rows and indicated the next open seat. When Brault was in the chair Atkins arranged him in a pose identical to his former colleagues. When he was satisfied with the result he turned to Fisher and said, "Let's get the others."

It took forty minutes to unload the Explorer. Fisher guessed it would take considerably longer to wipe up the blood left in the SUV's storage area. There were still a few unoccupied seats in the last row of the auditorium and Fisher did not think he would be able to see them filled. They, mostly Atkins, had been lucky so far. Sooner or later they were going to go after someone who had quick access to a gun or a cop would pull them over for something and the jig would be up. That was assuming Fisher's nerves would hold up and he seriously doubted they would.

He pulled a cigarette from his pack but his hands shook so badly he dropped it. He picked it up and fumbled with his lighter but that, too, found its way to the floor. He reached down for it but Atkins beat him to it. He picked up the lighter and flicked it to life and held it up for Fisher. In all his life he had never needed a cigarette this badly. When he finished with it he was calm enough to light the second one himself.

When that one was done he pulled a third from his pack, but Atkins said, "Save it for later. I have someone who wants to meet you."

Fisher looked at him with the unlit cigarette dangling from his lips and he said, "Who?"

Atkins smiled. "She's downstairs. C'mon, I'll show you."

Fisher reluctantly pulled the cigarette from his lips and slid it back into the pack. He followed Atkins from the auditorium and back down to the lower level. He was absolutely certain he did not want to meet Atkins' friend, but his legs did not obey his commands to run like a crazy son of a bitch for the loading dock. His body seemed to be on autopilot and he did not know how to turn the fucking thing off. He followed Atkins past every door, every window, every means of escape.

Atkins led them down a long hall and by the time they entered the boys' locker room Fisher's cheeks were wet with tears.

****

Anderson sat on the rear bumper of the ambulance and held the icepack against the back of his head. Smith's house had become a beehive of activity since his phone call. Captain Lange was the first to arrive and Anderson fooled himself into thinking, if only momentarily, that he had showed up out of concern for one of his officers. It turned out he was on his way into the station when the call went in. His questions concerning Anderson's status had sounded sincere, but Anderson did not buy it. After a few moments Lange entered the house and waited for the forensic team.

The female paramedics were two people Anderson did not know very well. Their names were Piccarillo and Coussens, but he did not know which was which. They took his vitals and applied the icepack and hovered around him. They were at a loss to explain the frostbite on his arm, and he offered no explanation. One of them applied a salve and bandaged it. Both were eager to get him to DLH, but Anderson wanted to wait until the scene at the house played out. He watched the forensic team move equipment into the house and they took a sample of oil from the driveway and swarmed about the scene like ants on melting ice cream.

The street was not cordoned off but flares had been set on the asphalt in a crescent moon pattern in front of the house. Several cars drove slowly past and the people in them rubbernecked until they were several houses past. Anderson ignored them and instead concentrated on the dull throbbing in his head.

A blue Dodge pickup slowed as it neared the activity and Anderson glanced at it and saw Murphy behind the wheel. His eyes focused when he saw Anderson and he pulled the truck to the curb and got out. Anderson managed a weak wave and Murphy joined him at the back of the ambulance.

"What the fuck happened here?" He eyed the people moving in and out of the house.

"Doughnut sale," Anderson said drily.

His eyes went from the house to Anderson. "You okay? That doesn't look too good."

"I'll live," Anderson said and winced as he shifted his weight. "Just not gonna be happy about it for a few days." He nodded in the direction of the pickup. "Where'd you steal that?"

"Huh?" Murphy followed Anderson's eyes. "Oh. Customer car. Testing the new brakes. You gonna tell me what's going on?"

Anderson shrugged. "Got hit from behind. Lights out. But at least they came back on again. Looks like Mr. Smith won't be as lucky."

Murphy's brow furrowed. "Smith? From the school?"

Anderson nodded and winced again. The dull throb in the back of his head was upping the volume again. "Yeah. He was telling me about something but he never got to finish. Look, Murph, I don't know how much more I can say. It's a police matter now."

"Yeah, yeah." Murphy waved him off. "Think this is connected to Atkins?"

"One way or another."

Coussens, or maybe it was Piccarillo, approached him and said, "Officer, we shouldn't wait any longer. We have to get you to the hospital right away. If this is a concussion or worse, a fractured skull, timing is crucial."

"My skull isn't fractured," Anderson said, somewhat annoyed.

"Oh, I'm sorry. Forgive me for not recognizing you, *Doctor*."

Murphy looked at Anderson and burst into laughter. Anderson joined him a moment later, but stopped just as quickly when the back of his head threatened to explode. When the man with the sledgehammer stopped beating the inside of his skull, he said, "Murph, think you can pick me up at the emergency room later? I'll need a ride."

"Call me," Murphy replied.

"Will do."

Murphy took a few steps back and waved again. "I'll talk to ya later, Matt. Be careful, okay?"

Anderson waved back. "I'll be fine. And thanks." He returned his attention to the paramedic. "Waiting on you now."

The paramedic gave him a sour look and helped him into the ambulance.

****

Fisher opened the back of the panel truck and climbed in. Atkins followed him inside. If it had been cold inside the school, and frigid inside the boys' locker room, the interior of the panel truck was a blast furnace. The sun had crested while he was being introduced to Atkins' new friend. The panel truck sat fully in the sun and the inside was blistering. Sweat sprung up on his forehead and arms almost immediately. He barely noticed.

Atkins took a pry bar from its slot on the wall and handed it to Fisher. He took it and knelt beside the box marked TNT and jammed the bar's business end between the boards. The top came off reluctantly; the nails holding it in place were long and thick. When it was separated from the rest of the box Fisher tossed it aside.

He looked inside the box. He did not know how many sticks of dynamite it held, but it was more than he had ever seen in one place. His excitement caused his jeans to tighten and it took him a moment to realize he had an erection. *Hello old friend*, he thought, and laughed. His laughter died when he looked at Atkins.

Atkins' long hair was nearly plastered to his skull with sweat. He wore an unpleasant expression and it was directed fully at Fisher. "This isn't a game, Danny. I thought you knew that."

Fisher nodded soberly. "I know. Sorry, man."

"Do you know how to rig this shit?"

Fisher shook his head. "No idea."

"It's easy. Here, I'll show you." Atkins showed him.

Twenty minutes later Fisher followed Atkins out of the truck. The late-afternoon air was warm, but compared to the inside of the panel truck it felt like they had stepped onto the tundra. Fisher was relieved to feel the cool air and thought about how good a cold beer would be right about now. He doubted either Atkins or his new friend would allow him such a luxury. He resigned himself to the nearest water bubbler inside the school.

The sweat on his arms and in his hair froze before they exited the other side of the loading dock and emerged near the locker rooms. The sudden change in temperature made him nauseated and he stopped and leaned against the wall and tried not to vomit. It climbed up his esophagus and made it as far as the back of his throat before it retreated slowly back into his stomach. Fisher tasted bile and spat on the floor.

The water bubbler was on the wall between the girls' and boys' locker rooms. He thought about the water before he got a better idea. He took a step toward the boys' locker room but he stopped himself before he could reach for the door handle. It was just a little too close to *her*. He settled on the girls' locker room; school was not going to be in session until after sunset anyway, so it wasn't like he would get into trouble.

He entered the locker room and all but ran into the shower room and turned on the closest faucet. The water erupted from the showerhead and it was the single most joyous moment of Fisher's life. He had never felt such relief. He stood under the head and let the water rain down on him and, although he would not be aware of it for some time, he climaxed.

Twenty minutes later he had not moved a muscle. He opened his eyes long enough to see Atkins leaning against the tiled wall with his arms folded across his chest and the corner of his mouth turned up in a smirk. Fisher wiped the water from his eyes and looked again.

"C'mon, Danny, that's long enough," Atkins said.

Fisher turned off the water most reluctantly and said, "I guess you're right. Almost time to get a move on."

"Almost," Atkins agreed. "I'll walk you out."

They left the girls' locker room and Fisher heard his sneakers squeak all the way down the corridor. Water welled up with each step he took, but he did not mind. Before they reached the loading dock his clothes were frozen to his skin. "I hope I don't get pneumonia," he remarked.

Atkins smiled a bit. "I don't think you have to worry about that."

Fisher considered for a moment before he nodded his agreement. "Suppose not."

When they reached the loading dock he reached into his back pocket and pulled out his pack of cigarettes. It was soaked through and frozen solid. He stared at the pack longingly before he tossed it away. He looked hopefully at Atkins.

Atkins shook his head. "Sorry, man. I haven't touched a cigarette since that day my dad beat my ass for smoking. You remember that?"

Fisher nodded, but he could not hide his disappointment. "Yeah."

"Besides, she doesn't want us to smoke." He inclined his head in the direction from which they had come. "She wants us to be healthy."

"Yeah," he said again. He looked out through the open door to the panel truck. "I guess I'd better hit the road. Emergency room's east entrance, right? Around eleven."

Atkins nodded. "*Before* eleven. Just to be safe."

"Okay." Fisher exited the school and climbed into the cab of the panel truck. He looked at the dashboard clock. It flashed 4:11 at him. He sat back and rolled down the window. There was not much of a breeze but what little there was felt good.

The sun hovered just above the treetops in front of him. It would continue to beat through the windshield for perhaps another fifteen minutes. He felt confident he could withstand it for that long.

He sat back and turned the ignition back one slot. He turned on the radio and his favorite song greeted him. He sat and tapped his fingers in rhythm until he caught sight of himself in the rearview. He was forced to cut his hair when he took the security job. That was bad enough. It was white now, as white as snow. He might have let his body turn to shit over the years, especially since his divorce, but he had always prided himself on his thick, black hair. When time seduced some of those strands to turn against him they were quickly plucked before they could corrupt those around them. And now...

He ran a hand through it forlornly, as if he had come across the body of an old and dear friend. *When did it happen?* he wondered. *Wasn't it still black when I was looking in the mirror and shaving yesterday morning?*

He sat back in the seat again and mourned his lost color when it occurred to him to check the glove compartment. He found the truck's registration and insurance information, a wad of napkins from McDonalds and a pack of American Spirits. He gasped with delight and took the cigarettes. He checked the side mirror and saw Atkins carrying the TNT box from the loading dock into the cafeteria. He would no doubt be busy for some time before he returned to the locker room to be with her. That was good. They would distract each other while Fisher sneaked in a few smokes.

There were only two in the pack but that was okay. He'd chain them and that would hold him over for a little while. He pushed in the truck's lighter and a moment later it popped out quite happily. Its heating element glowed the most beautiful shade of orange he had ever seen.

Fisher sat and smoked with the sun in his eyes and hoped he did not get caught. When his favorite song ended it started right back up again. He even managed to forget about his hair. Life was fucking good.

Chapter Fourteen

Extra Credit

Holly waved as Luciana pulled away from the curb. She remained at the front door until her friend's car disappeared into the darkness and then she closed the door. She walked back to the kitchen and cleaned off the table. The dishes and glasses went into the sink, the wine bottle went into the fridge and the joint went between her lips. She walked out the sliding glass door to the back porch and sat in the lounge chair and fired it up.

It had not been her intention to smoke. She did not ask Luciana if she had anything with her, and Luciana had not volunteered any information. When she walked Luciana to the front door the woman had turned and slipped it into Holly's hand with a conspiratorial grin. Holly opened her hand and looked at it and her first reaction was to give it back. But she kept it and thanked Luciana and watched her leave.

She had to admit, she missed it. It had been eight years since she had indulged, not counting the other day, and it felt like welcoming home an old friend. She hit it a few more times before she let it go out. She sat in the lounger and felt the cool night air on her arms and her legs and she felt good. With her head pleasantly in the clouds she reentered the house and closed and locked the back door.

She eyed the dishes in the sink but she felt too good to waste her time with them. She took the stairs two at a time and opened Cassandra's door a crack. Her daughter lay in her bed half under the covers with the ceiling fan providing a pleasant breeze. She held her stuffed penguin tightly to her chest. Holly entered as quietly as she was able and kissed her daughter's cheek.

She was halfway to the door again when she noticed Cassandra's *Hello Kitty* book bag hanging from the post on the footboard. Holly stopped and regarded it. The last she had seen of the book bag it had been tossed in the closet after her mother had bought it in anticipation of Cassie starting grade three in the fall. Had Cassandra been playing with it? She had expressed excitement at the first mention of school, but her enthusiasm had dwindled as the day approached. Perhaps she had changed her mind again and school was once more a good thing. Holly smiled at the thought. She left her daughter sleeping contentedly and returned to the kitchen.

She felt the munchies coming on and she rummaged through the cupboards until she came across the chocolate chip cookies. She carried the box into the living room and plopped down on the couch. She turned on the television with the remote and flipped through the channels until she found the one that showed old music videos for late night insomniacs. She sat back and ate the cookies and watched the heavy metal heroes she had worshipped as a young girl.

She had forgotten how tired she got when she was high. Some people became paranoid or got dry-mouth but Holly suffered neither of those maladies. She simply became tired. She struggled to keep her eyelids open, but they had increased in weight by a factor of one thousand. Quite against her will, she closed them.

The clock on the cable box read 10:14 when she nodded off.

****

Anderson exited the emergency room to the sound of thunder. The rain that had threatened to arrive all day had finally done so. It was not a downpour, not yet, but he got the distinct impression it would be before long. It beat a steady rhythm on the overhang that protected the emergency room entrance and the parking spaces for the ambulances. A couple of ambulance jockeys were present chatting up the nurses and orderlies who came outside to smoke. They were clustered in a group away from the doors. Anderson regarded them for only a moment before he looked into the street for his ride.

A bright yellow Wrangler beeped its horn twice and Anderson could see the driver wave to him. He descended the steps to the sidewalk and opened the Jeep's door. He shook Murphy's hand as he slid into the seat and closed the door behind him. "Thanks, Murph. I appreciate it."

"It's all good," Murphy replied. He shifted into gear and released the clutch and they pulled away from the curb. "Not like I had anything else to do tonight. How are ya feeling?"

Anderson sighed. "Like shit. Head's still pounding, but nothing's fractured. Don't even have a concussion. Just a five-alarm headache."

"Sounds like you got lucky."

"I guess," Anderson replied. He watched the windshield wipers travel back and forth across his field of vision and listened to the staccato rhythm of the rain on the Wrangler's canvas top. "Where's the Chevelle?"

Murphy snorted. "That car doesn't see rain. Or snow, for that matter. It's at the shop nice and dry." He paused for a moment. "Where to?"

"Home," Anderson replied. "Bradley stopped by a little while ago and said they brought my car home for me."

"That was nice of the prick."

"Yeah, I thought so."

"Just do me a favor and don't look in the glove compartment, okay?"

Anderson would have laughed if he knew his head would not threaten to explode. "Don't worry about it. If you get pulled over you have a get out of jail free card tonight. Just so long as it's nothing too serious."

Murphy shook his head. "Nah. Just a half-ounce of weed. I forgot to leave it at home before I left to come get you."

"Don't' sweat it."

They rode in silence for a few more moments before Murphy said, "You gonna tell me what happened at Smith's? Or do I have to wait for tomorrow's paper?"

Anderson stroked his chin. "I'm not even sure where to begin. He was telling me about Ann Carlson and what went down back in eighty-five before she disappeared. He seemed to think Mr. Ford was involved."

"The teacher from DLES? The one who killed the dancer at Lucky's?"

Anderson nodded. "The one and only."

"No shit," Murphy said.

Anderson paused, not certain of how much of the story he should relate. It *was* an ongoing investigation, after all. Then again, Murphy was not a reporter and, as far as Anderson knew, did not have a reputation for telling tales out of school.

He began to go into greater detail as they turned onto West Main Street.

****

Fisher did his best to keep a car or two between himself and the yellow Wrangler. He doubted Murphy would notice the tail he picked up at the hospital but Anderson was another matter. He was not driving the most inconspicuous vehicle in town and Anderson was a cop. He was trained to notice what was going on around him. So he did his best to stay far enough away as to avoid being noticed. When the cars between them turned down a side street Fisher backed off even farther but remained close enough to see the Jeep's taillights.

He had been surprised to see Murphy pull up outside the emergency room. He was told to look for the

Wrangler, but she had neglected to inform him of the driver's identity. Had she known? Probably. She knew which vehicle to look for and even its color. It dawned on him that she had known the identity of the driver and did not consider it worth mentioning. That gave Fisher some confidence. It told him she did not consider Murphy a threat.

The sight of his old nemesis brought a smile to Fisher's lips that was impossible to shake. Murphy had never gone along with the established order of Atkins and his group being the ultimate badasses in school. He had fought nearly everyone in Atkins' group at one time or another, including Atkins himself. And the one time he slugged it out with Murphy, Fisher walked away with a bloody lip and two loose teeth. He considered Murphy's presence a bonus to his evening.

He gripped the steering wheel a bit tighter and decided to savor the moment.

****

Holly dreamed of seeing Cassandra off on her first day of school. She came down to the living room in her nicest outfit and Holly fussed with the girl's hair and straitened her skirt a bit. Cassandra stood still for it all, but Holly could sense her willingness to be off. She smiled in spite of herself. Holly had never been very enamored of her time in the classroom and she took it as a good sign that her daughter did not share her attitude. *At least for now*, Holly thought in the dream. When Cassie got older and the rebellious streak Holly was certain was there manifested itself it might be a different story. For now, however, the girl was excited.

Holly walked her to the front door, but Cassandra made it very clear she did not wish to be escorted all the way to the school bus parked at the curb. Holly opened the door for her and Cassandra skipped down the walk. Holly wished she had noticed the rain before she let her daughter past her, but it was not coming down too hard and it was a short walk to the bus. If it was still raining when the bus dropped her off, Holly would wait at the end of the driveway with an umbrella. The bus's door opened and Cassandra took the steps slowly. Holly waved, but her daughter did not look back. The bus's door slid closed and the flashing red lights went dark and the bus pulled away from the curb.

Holly's hand dropped slowly to her side and her smile faded. The inside of the bus had been dark and she could see almost nothing. She got the impression the bus was almost fully loaded with children but she had seen no one. It bothered her and she did not know why.

The bus continued on its way down the street and was lost from Holly's line of sight. She closed the door slowly, reluctantly. She felt, quite suddenly, that something was drastically wrong. She leaned back against the front door and tried to put her finger on the reason for the feeling. Nothing came.

She walked slowly back to the sofa and sat down. She was certain beyond any doubt that something terrible had happened or soon would. She was incapable of knowing why, just as she was incapable of shaking the feeling. She tapped her fingers on the sofa's armrest for several moments, but the answer remained elusive. She looked at the television. Scandal's video for their hit "The Warrior" gave way to Katrina and the Waves.

They don't play videos in the morning, Holly thought. *This shit is late-night only. And "Walking on Sunshine"?* Absently she scratched an itch that took up residence on her arm. She watched the video and Katrina herself was dancing in what looked to be an old apartment building or perhaps a factory. As Holly watched, the old brick building began to take on a form familiar to her. It looked less like an apartment building and more like a school. A *specific* school. A school which, the last time Holly saw, was in flames.

She sat bolt upright on the sofa and looked through the picture window. The streetlights shined and bounced their light off the wet pavement. The rain had intensified and she could see it even in the darkness. She became aware she was scratching her arm hard enough to draw blood. She stopped and looked at it and gasped. The handprint she had picked up inside the funhouse had faded somewhat, but she had aggravated the wound. Beads of blood trickled down her arm and dripped onto the sofa.

Her head snapped in the direction of the bedrooms upstairs. She vaulted off the sofa and took the stairs three at a time. She stopped in her tracks at the top. Cassandra's door was open. Holly ran to it and turned on the light and saw her daughter's empty bed. Her eyes fell on the footboard and saw the girl's book bag was gone.

"Cassie!" She threw open the closet, but found it uninhabited. She ran to her own room but her daughter was not there. She shouted her name again. Cassie did not answer.

Holly screamed and ran back down the stairs. She picked up the kitchen phone but it sailed out of her hand and landed in the sink. She heard the wine glasses shatter.

The plastic panel that held the battery in place bounced out of the sink and landed on the counter. She took a single step toward it before she reversed course and grabbed her car keys off the kitchen table.

She bolted out the front door and ran for her Honda. Her hair and clothes were soaked in the time it took her to open the door.

****

They drove past Murphy's shop and the other storefronts in silence. Anderson allowed Murphy the time to process what he had been told. It could not be easy for him and Anderson could relate. He still had a difficult time wrapping his head around what Smith had told him. He left nothing out despite the threat of what Lange would do to him for sharing such information. He no longer cared. *Besides*, he reasoned, *I need someone else's perspective on this. Someone who was there that day.*

Murphy cleared his throat. "So you think Mr. Ford killed Dark Annie. Okay, if you say so. I still don't see what this has to do with what's been happening around town lately. And how does Atkins fit in?"

"I don't know," Anderson admitted. "There's the connection between Ann Carlson and Atkins Sr., but beyond that..." His voice trailed off. He shook his head. "I don't know. Between the bump on my head and the painkillers I can't think straight. Maybe in the morning I'll see it better."

"I hope so," Murphy replied. "Then you can explain it to me because I'm fucking lost."

They drove in silence for two more blocks. Anderson listened to the rain and watched the wipers sway back and forth in front of him. Combined with the powerful painkillers the doctors had pumped into him the affect was nearly hypnotizing. He shook his head to clear it and groaned as the pain flared.

"What the hell is this?" Murphy asked.

"Hmm?" Anderson had closed his eyes but he opened them again and knew what had caught Murphy's attention.

A school bus was stopped at the light in the opposing lane. As Murphy came to a stop at the same intersection he pointed at it. "Since when do busses run this late?"

"They don't." Anderson leaned forward in the seat and wiped at the fog on the inside of the windshield. "Maybe it was being repaired someplace."

Murphy shook his head. "No. The only shop in town that works on school busses is Kyle Brothers. I know because they underbid us on the contract. And they don't work this late."

"Someone coming back after a sporting event somewhere?" It sounded like bullshit and Anderson regretted mentioning it. "Never mind."

They sat and watched the school bus. It was dark inside but the streetlights succeeded in penetrating weakly through the windows. "Are those people?" Murphy sounded incredulous. "Christ, they look like little kids."

Anderson's eyes went to the front of the bus. He could see the silhouette of the driver, but the rain and the darkness prevented him from seeing any detail. He thought he saw the driver's head turn in their direction, but he could not be certain.

All at once the bus driver mashed the gas pedal. The bus lurched forward and its diesel engine roared. It surged across the intersection. Anderson saw the red traffic light reflected in the bus's windshield. He was thankful there were no cars crossing the intersection at that moment.

"Jesus," Murphy said. "What the fuck is that guy—" Murphy stopped and stared after the bus. He turned in the seat and looked at Anderson. "That was Atkins!"

The hair on the back of Anderson's neck stood at attention. *"What?"*

"That was Atkins! Driving the school bus! I'm sure it was him." Murphy spun the wheel hard to the left.

The Wrangler was jolted hard from behind and Anderson threw up his hands to prevent his head impacting the windshield. The airbag deployed and for a moment he could see nothing. The Wrangler jolted again and he felt the tires jump the concrete lane divider. He grabbed at the airbag and wrestled it away from his head. The Jeep's horn came alive and stayed that way. He looked at Murphy with wide eyes and saw him struggling to keep the Jeep under control. He turned in his seat and saw a large white truck behind them. Its front bumper was marred by a streak of bright yellow paint.

"Christ!" Murphy shouted and fought the steering wheel. "What the fuck is this asshole doing?" The Wrangler rolled off the concrete divider and its engine died.

Anderson looked out the back window, but it was hard to make out anything except the truck's headlights closing on them. "Murph, get us outta here," Anderson said. His voice was surprisingly calm. "Punch it."

Murphy turned the key. The engine whined for a moment before it roared to life. Murphy jammed the transmission into second and popped the clutch. The wounded Wrangler shot forward. They nearly clipped a white car as it sped past. Murphy spun the wheel to avoid the collision and succeeded by what Anderson guessed was inches.

The truck's leading edge caught the Wrangler and spun it around into the opposing lane. Murphy hit the brakes and for a moment the sound of squealing tires outshouted the horn. He slammed his foot on the gas pedal and they started back the way they had come.

Anderson looked behind them again and saw the white panel truck with **Baribeau Bros. Industrial**

Construction stenciled on the side make the wide turn. A moment later it was directly behind them again.

"He's coming on fast," Anderson said.

"I see him," Murphy yelled. "I can't shake him in this. He fucked something up. I can't get any power."

The truck hit again and the canvas top broke free and shot away into the darkness behind them. Rain pelted them and Anderson wiped at his eyes and watched Murphy do the same.

"Matt, he's gonna run us off the road! Shoot this piece of shit!"

"With what? I'm unarmed." He looked back over his shoulder and saw the truck bearing down on them again. He looked around them and got his bearings. "Police station is up ahead on the right. Turn in there."

Murphy shifted again. "I don't think we can make it that far. I can't get any speed."

The truck hit again and Anderson grabbed onto the roll bar for all he was worth. The Jeep spun hard to the right. Murphy hit the brakes again and turned the wheel but he had become a spectator in this particular contest. The Wrangler jumped the curb, hit a concrete wall and bounced back onto the blacktop. The truck caught it again on the way past and Anderson felt the wheels leave the ground. The Jeep crashed onto its side and skidded along the pavement. Murphy leaned away from the street as much as his seatbelt would allow.

The Jeep continued along its path until its momentum was exhausted. It came to a stop in the middle of the road and facing the wrong way.

****

Fisher did not have a good enough view of the remains of the Jeep or its two occupants; the rain blurred the image in the side mirror. He stuck his head out the window and giggled at the wreck. The Jeep's remaining functional taillight stared back at him like the eye of a dead man. He looked at it as long as he dared before he returned his eyes to the road ahead.

"I did good, didn't I, Miss Carlson? Just like you said. And that prick Murphy was an added bonus." His eyes brightened when the proper term came to him. "He was *extra credit*!" He laughed again.

Out the windshield he could see the entrance to the police department. Fisher floored the accelerator and sang along with his favorite song on the radio.

****

Anderson released a breath he did not know he held and looked at Murphy. The man behind the wheel opened his eyes slowly and realized the Jeep had stopped. He lowered his arms and looked, stunned, at Anderson.

"You okay?" Anderson shouted. The rain had intensified and the wind had picked up. Anderson could barely hear himself. The Jeep's horn, thankfully, gave up the ghost the same time the wreck came to a stop. He still needed to shout to be heard. His head threatened to explode and the pain teamed up with the wind and the rain and nearly blinded him.

Murphy looked at him and gave him a thumbs-up. He had apparently come to the same conclusion about the noise level around them.

Anderson looked through the remains of the windshield. He expected to see the truck coming back at them and he started working on his seatbelt in anticipation of the next impact. He was utterly surprised by what he saw instead.

The truck sped away from them and it blacked out its lights. It seemed to pick up speed with each passing second. He fancied he could hear its engine screaming but it would be impossible over the rain and wind.

Anderson unlocked his seatbelt and stopped himself from falling on Murphy by grabbing onto the roll bar. His head pounded and the pain had become almost a physical presence. He tried to ignore it and he pulled himself onto the Jeep's side. He stood and watched the truck make a hard right turn off the road and into a parking lot. It never broke speed. A moment later the sky above where the truck had gone brightened considerably.

The explosion was loud and drowned out the noise of the storm. The fireball was larger than anything Anderson had ever seen before. It climbed into the night sky and blossomed into an ugly, orange and black cloud. The ground beneath them shook with enough force Anderson nearly lost his balance and tumbled off the Jeep's side. He squinted against the sudden brightness and shielded his eyes. He could see pieces of debris, large and small, shoot skyward against the bright backdrop of the fireball and then they were gone.

"Holy Jesus," Murphy said.

Anderson looked away from the fireball and saw Murphy struggling to pull himself from the wreckage of the Wrangler. He reached down and helped him. Together they dismounted the ruined vehicle and regarded the scene a short distance away. The fireball was gone but the red-orange glow of raging flames just beyond their sight chilled them. Black smoke rose from the scene but the wind took it and whipped it in every direction.

"What the hell was that?" Murphy asked.

It took a moment for Anderson to find his voice. When he did it was barely above a whisper. "The police station."

****

Holly tried for the fifth time to dial 911, but the road was slippery and her visibility was nil. She could not quite get the right numbers, so she gave up and tossed the phone onto the passenger seat.

She had lost sight of the bus only once after she tracked it down. It turned onto West Main and she was stuck behind an old Monte Carlo that simply refused to run the light. She swore and hammered at the steering wheel but the light was not red for long. As soon as it changed she laid on the horn until the Monte Carlo was out of her way. She punched the gas and swerved onto West Main.

She could not see the school bus but she had a good idea of its destination. She drove faster than she should have and nearly wrecked more than once, but she kept the Honda on the road. She spotted the school bus stopped at a red light ahead. Perhaps the driver spotted her because the bus suddenly shot forward through the intersection and against the light. Holly's eyes narrowed in anger and she white-knuckled the steering wheel and floored the accelerator.

She blew through the light and the intersection and caused a collision between a yellow Jeep and a large white truck. Instinct made her hit the brakes and she gasped at the unintended consequences of her actions. Her Honda swerved to the side and it was all Holly could do to stop it from jumping the curb. She glanced in her rearview and the truck and the Jeep had separated. The school bus was pulling farther away from her. She said, "I'm sorry, I'm sorry," and sped after it.

The bus turned onto Piedmont Street and confirmed her suspicion regarding its destination. She eased off the gas a little, just enough for her to regain positive control of the car. She kept it in sight although she knew she had no chance of catching it before it reached the school. That was all right. It would not arrive more than a minute before she did. Not enough time for the driver to take the children into the school before she got there.

There was a loud and powerful explosion from somewhere back the way she had come. The Honda rocked on its suspension and it startled her and she hit the brakes again. She looked in her rearview and saw the fireball rise into the dark sky above the nearby trees. Tears began to spill from her eyes. She turned and looked out the rear window and hoped the mirror had lied to her. It had not; the fireball was real and she thought she could feel the heat even from a few blocks away. "What is happening?" She watched the pyrotechnic show burn itself out and then she saw the thick black smoke rise into the air. She almost put the car in park and stepped out but she remembered the school bus and that snapped her back to the present.

She hit the gas again and made the turn at the Seven-Eleven. She stole glances at the rearview, but she was too far away now to see anything other than a bright orange glow behind the trees. She refocused on finding her daughter and the fucker who stole her.

(Where are my children?)

And when she did catch up to the son of a bitch God had better have mercy on him because Holly had no such intention. She had no idea how her daughter had come to be on the bus, nor did she care.

(You took them from me.)

What she did care about, all she cared about, was getting Cassandra back in her arms and taking her daughter home. If the bus driver made any move to come between them, well, he would be the sorriest piece of shit child abductor in history. Holly would see to that personally.

(I want them back!)

The itch returned to her arm. Holly scratched it raw without knowing she did so.

Chapter Fifteen

Serious Fun

Anderson reached the end of the police station's driveway, Murphy on his heels. He stopped dead in his tracks and stared open-mouthed at the scene. The station's façade was gone, aside from a few stubborn bricks that held fast to the building's foundation. The roof was missing. The inside of the structure was nearly leveled. A few walls remained standing, including the two holding cells, but most of the building had vanished as if it had never been there. He could see into the records room and it seemed much of the station's top floors had pancaked down into it. Pieces of debris, from desks and chairs to the blackboard from the assembly room, littered the driveway and parking lot.

Several cars were ablaze. One of them, Lange's pickup, was on its side. Flames consumed the truck's interior. The vehicles in the impound area, most of them towed from Misset Park, fared only slightly better; the fence had come down and lay draped across two of them. Burning debris had landed on most of them and one of the impounded cars burned furiously.

There was almost nothing left of the panel truck. Its rear axle and tires remained, but Anderson could identify no other pieces of the truck. The tires burned noisily and popped and sputtered in the rain.

"Christ, Matt," Murphy said from behind him. "Jesus H. Christ."

Anderson looked over the destroyed cars in the lot. Beside Lange's he recognized four others. Anderson hoped most of them were on patrol, but he knew that was most likely not the case. Coming up on 11:30PM on a Tuesday night in Deacon's Landing with a strong summer storm to keep the residents inside, it was possible all the on-duty officers were inside the station. He swallowed and hoped he was wrong.

"So much for the cavalry," Murphy said breathlessly.

Anderson reached into his back pocket and pulled out his cell. He started punching in Bradley's home number before he realized the screen was cracked and dark. He tried it again before he spiked it on the ground in disgust. "Give me your phone."

"It's back in the Jeep," Murphy said. "I had it on the console between the seats. God knows where it is now."

Anderson stood and watched the flames consume his place of employment. He tried to ignore the itch which had taken up residence on his arm. It felt like a mosquito bite in the shape of a woman's hand. "We have to get to the school."

"Huh? What for?"

Anderson continued to watch the flames through the rain and wind. "You forget about Atkins and the school bus? Where do you think he was taking those kids?"

Murphy wiped water from his eyes. "Okay, I see your point. But it'll take too long to get there on foot. The shop is just down the road. Let's grab some wheels first."

Anderson could not argue the logic. Murphy started away. Anderson remained for a few moments. One of the interior walls collapsed and sent burning embers into the air before the rain claimed them. He swallowed hard and ran after Murphy.

****

Holly pulled into the driveway of Deacon's Landing Magnet School at a high rate of speed. The Honda swerved on the wet pavement but she kept all four wheels on the ground and that was enough for her. She could see the school at the top of the hill and, more importantly, the school bus parked across from the main entrance. She gunned the engine up the driveway until she came up behind the bus.

There was a man with long white hair standing near the bus's rear emergency exit. He spread his arms wide and smiled into her high beams. Holly gasped and turned the wheel hard to the left. The Honda's traction control system could not compensate quickly enough and she slid sideways toward the man. She closed her eyes and stood on the brake pedal and braced herself.

The sound of the impact was loud and jarring. Both windows on the right side of the car shattered and pelted her with small shards of glass. The airbag erupted from the center of the steering wheel and knocked her back into her seat. For a moment she was aware only of the sound of bits of glass bouncing around the inside of the car.

She almost blacked out but somehow she remained conscious and aware. She opened her eyes slowly. The passenger doors on the other side of the car were bowed in. Bits of glass littered the seat and the floor. She felt it in her hair and in her lap. The overhead console hung by its wires from the ceiling like the dead man at the end of a hangman's rope. The windshield was cracked but remained in one piece. Holly looked through the cracks and expected to see the man sprawled across her hood and a great deal of blood. There was no one there.

She moved to unlock her seatbelt and grimaced and clutched the side of her head. Her hand came away with flecks of blood on it and she looked at the window next to her. A spider web crack originated from the spot where her head must have impacted the glass. Strands radiated out from the center of the crack but the window was intact. She felt around the wounded area and decided it was not serious. Certainly not serious enough to keep her from finding her daughter.

She unlatched her seatbelt and threw open the driver's door. Rain pelted her but she paid it no mind. She stepped out of the Honda and collapsed to the pavement with a yelp. Pain shot through her right knee and she clutched it with both hands and writhed on the wet blacktop. She pounded the ground with her fist and gritted her teeth and got her hands under her. She pushed herself to a standing position and leaned against the Honda and rubbed her knee.

After a moment during which she determined there were no broken bones, she turned toward the school. "Cassie!" she screamed into the storm. "Cassie, Mommy's coming!" She limped around the back of the Honda.

The man rose up suddenly in front of her.

Holly had enough time to register his presence before his backhand caught her jaw. She spun around. Her knee gave and she went down again. She had enough presence of mind to protect the injured knee, but she could do nothing else. She tasted fresh blood and turned and looked over her shoulder.

The rain made it impossible to focus on his features but she recognized him anyway. "Atkins," she said. "What did you do with my daughter? If you hurt her in any way—"

"Hush, now," Atkins said. His voice would have been soothing under different circumstances. "I didn't plan to deal with you for a while, but you forced my hand."

He reached down and lifted Holly from the ground. With her arms pinned to her side, he brought her within inches of his grinning maw. He tilted his head to the right and Holly followed his eyes. "Right over there. Remember that day I tried to teach you a lesson? If that piece of shit Murphy hadn't gotten involved maybe you would have learned your place. Then you wouldn't have to make a living by taking your clothes off in front of strangers." He pulled her in closer until their noses nearly touched. "You fucking whore."

Holly reared back and slammed her head forward. She felt Atkins' nose explode against her forehead and warm blood splashed onto her face and into her hair. Atkins screamed and dropped her. Holly kept her feet under her and watched him stagger back. His hands covered his broken nose and blood flowed between his fingers. Holly braced herself and brought up her foot with all the speed and strength she could muster. She connected solidly with Atkins' testicles and he screamed again and collapsed. Holly nearly joined him. Her knee was on fire and could not support her full weight. She managed to remain standing only because her car was close enough for her to lean upon.

She gasped, out of breath with fear, anger and adrenaline. She looked at Atkins. He had folded himself into a fetal position and cradled his injured manhood with both hands. His nose bled freely and she noticed for the first time she had knocked out one of his front teeth. "Fuck you!" she screamed. Atkins did not reply.

She returned her attention to the school. "Cassie!" She limped past the bus and her mangled car and moved to the building's front entrance as quickly as her knee would allow. Her heart sank when she tried the first door and found it locked. She tried the second and it opened easily. Holly threw it open and stumbled into the building.

The foyer was dark. The exit signs were illuminated and glowed a soft red. The office was to her right and the glass doors and walls of what looked to be the gymnasium stood twenty feet in front of her. "Cassie," she called out. Her voice echoed along the deserted corridor. Her breath frosted the air and she became aware of the temperature inside the school. She shivered and pulled her wet clothes closer to her skin. That made her colder and she whipped off her outer shirt. She used it to wipe the blood from her face and then tossed it aside.

"Cassie, where are you?" She listened intently. She could hear nothing; the school was silent as the grave. She could see several posters and banners. All bore slogans encouraging the students to do well in their studies. She swore under her breath and tried to quiet her barking knee.

The hallway opened to her left. Ahead and to her right was an open staircase leading to the second level. Holly approached the staircase slowly. It was made of concrete, but a new strip of green carpet ran up its center.

She took the first step and her knee barked at her some more. She grunted and gritted her teeth and took the second step. "Cassie! Where are you, baby?" She stopped and listened to the silence. "Mommy's here."

She reached the halfway point on the staircase when she paused and rubbed her knee. It still felt unbroken but it hurt like nothing Holly had experienced save the twelve hours she spent in labor with Cassandra. She eyed the top of the stairs. The second level was as dark as the first. She used the rail and pulled herself up a few more steps.

"Hello again," said a male voice from behind her.

The sound startled her. She gasped and screamed as she turned.

Atkins laid a haymaker across her jaw. Stars exploded across her field of vision. She lost her grip on the rail at the same time her knee gave. She tumbled down the stairs, but she was barely conscious enough to note each impact. She came to a rest in the foyer, flat on her back and one foot on the first step.

She opened one eye and saw Atkins limp down the steps. He stopped and loomed over her with his hands balled into fists and blood coating his lips and chin. "You are *so* fucking lucky Miss Carlson wants you," he said. The absence of the front tooth added a whistle to his words. "If it were up to me..." He allowed his voice to trail off. He smiled and more blood tricked from the corners of his mouth. It dripped from the space vacated by his front tooth. "Ooh, we would have some *serious* fun."

He dismounted the staircase and stood behind her and took her hands in his. The last thing of which she would be aware before the darkness took her was Atkins dragging her down the corridor.

****

Anderson pressed the red button on the wall panel and watched the garage door pull open. He turned back and saw Murphy slide behind the Chevelle's wheel. When the door was fully open he ran to the car and opened the passenger door. Murphy did not wait for him to close the door. He fired up the 396, turned on the headlights and smoked the tires on the way out.

The rain immediately obscured their vision and Murphy swore and turned on the wipers. He sighed with relief and said, "I was hoping they'd work. I really had no idea until just now."

Anderson would have laughed if the situation was different. "You're a mechanic and you didn't know if the wipers would work?"

"I told you," Murphy said as they pulled onto West Main Street, "this car doesn't see rain." He paused for a moment and frowned. "First time for everything."

They made it one block west when Anderson saw a police unit, lights and siren blazing, tearing ass toward the station. He whipped his head around and watched the car recede into the distance. Smoke continued to rise into the dark sky and he could still see the orange glow where the police station used to be. It had diminished considerably from when the explosion occurred but it was still visible. "Somebody made it," he said. "Thank God."

"Wanna go back?"

Anderson turned and faced the windshield again. He shook his head. "No. Not while Atkins has a school bus full of kids. If it's just him, we can handle it."

Murphy made the turn onto Piedmont. "What do you mean, 'if it's just him'? You think he has help?"

"C'mon, Murph, you think he could have engineered all this on his own?" Anderson shook his head again. "He was never that bright and you know it. And how'd he get those kids on the bus? You think he just pulled up to their houses and beeped the horn?" His lips compressed into a thin line. "I think *she* got the kids on the bus. I think Atkins is working for her. I think he has been since he got into town, maybe even before then. I don't know how, but I'm going to ask him first chance I get."

"Wait a minute. Who's *she*?" He slowed when they approached the stop sign near the Seven-Eleven then gunned the engine through the turn. "Tell me you don't mean Ann Carlson."

Anderson swallowed. "None other."

Murphy shifted into fourth and the Chevelle sped up the soft grade of the hill which led to DLMS. "Oh, c'mon, Matt. That's just a local legend. Nobody actually believes in her."

"I wouldn't say nobody. Everything I've seen for the last week and a half, everything I've heard, it all points to her."

"Matt, she disappeared, when? Twenty-nine, thirty years ago? Even if she's still around she'd be in her fifties, at least. How's she going around collecting kids? And why bring them to the school?"

The corner of Anderson's lip turned up in a wry smile. "If you're looking for a teacher, where better to start than a school?" He paused to glance at Murphy. "And I never said she was still around. Smith thought she was dead and he implied that Ford killed her. But her body is inside the school."

"Okay, that's just plain nuts." Murphy turned up the school's driveway. The Chevelle fishtailed on the wet pavement, but Murphy corrected the drift and floored the accelerator up the hill. The tires screamed their protest. "How on earth did you come up with that?"

"It makes sense. In a fucked up way, I admit, but it makes sense. Ford kills her, either by accident or on purpose. Hell, maybe he doesn't kill her. Maybe he just beats the shit out of her. Who knows? The bottom line is, he fucked up big time. He's going to death row if she's dead, maybe he only loses his job and spends some time in prison if she's alive. So she has to disappear, one way or another."

"Okay. But why the school?"

Anderson did not reply. He took a deep breath and shuddered. He looked out the window, through the lessening rain, and saw the building formerly known as Deacon's Landing Elementary School loom before them. It rose from the ground and looked like nothing so much as a red brick tombstone. A chill worked its way down his spine and it had little to do with his soaked clothes. He saw the school bus parked across from the main entrance and he pointed to it. "There."

They sped up the driveway until they crested the hill and the pavement leveled. The Chevelle's engine reduced its bestial roar to a dangerous growl as Murphy downshifted. They approached the front of the school slowly.

"Jesus, is that Holly's car?" Murphy asked.

Anderson leaned forward and tried to see through the rain. The white Honda looked as if it had grown out of the back of the school bus. The Chevelle's headlights reflected off bits of broken glass on the blacktop. Anderson could see no one inside the wreck; the driver's door was open and both front seats were empty. He saw the driver's airbag hanging from the center of the steering wheel. Murphy brought the Chevelle to a stop and applied the emergency brake and killed the motor.

Anderson unlocked his waist belt and stepped out of the car. He ran to the wrecked Honda and looked inside. A small pattering of blood stained the driver's seat, but the car was unoccupied. "She's not in here," he said over his shoulder.

Murphy joined him and looked at the Honda. He whistled through his teeth. "Fuck me. What the hell happened here?"

Anderson ignored him and turned his attention to the bus. He walked slowly along the side of it until he came to the doors. They were open and Anderson stepped inside and looked about. "Bus is empty, too." He stepped back out into the rain. "They're all inside."

"Holy shit," Murphy said. His voice was flat and emotionless.

Anderson looked at Murphy and followed his gaze to the front entrance of Deacon's Landing Magnet School.

It took his mind a moment to reconcile what his eyes saw with what he knew. The front entrance area of the school had changed. It was no longer Deacon's Landing Magnet School. It appeared much as it did on the last day of classes when it was known to all the residents of the town as Deacon's Landing Elementary School. The newly remodeled front entrance was replaced by the double doors that always made Matty Anderson think of oblong eyes watching his approach. The red brick of the façade was darker than it had been the night Anderson found Murphy parked in the same spot in which they now stood. The red brick of the old façade had discolored to dark brown by the time Matty Anderson enrolled as a student. The same color now stained the new bricks like cancer on the lungs of a lifelong smoker. Matty Anderson never gave much thought to the color of his school; Matt Anderson recognized it and hated it immediately.

"This can't be real," Murphy said.

"I don't suppose you have any weapons in your car?"

Murphy shook his head. "Maybe a tire iron in the trunk. That's about all."

Anderson did not take his eyes from the school. "Get it. And a flashlight wouldn't be a bad idea, either."

He heard Murphy retreat to his car and a moment later the Chevelle's trunk sprung open. A moment after that Murphy returned to Anderson's side. "I forgot about this," he said and held out a sledgehammer with a short wooden handle. "Used it to get the brake drums off. I've been looking all over for this fucking thing." He hefted the tire iron and the hammer. "Which one you want?"

"Doesn't make a difference. Either or."

Murphy slid the tire iron into his belt and held the hammer out to Anderson.

Anderson took it and felt its weight and it made him feel marginally better. He looked again at the school's entrance. "You have a flashlight?"

Murphy pulled it from his back pocket. It was small and plastic and cheap, but it came to life when Murphy pressed the button. "Just this. It ain't much, but it works."

"It'll do. Let's go."

Anderson took his first steps toward his old school. By the time they reached the double doors his skin was coated with a thin sheen of sweat.

****

Holly did not want to wake up but the voice in the back of her mind would not shut up. It sounded suspiciously like her mother's voice. Her tone was one Holly had not heard in years, since she was a teen and firmly in the midst of her rebellious phase. She tried to shut out the voice, as she had back then, with the same result. It forced her back to consciousness and Holly reluctantly went along for the ride.

The first sensation of which she became aware was the pounding in her head. It felt as if her brain was trying its best to escape her skull. She groaned and pressed a hand against the side of her head. She winced and mumbled a protest against the pain.

Beyond that, she became aware of the temperature around her. Was it not mid-August? Why was she so fucking cold? Her tank top and jeans felt stiff and abrasive and she realized they were coated with ice and frost. In the end it was this conclusion that forced her eyes open.

Holly lay on a tiled floor. The wall across from her was made of cinderblock and painted baby blue. A wooden bench was bolted to the tiled floor and a row of lockers stood behind her.

She got one hand under her, but its twin refused to move. Holly tugged at it before she realized it was frozen to the floor. She tried to turn her head and confirm her theory but her right cheek was likewise frozen in place. Holly sucked in a deep breath and tore her right hand free. Her howl of pain echoed off the cold cinderblock. She brought her hand up to her eyes. Her palm and fingertips were red and raw and the cold air stung the wounds. Pinpricks of blood welled up from the red areas. Tears stung her eyes but she blinked them back.

Cassandra was here somewhere and the thought of her daughter made her narrow her eyes and grit her teeth. She braced herself against the floor and pushed up for all she was worth. The floor seemed reluctant to let her go and Holly struggled against the ice and the pain. She felt her skin begin to tear and she screamed and put everything she had into the next push.

Holly tore free of the frozen floor and her scream echoed off the walls again. She had the presence of mind to hurl herself onto the nearby bench before her injured knee gave way under her weight. She worked herself into a sitting position and felt gingerly around the wound to her cheek. It stung like a son of a bitch, but the area of missing skin did not feel large. Holly looked at where she had lain and saw a thin strip of skin welded to the tiles. She spat blood on the floor.

She wrapped her arms around herself and tried to stop her muscles from trembling. The cold saturated her body and she had to grind her teeth together to keep them from chattering. She brought her legs up, ignored the pain from her wounded knee, and hugged them to her chest. Holly teetered on the bench and nearly lost her balance more than once. She did not tumble to the floor and that was due mostly to willpower.

Her throat was dry and she produced nothing but a weak croak when she tried to call to Cassie . She looked about the locker room and froze when she saw Atkins leaning against the closed door. His arms were folded across his chest, but it did not seem to be because of the temperature inside the room; his stance was purely casual. His smile was wide and it reached his eyes. Blood had crusted on his chin and the sides of his mouth. It glistened beneath a thin sheen of frost.

"About time, sleeping beauty," he whistled amicably. "I didn't think I hit you that hard."

Holly stopped grinding her teeth together long enough to say, "Fuck you." Her breath frosted the air. She shook with cold, but anger began to seep its way into her muscles. Her lips trembled. "Where's my daughter?"

"Before we get to that, I wanted you to know it's nothing personal." He unfolded his arms and laced his fingers behind his back. The move was casual, absentminded, as was his pace as he moved away from the door. "Well, that's not entirely true, is it? You kinda had this coming."

He walked past her, hands still behind his back. Holly eyed the door and calculated her chances of making it through before Atkins caught her. She realized she could not hope to make it, not with her knee in its present condition. She sat and hugged her legs closer to her chest.

"You know, my dad had it coming, too. You heard about what happened to him?"

He stopped and looked back at Holly as if he expected an answer. He received none. She did not even look at him. He waved a hand dismissively through the air. "I guess it doesn't matter. But like I said, you had this coming. You're just lucky she wants you."

Holly continued to look straight ahead. Atkins passed in front of her again and Holly forced herself to remain on the bench. She wanted nothing more than to launch herself at him and tear out his eyes. She remained in place and shivered.

"Kenny, please. Where's my daughter? Whatever you have against me, it doesn't have anything to do with her. Let her go. Please, Kenny."

Atkins shook his head. His hair might have whipped back and forth were it not frozen against his skull. "Haven't you been listening? It's not me you have to worry about. It's her."

"Who is *her*?" The anger crept into her voice and Holly found she had no interest in evicting it. "You keep talking about *her*. You mean Ann Carlson? She's gone, Kenny, disappeared without a trace when we were still kids, for Christ's sake!" She swept her arm in a gesture that took in the locker rom. "There's no one else here. It's just *us*."

Atkins ran back to her and planted his hands on the bench to either side of her trembling form. "You'd like to think that," he hissed. "You'd certainly be in a lot less trouble if you were right. But you're wrong. Dead wrong."

He leaned in and planted a kiss on her cheek. Holly shrunk away, but her hands remained wrapped around her legs. She squeezed her eyes closed and tried not to vomit. He avoided the raw area on her cheek and planted his lips closer to her temple.

"I have to go now, babe. She's here now and she wants to talk to you in private." He smiled and turned from her. He walked toward the door and did not look back.

Holly watched incredulously as Atkins slipped out the door and left her alone. She remained on the bench for several moments. The door remained closed and Atkins did not reenter the locker room.

Slowly, Holly unfolded herself. She flexed her knee, but the cold must have numbed the pain. It still throbbed but nothing like it had even a few moments before. She stood slowly and remained in place until she felt confident she would not tumble to the floor. She tested her knee again and decided it was good enough to get her on the move.

Atkins was certainly on the other side of the door, waiting for her to make a break for it. She would have to hit the door hard and hope her momentum was enough to carry her past him. *Go for the balls again*, she thought. *And this time don't settle for one shot. Jump up and down on those fuckers until he passes out or dies.* It was not much of a plan but it was all she had. She took her first hesitant steps toward the door.

She stopped when she felt the breeze. It was slight and colder than the air around her. She felt something behind her, enough to make the hair on the back of her neck stand up and take notice. Her arm began to itch again.

She turned slowly, reluctantly. Tears began to well up in her eyes. Her breath hitched in her throat. She completed the turn and looked at the wall.

The woman stood, hovered, really, in front of the baby blue cinderblocks with her arms outstretched as if awaiting an embrace. Her long black hair whipped behind her as if she stood in front of an invisible fan. She wore a long black dress that stopped at her ankles; it ruffled in the breeze. Her feet were bare. Holly noted absently her toenails were painted hot pink.

What caused Holly's heart to skip a beat and the blood to blossom from the wound on her arm was the ethereal transparency of the apparition. Holly could see the cinderblock wall through her body. It wavered like the image on an old television screen.

Hello, sweetheart, Dark Annie said. *Welcome back.*

Holly found her voice at last. She screamed.

Chapter Sixteen

A Bad Place Now

Murphy opened the front door to Deacon's Landing Elementary School and entered the main hallway before he realized Anderson remained outside. He turned and saw him frozen in place, hand outstretched for the door handle. Murphy walked back and opened the door. "You okay, Matt? You don't look so good."

Anderson swallowed several times. His eyes went from Murphy to the doors to up the facade of the building. His hair and clothes were soaked and Murphy got the distinct impression not all of it was rain. He lowered his voice, tried to sound calm despite his own rapid heartbeat. "Matt, Holly's in here. *Kids* are in here somewhere. C'mon, let's go."

Anderson swallowed again and looked at Murphy. He hefted the hammer and its weight seemed to make him feel better.   He took his first steps inside the old school. Murphy stepped aside and let him through.   Anderson stood just inside the doors and seemed to take in the open hallway. "Just like I remember it," he whispered.

Murphy looked about. It was dark inside the school, much darker than it was outside. He found a light switch on the wall next to the door and turned it on. The school remained dark. He flicked it a few more times before he gave up. He activated the flashlight and shined the beam in front of them. "That's better." He regarded Anderson for a moment before he nodded. "Yeah.   That's Mrs. Santos' room right there. I had her in third grade. Mrs. Cavanaugh across the hall from her." He indicated the next door on the right. "The main office, where Mrs. Lockwood held court." He looked about again before he said, "Okay, I admit, I thought you were off your ass before with all that Dark Annie shit. Now, I'm not so sure."

Anderson continued to look about as if Murphy had not spoken. "Just like it was back when we were kids."

Murphy grinned despite himself. "Who says you can't go home again?"

"This ain't home," Anderson said immediately.

Murphy cringed. "You know what I meant. C'mon, let's find the kids and Holly."

They walked in silence down the main corridor. They passed the front office. Murphy peeked through the windows but it was far too dark for him to see anything in detail. He fancied he could see the door to Miss Renna's office but it was wishful thinking. He remembered her only because he had had a crush on her when he was twelve years-old. Absently, he wondered where she had disappeared to since the fire.

Their wet shoes squeaked against the old tiles. The sound echoed off the walls and Murphy was struck by just how eerie a school could be after hours. It had never occurred to him, mostly because he had never walked through a school at night. Minus the noise made by children and their teachers, it more closely resembled a morgue than a place of learning. The thought sent a chill down his spine and he swallowed and continued forward.

The corridor continued past the main office. More doors stood closed on either side. Murphy remembered the library was on the right and the teachers' room was directly across from it. More third and second grade homerooms lay ahead of them but Murphy could not remember the names of all the teachers. *Three decades and pounds of weed later the memory isn't what it used to be*, he thought.

Motivational posters and banners hung on the walls. Murphy shined the light on them and read a few aloud. "Hey, I forgot all about these."

"I didn't," Anderson replied. His voice remained flat.

The corridor ended ahead of them. The boys and girls lavatories were nestled in the corners between the staircase that led up to the second floor and down to the gymnasium and locker rooms.

"Hang on, Matt. Auditorium on the left. I wanna check it out. Kids might be in there."

"I don't hear any kids," Anderson said, but he followed Murphy to the doors.

Murphy shined the light on the sign next to the old double doors and it confirmed his memory. He pulled on the handle and the door opened silently. The room was black as midnight. The small flashlight did little to illuminate the space. Murphy felt along the wall for a light switch. When he found it he flicked it and received the same result as he had in the foyer.

"Murph, to the left," Anderson said from beside him.

Murphy directed the flashlight beam in the desired direction and the breath caught in his throat. Most of the back row was occupied by corpses. They sat in the chairs and looked straight ahead. Murphy nearly lost his grip on the flashlight and the crowbar. He moved slowly past the corpses, turned, and shined his light at them.

They were men and women. Their apparent age ranged from the fifties to the seventies. They had died in various ways from head trauma to chest wounds, but most appeared to have had their throats cut. Murphy did not spend much time on any one corpse but those he looked at were uniformly covered with blood.

"Jesus, I think that's Mr. Ruiz."

"And LaVallee next to him. Wallace, Zylali, Verrastro." He swallowed loudly. "Smith."

Murphy looked at Anderson. "Dark Annie did all this?"

Anderson shook his head. "No. This was Atkins."

Murphy swore. "And he has a bus full of children in here somewhere." He shined the flashlight around the room, but aside from them and the former faculty of DLES, they were alone. "At least Holly isn't in here."

"I think they're all downstairs. With her."

"You said that before. I still don't get why you think she's here. Buried, I mean."

Anderson said, quite matter-of-factly, "Remember before she disappeared? Before the school burned? They were remodeling downstairs near the locker rooms. There were construction guys all over the place. Remember that?"

"Vaguely."

"I think Ford brought her here, dead or alive, and hid her down there. Maybe he had help, I don't know. His brother was the head of the local contractors' union back then. He could have hidden the work from his employees or maybe threatened them into silence if they noticed the work had been done. I'm just guessing here, but it all adds up."

"It does?" Murphy could not keep the skepticism from his tone. "What work? What the hell are you talking about?"

"Ford takes her back to his place or somewhere else where he thinks he can have sex with her. Things go bad, he fucks her up. Now he has to get rid of the body. He knows the police will dredge the ponds around here and the wooded areas are too popular with the kids. So he brings her body to the only place he can think of where it'll be easy to conceal her. I think she was buried down there. Or left to die. If you put a gun to my head and make me guess, I'd say she was walled up."

"Get the fuck—" Murphy did not finish his sentence.

Thin arms that might have belonged to a corpse descended from behind Murphy and pulled him back violently. He yelped his surprise and lost all semblance of balance. The flashlight and the crowbar flew from his hands and he was pulled back into the corridor. The flashlight bounced once on the floor and the auditorium was plunged into darkness. The double doors slammed closed as if pushed by hurricane winds.

The arms yanked back hard and Murphy felt his feet leave the floor. He sailed through the air and crashed into a row of lockers that lined the wall. He spun around, still off-balance, and fell against the lockers. He pushed himself back onto his feet and peered into the black around him.

"Hello, Murphy. Been a long time," said a musical, whistling voice from the black. It echoed off the walls and created the illusion it came from everywhere.

"Atkins," Murphy said.

"You shouldn't have come back," the voice whistled from all around him.

Murphy tried to see into the darkness but his eyes had yet to adjust. There was a faint red light from outside, from the brake lights on Holly's car. It was not enough. He tried to listen for any sound of movement, but he heard nothing but his wet boots squeaking on the floor and

Anderson pounding on the auditorium doors somewhere behind him. "Where are the kids, Atkins? What did you do to them?"

"You should be more worried about what I'm going to do to you," the darkness answered.

Too late Murphy heard the rapid footsteps to his right. He turned in that direction and felt sharp pain dig into his arm. He gasped and instinctively covered the wound. The blade had not cut deep but blood welled between his fingers. It felt hot against the cool air in the corridor. He listened to it patter on the floor.

"Murph!" Anderson shouted. The pounding on the doors was joined by the squeak of the handles being turned. "Unlock the door!"

"He can't help you, Anderson," Atkins called out. "And you can't help him."

Murphy closed his eyes and tried to tune out everything but the sound of footsteps. He heard them too late again. The blade felt more like a sword this time and it sliced across Murphy's shoulder. He screamed in surprise and backed up until he felt the lockers behind him again. His back was wet and hot with blood.

"What's the matter, Murph? Can't see in the dark?" He laughed before his tone became serious. "You beat me once. That's not gonna happen this time."

Murphy braced himself for another attack.

****

Anderson pounded on the doors for another moment before he gave up. He felt blindly along the doorframe until he found the deadbolt at the top. He stopped when he realized it was in the open position. "Not locked," he whispered. He backed up a few steps and threw himself at the doors. They did not move an inch and his shoulder shouted at him and promised him pain by morning. He backed off again, braced himself for another try, and then thought better of it. The doors would not open until *she* decided to open them. He was certain of this even if he did not know how he reached the conclusion.

He walked down the center aisle and got down on all fours and felt around for the flashlight. The carpet beneath his fingers was old and well-worn. He felt dirt and sand and sniffed dust. He came across a pen and discarded it. The next object he found felt like a girl's hair barrette. It was small and plastic and he imagined it was pink although he could not see it. This, too, he discarded.

He found the flashlight next to the outermost seat a few rows down. He rose to his knees and hit the button. Nothing happened. He rapped the flashlight on his open palm a few times and tried it again. The beam was weak for a moment before it returned to its former strength. It winked out momentarily and came back on.

He directed the light back at the double doors, over the heads of the corpses in the back row, and narrowed his vision to the deadbolt at the top of the doors. It was unlocked as he had guessed. He took a stride toward the doors before he thought better of it.

Anderson shined the light toward the stage. It was sixty feet away and he could just make out its outline. He limped toward it. The last time he had seen the stage it was full of his classmates putting on their version of *The Wizard of Oz.* He remembered how pretty Nathalie Merrill had looked as Dorothy with her hair in pigtails and the stuffed Toto poking out of her basket. He had wanted to ask her on a date, but his nerves failed him. He cast aside the memory and pulled himself onto the stage.

The curtains were spread open and Anderson advanced into the backstage area. The flashlight beam swung in a slow arc in front of him. He found the stage door which led to the side parking lot. It was locked and chained. He tugged on the chain and although it appeared old it did not give. Anderson swore and turned in the opposite direction.

There was a single door on the far side of the backstage area. He crossed to it and shined his light on the dead EXIT sign above the door. He tried the handle and it moved easily. He pushed the door open slowly and looked inside. The staircase was narrow and descended into darkness.

Anderson kept the light on the stairs and his free hand on the rail. At the first landing the stairs continued down. He followed them until they ended at a small alcove. A single door stood in front of him. Anderson licked his lips and tried it. The door creaked open.

Bright light and a blast of frigid air invaded the alcove and Anderson stepped back involuntarily. He squeezed his eyes shut against the unexpected assault and held up a hand to protect his face. The light was oppressive after the darkness of the auditorium and the staircase and it made his head pound. He squinted into the light spilling into the alcove and waited until his eyes adjusted.

The first thing he noticed was his breath frosting the air. It had been chilly upstairs, but the basement level felt like mid-January in Toronto. He shuddered and felt his wet clothes constrict a little around his body. He leaned on the door and opened it slowly.

He was at the end of a long and brightly lit corridor. The walls were cinderblock and coated with frost. The floor tiles were off-white but they too were frozen. He looked up the corridor, in the direction of the boiler room and the locker rooms and pictured Mr. Mitchell. His coach's whistle was around his neck and he walked unknowingly to his death. Anderson found he could almost see the man who had saved him once from a beating at the hands of Atkins and his cronies.

The walls were adorned with colorful scenes painted by the students. They showed crudely-drawn figures playing baseball and soccer. A group of three faceless cheerleaders dressed in the school's colors performed acrobatic stunts worthy of Olympic-level gymnasts. The paintings were muted by the frost that seemed to cover every inch of the lower level. On the wall above the cheerleaders was a framed sheet of paper which read: "Illustrations by Miss Carlson's 8th Grade Class."

A thin cord hung a few inches from the ceiling. Anderson followed it with his eyes. It led back to the end of the corridor perhaps twenty feet behind him. The corridor ended at another set of glass doors with another dead EXIT sign above them. What caught and held his interest and made his eyes widen was the object at the end of the cord taped above the sign.

His shoes crunched on the ice crystals beneath them. He remembered the flashlight in his hands. He shined it on the object on the wall as if the added illumination would reveal he had been mistaken. He was not. The single stick of TNT looked to be secured to the wall with blue painter's tape. "Holy Jesus," he whispered. Absently he turned off the flashlight and shoved it into his back pocket.

Be careful, honey, Jen chimed in. *This is a bad place now. It's* her *place.*

"You don't have to tell me," Anderson replied.

He turned and took a few quick steps down the corridor, but stopped when he nearly lost his footing. He thought about Murphy upstairs but the dynamite took precedence. He kept his eyes on the cord and followed it down the corridor. It disappeared into the first door he found. He looked at the stenciled lettering on the door. BOILER ROOM, it read. Naturally. Anderson tried the door, but found it locked. The door handle was cold enough to cause him to gasp and pull his hand back. He looked at the flesh on his palm and found it red and painful. He flexed his hand a few times until the pain subsided.

The cord reappeared on the other end of the door and continued down the corridor. Anderson kept his eyes on it. It disappeared and reappeared into the next door he saw, as well. This one read GIRLS LOCKER ROOM. There was no handle, simply a push plate on the door. Anderson used the sledgehammer to nudge the door open.

You always wanted to see the inside of this room, didn't you? Jen asked. Her tone was musical, amused. *Well, now's your chance. Get an eyeful.*

"Thanks." He stepped across the threshold and shivered. The air felt twenty degrees colder than in the corridor. Two separate rows of lockers stood in front of him. A small office once used by the girls' gym teacher, Mrs. Baker, was to his right. He found the light switch and flicked it up. The fluorescents in the ceiling blinked to life. They, too, were covered with frost.

He found the cord along the ceiling and followed it into the shower room. Ice coated the floor to a depth of a few inches. Stalactites of ice protruded from one of the showerheads. He remained on the edge of the shower room and followed the cord to another stick of dynamite taped to the wall near the corner. The cord ran through it and out the opposite end. It continued along the wall and past him and out the door.

Anderson turned and walked slowly and carefully toward the exit. He reached the start of Mrs. Baker's office when he felt a stiff and frigid breeze on his neck. He turned quickly. His feet threatened to skid out from under him but he steadied himself at the last moment. He nearly dropped both the flashlight and the hammer.

The woman with the black hair and black dress levitated a few inches above the tiled floor. Her arms were outstretched, her mouth opened wide and her eyes full of fury. Anderson gasped and two thoughts repeated themselves in his mind. The first was that he had seen this woman before, and not while he was unconscious on Smith's kitchen floor. She was, without doubt, the woman he had seen in the upstairs corridor the day Deacon's Landing Elementary School burned.

The second thought, which struggled to be heard above the first, was that he was correct about what happened to Ann Carlson.

The apparition screamed and catapulted herself through the air directly at him.

Run, baby, run, Jen shouted.

Anderson let out an involuntary scream and backed up too quickly. His feet flew out from under him and he crashed into the window of Baker's office. The glass shattered and rained everywhere. The frost on the floor and the wall provided no traction and Anderson landed in a heap. The flashlight flew from his hand and skittered across the floor. He sat against the wall and waited for Dark Annie to grab him.

She never did. The sound of her scream faded and Anderson opened one eye and looked about. The locker room was empty. He turned and grabbed onto the window frame above and pulled himself to his feet. He used it to steady himself and reached down and scooped up the hammer. He scanned the room for the flashlight but before he could find it the fluorescents winked out and the room went dark.

He could hear nothing but the sound of his own breathing and the blood pounding in his ears. It nearly deafened him. He felt along the wall until he came to the corner. The next breeze he felt on the back of his neck was colder than anything he had felt in his life. He became acutely aware she was standing (*levitating*) beside him in the darkness.

You can't have my children, Dark Annie told him. *They're* MINE!

Anderson felt cold hands on his arms. The wound on his forearm froze instantly and he screamed again. He took two quick steps forward and his leg impacted one of the benches. His scream became a howl of pain. His right shin throbbed and threatened to take him to the floor again. Anderson ignored it and tried for the door.

The hands on his arms tightened their grip until Anderson thought his bones would pulverize. His feet left the floor. He felt suddenly lightheaded and dizzy. He imagined the room spinning around him. When he felt her cold breath on his face he was thankful all was darkness.

Come with me, Dark Annie said.

Chapter Seventeen

The Live Woman and the Dead Woman

Murphy threw what he considered to be the best haymaker of his life. It glanced off Atkins' shoulder. He heard a short grunt of pain from Atkins, but nothing more. Murphy's feet slipped on something wet and he knew it was his own blood. Atkins had cut him perhaps fifteen times since pulling him from the auditorium. None of the cuts felt deep and none were close to his organs or arteries. He knew Atkins was doing it on purpose, keeping him alive and savoring the moment. What he did not know was how Atkins could see him in the dark corridor. Murphy was going on sound alone and each time he heard Atkins close in the attack would come from a different direction. He did not know how much blood he had lost but he already felt lightheaded. *Can't keep going like this, Murph*, he told himself. *Need to introduce some changes to this particular paradigm.*

He kept his sense of direction only because he could still see the faint glow of the taillight on Holly's Honda outside. The double entrance doors were perhaps sixty feet away. The light did nothing to help him find Atkins; if anything, it seemed to mock him with its monocular red gaze.

Murphy's breathing was coming faster and shallower with each moment. He felt the cold in his fingers working its way into his hands. He wondered how long it would be before he passed out. However long it took would make little difference. The moment he hit the floor Atkins would finish him off. Of this he was certain.

The blade cut across his arm and Murphy screamed and clutched the wounded appendage. Blood seeped from the wound, but it did not feel like much. "Fucking coward," he hissed into the darkness.

"I'm rubber, you're glue, Murphy," Atkins said. "I forget the rest."

"You never were that smart," Murphy grunted between gasps of breath. His foot slipped on more blood and he sank to one knee. He placed one hand on the floor to stop from going down all the way. His hand slipped in the blood, but he saved himself with the other. The world started to go black around the edges, even more than the darkness around him. His heartbeat was slow, much too slow considering all that had happened and was happening.

He lifted his head and eyed the exit. It was his only option and he knew it. He threw himself in the direction of the mocking red glow. He got his feet under him and it took only a moment for him to feel dry floor beneath his boots. He staggered more than ran for the exit. More than once he leaned to the side enough to crash into the lockers. He heard Atkins gasp in surprise and his rapid footsteps coming up behind him.

"Where do you think you're going?"

"Not far," Murphy admitted.

He reached the double doors and pushed them open with his own momentum and body weight. He was through them and tasted outside air before Atkins tackled him around his knees. They went down in a tangle of arms and legs, Atkins on top. Murphy rolled onto his side and threw his arm out with little hope. He surprised himself and Atkins when he landed a solid, satisfying blow to the latter's jaw. Atkins squealed and rolled off him.

Murphy struggled first to his knees and then pushed himself onto legs that threatened to buckle at any moment. The air outside was warm, nearly tropical after the time he spent inside the school. It refreshed him and made him more alert. The rain had stopped as well. He saw the school bus and Holly's car growing out the back of it. Beyond that the dark blue silhouette of the Chevelle. Murphy staggered toward it.

He heard Atkins swear from somewhere behind him. He spared a single glance over his shoulder. Atkins was on all fours and reaching for his knife only a few feet away. Murphy gauged the distance to the Chevelle and decided he could make it. He willed himself to stay upright for just a few more moments.

Murphy reached the Chevelle in time to see Atkins leap to his feet. The scrawny man saw Murphy and screamed. His features contorted into a mask of rage and hate and he sprinted at the Chevelle. Murphy got the door open and collapsed into the driver's seat. He had enough presence of mind to slam the door shut and punch the lock. He leaned back against the seat and looked through lidded eyes at Atkins on the other side of the window.

Atkins tapped gently on the glass with the tip of the blade. His rage became a smile. Fresh blood dripped from inside his mouth. "You're done, Murphy. You got nothing left. Come on out and take it like a man, you piece of shit."

Murphy looked away before he closed his eyes. He summoned what strength he had left and pulled the keys from his pocket. He reached as far as he was able and managed to slide the ignition key into the slot. His fingers were numb and he lost his grip and his hand fell away. The keys dangled from the ignition and caught the light reflected off Atkins' blade.

Murphy slumped back into the seat and was still.

****

Atkins tapped on the window again. Murphy did not react. Atkins repeated the gesture. "Murphy." He cleared his throat and raised his voice. "Murphy!" The word whistled from him and made him angry. He banged on the window with the side of his fist. "Fuck you, Murphy, wake up! You've had this coming a long time." He banged on the glass again. Murphy did not flinch. The smile vanished and Atkins snarled and screamed at the night sky. "You won't take this from me. I waited too long for this. Wake up! Wake up *right now!*"

Murphy remained silent and still.

Atkins hit the window with the knife handle. The glass held. He screamed again and slammed his elbow against it. Pain shot up his arm and made him drop the knife. He clutched his elbow and howled and danced on the blacktop. His rage pushed the pain into a small corner of his mind and he threw himself at the window again. He stopped himself just short of impact and stared daggers at the glass.

Slow down, idiot, said the voice in his head. It sounded suspiciously like his father's. It certainly held the same tone. *You still have Anderson locked in the auditorium.*

And so he did. Murphy might have robbed him of the ecstasy of the killing stroke, but if he played his cards right he could redeem himself with the cop. And Anderson would have to pay the price for Murphy's escape as well. Atkins suddenly felt pity for Anderson, as much as he was capable of such an emotion. His death would be doubly brutal. The rage vanished and the smile returned.

Atkins scooped up the knife from the pavement and turned back in the direction of Deacon's Landing Elementary School.

****

The first sensation of which Anderson became aware was the cold. It saturated his being and made his muscles tremble. His clothes were caked with frost and ice and it scratched his skin. His hair was frozen to his scalp. He groaned and tried to open his eyes. For a moment he feared they had frozen shut. They opened reluctantly and he blinked and turned away from the bright lights in front of him.

He was seated in a chair much too small for his frame. The armrests squeezed his sides and made it difficult to breathe. He lowered his head and opened his eyes and allowed them to adjust to the light. He could hear murmuring from in front and around him. His eyes worked better and he raised his head and looked about.

He was seated in a chair in the cafeteria. Several tables were lined with children, perhaps as many as seventy or eighty. *As many as could fit into a single school bus*, he thought. They spoke to each other in hushed tones. Their eyes were wide with fear; more than a few cried openly if silently. They shivered and wrapped their arms around their small bodies and rocked back and forth.

He turned his head to the side and found he was not the only adult in the room. Holly sat in the chair next to his. Like him, she was much too large for the chair, although it fit her better than it did him. Her head was down, her eyes closed. Anderson thought for a moment she was dead until he saw her breath frost in the air.

"Holly," he whispered. He looked about, saw no one but the children. Their teacher had yet to present herself. "Holly, wake up. We're in trouble."

Holly's eyes fluttered, but she remained otherwise unresponsive. Her chest expanded and contracted shallowly. Her eyes remained closed.

"Holly, goddammit," he hissed. "Wake up now. I need you." He scanned the faces of the children until he located Cassandra Wayne. She was at the opposite end of the nearest table. She sat next to a blonde boy and shared the same terrified expression as the other children. He leaned in as close to Holly as his chair would allow. "Your daughter needs you."

Holly mumbled something and her eyes fluttered again. Her head lolled on the end of her neck and she began to sway back and forth in the chair. All at once her eyes snapped open and she screamed.

The children jumped and screamed as well, startled out of their silence. The few who were not already crying burst into tears and sobbed loudly. Several called for their mothers. Anderson shot a quick look at Cassandra and saw the child crying hysterically and stealing glances at her mother. Her lips moved, but Anderson could not hear her above the cries and screams of the other children.

Holly shook her head to clear it and looked about the room. Her half-lidded eyes focused on Anderson. Her lips parted and she said, "What...?"

"Stay with me, Holly," Anderson said.

Her eyes left him and went to the other occupants in the room. Her eyes opened fully when she saw her daughter. "Cassie!" she shouted.

Cassandra's reply of "Mommy!" was loud enough to rise above the other children. The child held her arms up and her eyes pleaded.

Holly sprung from the chair and ran to her daughter. She tore the little girl from the bench and hugged her tightly.

Anderson squeezed himself out of the chair and joined them. They seemed oblivious to his presence until he placed a hand on Holly's shoulder.

She snapped her head in his direction and said, "Matt Anderson?"

Anderson nodded. "We have to get these children out of here right now."

She looked about the room as if seeing it for the first time. "Where are we? My God, is this the old cafeteria?"

Anderson pointed to the doors thirty feet away. He could see the outline of an SUV of some type parked outside. "There, through those doors. Let's get these kids outta here."

"Miss Carlson won't like that, mister," Cassandra said. She seemed to have gotten her tears under control, but her breath still hitched. "She told us we can't leave."

Anderson stroked her hair. "It's okay, honey. I'm a police officer, remember? And I say we *can* leave."

"Matt, I saw her." Holly's eyes were wide, but she kept her voice level. "In the boys' locker room."

"She came at me in the girls' locker room." And it fell into place for him. He nodded his understanding.

He took a step away from them and looked at the children seated at the long table. "Children, my name is Officer Anderson. I'm a policeman. We're all going to go outside now, okay? I want you all to stand up and follow Miss Wayne here to the doors."

A few of the children stood slowly, but most remained on the benches. They looked at him, at each other. Tears continued to flow. The few brave enough to climb to their feet looked hesitant and scared.

"C'mon, children, we have to move right now." He waved his arm in the direction of the doors. He stopped in mid-motion when he saw the open box labeled TNT on the floor. He approached the box slowly and looked inside. It was a large box and nearly empty. Two sticks of dynamite remained. He thought of what he had seen in the corridor and the girls' locker room. *Two sticks out there, and only two here. Where are the rest?*

Oh, I think you can figure it out, Matty, Jen said.

He returned his attention to Holly. She must have read his expression because her eyes widened and she whispered, "What?"

Anderson swallowed. He lowered his voice as much as he could. "This whole place is rigged with dynamite. We need to get these kids out those doors right now."

Holly gasped and looked about the room. Suddenly every shadow contained a pile of explosives...and there were *lots* of shadows. She put Cassandra back down.

Anderson moved along the table and lifted each child not already on their feet into a standing position. His knee still hurt but the cold seemed to have taken off some of its edge. "Let's go, children. We have to go outside now. Single file, like a fire drill. And when I say run, we're all gonna run just as fast as we can."

The children seemed skeptical but they stood and walked slowly away from the table. They lined up in a single file and faced the double doors. Most of them looked back over their shoulder, their eyes wide and wet. Holly walked to the doors and found the first one unlocked. She turned and nodded to Anderson. Cassandra remained next to her.

"Okay, let's go!" Anderson said.

The children began to move.

Holly opened the door and took one step outside when she halted and screamed. Cassandra imitated her mother. The children ran as quickly as their legs could carry them back to their places at the table.

Anderson looked outside and saw the woman hovering in the air in front of Holly. She wore the same mask of rage he had witnessed in the locker room. Her black hair whipped back and around her. Icy winds tore through the open door and into the cafeteria. Holly huddled against the onslaught, but she retreated out of the path of the sudden gale.

Dark Annie glided through the open doorway. The door slammed shut behind her hard enough to shudder in its frame. *Children, return to your seats, please. I'll be with you in a moment.* The teacher's voice was calm, almost tender, but there was an undercurrent that chilled Anderson more than the temperature in the room.

He backed up when Dark Annie turned her attention to him.

****

Murphy opened one eye just enough to see Atkins was no longer at his window. He lifted himself up and saw the thin man with the blade nearing the front entrance. He sat up the rest of the way and took a long, shallow breath. He was still lightheaded, still on the edge of unconsciousness. The leather driver's seat was slick with blood. The black edges in his vision were beginning to expand.

"Not much time left." He had not intended to whisper, but it seemed he was no longer capable of speaking at his usual volume. He needed to use his hand to push down on his left leg to work the clutch. *Thank God we won't need the brakes on this trip.* He turned the key in the ignition.

The big block V8 roared to life. He looked up in time to see Atkins whirl in his direction. Murphy spun the wheel and hit the gas with everything he had left. The Chevelle turned a tight circle and narrowly avoided the front end of Holly's Honda. He straightened the wheel and the Chevelle surged forward. It jumped the curb and Murphy screamed with the effort of working the clutch one last time.

Atkins looked incredulous. He stood in front of the double doors with the knife still in his hand and shouted something Murphy could not hear above the scream of the 396. At the last moment he pulled the headlight knob and bathed Atkins in the sealed beams. Atkins raised the knife above his head as if he were preparing to deliver a death blow to the more than thirty-five-hundred pounds of solid steel racing toward him.

Murphy smiled behind the wheel and gave him the finger.

The Chevelle crashed into and through the double doors of Deacon's Landing Elementary School. The tires stop-stuttered on the raised doorframe, but only for a moment. In the space of a single heartbeat the old muscle car was through the doors and the foyer and screaming down the main corridor. It shot past the library and the conference room and the auditorium with its assembly of corpses. The one remaining headlight showed the end of the corridor ahead. Murphy was past being able to do anything about it and the Chevelle crashed headlong into the wall between the boys' and girls' lavatories with an explosion of dust and debris. Old ceramic tiles cracked and shattered and rained down on the hood. The Chevelle bounced back a few feet and came to a stop. The engine died and the last of the exhaust drifted slowly from the dual tailpipes.

What remained of Kenny Atkins lay plastered on the hood. His head rested on its side and his eyes stared sightlessly into the car. The knife remained in his right hand. Carved into the hood's three coats of blue and five coats of lacquer were the letter **D** and **A**.

****

Holly retreated slowly from the doors. She held her daughter's hand tightly and tried to shield the girl from the blast of Arctic air. The wind ceased suddenly when the door slammed closed. Holly saw the apparition float slowly in Anderson's direction. Anderson was backing away. He took his eyes from the floating woman and shot a look at Holly. He tilted his head almost imperceptibly toward the open box labeled TNT. He looked at Holly again before he returned his eyes to Dark Annie.

Holly nodded her understanding although Anderson was no longer looking in her direction. She turned and ran back to the table where the children were retaking their seats. She knelt down and put Cassandra on the bench and brushed the girl's hair from her eyes.

"Cassie, baby, Mommy has to do something. Don't move from this table until I tell you to. Okay?"

Cassandra was crying and the tears melted some of the frost which coated her cheeks. "Mommy, I don't want you to go," she cried. "Please don't go, Mommy!"

Holly tried to choke back her own tears, but she was unsuccessful. Her hands shook as she cupped her daughter's face and kissed her forehead. "Just stay here, baby. I'll be back, I promise."

Cassandra cried loudly and the other children followed her lead. They sat on the bench and shivered and cried. Dark Annie paused her advance toward Anderson and looked over her shoulder. Her eyes narrowed and settled on Cassandra. Her expression was altogether unpleasant.

Holly stood and waved her arms in the air as if she were directing the landing of an invisible airplane. "Here," she shouted. "Here you *bitch!*" She looked about frantically until she saw her daughter's book bag on the floor at her feet. She picked it up and threw it with everything she had.

The book bag sailed through the air and would have hit Dark Annie squarely in the chest had it not passed through her. The dead woman turned around and faced Holly. Her features were twisted with rage and hatred. *How* dare *you*—

"Fuck you!" Holly screamed.

Dark Annie seemed to forget all about Anderson and the children. She glided quickly toward Holly.

Holly bolted for the doors at the other end of the cafeteria. She had no desire to venture deeper into the school, but she could find no other way to help Cassandra escape. She reached the double doors and stopped and turned. The dead woman was past the children's table and picking up speed with every moment. Holly cast a final look at Cassandra before she flung the doors open and ran into the corridor.

****

Anderson waited for Dark Annie to pass through the doors after Holly. When both the live woman and the dead woman were gone he ran back to the children's table. "Okay, kids, forget what I said before about the fire drill. Get outside and run as fast as you can. Stay together and go to the first house you see. Can you do that for me?"

The children looked at him, at each other. Many cast frightened looks at the double doors through which the ghost had disappeared. All were crying. Anderson looked there as well but the apparition did not return. Some called for their mother, their father, one small boy prayed.

"C'mon, kids, we have to go *now!*"

They remained on the bench. Many of them eyed the exit doors but they seemed to have lost the ability to move. Anderson swore and ran to Cassandra. She made no effort to hide her fear; her eyes were wide and tears streamed freely from them. Anderson took her by her hand and helped her to her feet. She screamed for her mother.

Anderson picked her up and ran for the exit. He threw open the door and braced himself for the icy winds. None came. The air outside was warm and damp and smelled like heaven. He eyed the Ford Explorer parked near the doors and considered it for half a second. He could not get all the kids into it and so he decided it was useless to him. And he could not leave, anyway. Not with Holly and Murphy still inside.

He placed Cassandra on the ground and waved his arm at the other children. "Let's go, kids, let's go. Now! *Move it!*"

Some of the older children slowly rose to their feet. The younger ones watched them and continued to look nervously at the doors on the other side of the cafeteria. The older children seemed to realize their teacher was not about to appear before them and they started for the exit. When they did the younger children followed them quickly.

They ran outside, past Anderson and up the short incline to the main driveway. "Keep going and don't stop," Anderson shouted. He grabbed a boy of about eleven as he passed. He took the boy's hand and placed it over Cassandra's. He looked down at Cassandra Wayne and patted her head. "It's okay, Cassie. Mommy will be fine. I'm going to go find her right now. You go with the other kids and stay with them. Okay?" He redirected his attention to the boy. "Stay with her and don't let go. Understand me?"

The boy nodded wordlessly and Cassandra wiped tears from her eyes. She looked at Anderson and he could see the hope and fear fighting for control behind her baby blues. She looked at the older boy holding her hand. She nodded at last and the two took off in tandem after the other children. Anderson watched them catch up to group before he looked back inside the cafeteria.

He strode purposefully to the box of dynamite.

****

Holly ran up the stairs as quickly as her legs would carry her. The adrenaline helped suppress the agony in her knee and she wondered how long it would last. She did not dare look behind her; it would slow her down and she had no desire to see the dead woman closing in on her. She reached the landing to the main level and threw open the doors and stopped dead in her tracks.

She almost did not recognize the Chevelle when she saw it. Its front end was crushed. Pieces of debris littered the floor all around the wreck. Smoke drifted up from inside the engine compartment and collected near the ceiling. The top half of Kenny Atkins was plastered to the hood. Blood dripped from his entrails and pattered on the tiled floor.

She approached the passenger door slowly and looked inside. Murphy lay slumped across the center console. There was quite a bit of blood inside the car. It had splashed onto the windshield and the dashboard. The seats were covered with it. Holly's hand went to her mouth to suppress a scream. She reached for the door handle with a hand that shook, but she pulled it back at the last moment. When she trusted herself not to scream she said simply, "Murph."

Holly heard something from far away. Her head whipped in the direction of the destroyed front entrance of the school. She could see nothing in the darkness, but she recognized the sound of scared children. She knew Cassandra must be one of them and her first instinct was to run after them. But that would mean leaving Anderson alone with...

Turning, she looked back the way she had come. The teacher peered at her through the window in the door. Her appearance had altered. She no longer looked young and beautiful; she more closely resembled a corpse. Her rotted lips pulled back from equally putrefied teeth and Holly lost the ability for rational thought.

She screamed and took a step down the corridor. Dark Annie passed through the door and moved rapidly in her direction. Her face was twisted into a mask of pure hatred.

Holly tried to duck, but she moved too slowly. Dark Annie passed over and through her and Holly screamed again. She felt cold like she had never felt in a lifetime spent in New England. Her clothes were instantly covered with frost and ice. Her skin turned blue. She gasped and collapsed to the floor. Her left pinky finger shattered like glass on contact with the cold tile and Holly stared at it with shock and horror. Tears spilled from her eyes and froze on contact with her skin.

She pushed herself to her feet. Cradling her ruined hand in her good one she ran for all she was worth down the corridor. In the part of her mind that still functioned was the knowledge she could not outrun the ghost. The school's main entrance was fifty or sixty feet away. She had no chance of reaching it. She also knew she could not survive any more physical contact with the dead woman.

The apparition was closing the distance between them. There were double doors on the wall to her right. She course corrected and crashed into them at full speed. They sprung open and Holly was on the floor once again.

She was in the old auditorium. Light from the remains of the Chevelle provided little illumination, but it was enough for Holly to see the tire iron lying on the floor in front of her. Her good hand managed to hold it when she grabbed it. She hooked her arm onto the closest seat and pulled herself up.

She turned toward the doors behind her. The tire iron fell from her suddenly-numb fingers. Corpses filled in the back row and the last functioning part of her mind shut down. Holly trembled, but did not retreat when Dark Annie entered the auditorium.

Chapter Eighteen

Help Me

After he was certain the children were far enough away Anderson ran for the box of dynamite. He grabbed the last two sticks. He ran as fast as he was able for the doors which led into the corridor. Holly had run left out the doors and Anderson knew she understood his intentions when he directed her eyes to the dynamite. He hoped she was okay.

He exited the cafeteria and turned right. His shoes slipped on the frost, but he kept them beneath him and made for the boys' locker room. Either would do, he was certain, but the boy's room was closer and he and he did not know how long Holly could last. The corridor was clear of floating apparitions and he took that as a good sign. He reached the door to the boys' locker room and for a moment he thought it was locked. Ridiculous. There was no handle on the door and no lock. *Frozen shut.*

He braced himself as best he was able and threw his shoulder into the door. His shoes skidded on the floor, but the door opened with the sound of cracking ice. The corridor was cold, freezing, but the locker room was much worse. Ice covered everything, from the walls and lockers to the floor and ceiling.   He felt the cold air invade his lungs and he coughed. The lockers and benches stood in front of him in three rows. Mr. Mitchell's office was to his right. The window through which Mitchell would keep an eye on his students was opaque with ice.

Anderson walked slowly around the lockers until he came to the area between them and the shower room. He closed his eyes and he could see his younger self emerging from the showers after a particularly sweaty basketball game with his towel around his waist and his hair dripping onto the tiles. He followed the child to his locker and watched him remove his school clothes and run the towel over his head. It occurred to him the last time he was within the room his parents were still alive and Ann Carlson was still dead. He was not enamored with the trade-off.

He eyed the wall which separated the boys' and girl's locker rooms. The ice covering it did not appear to be thicker than anywhere else in the room, but he felt he had indeed reached the correct spot. He knelt in front of the wall and placed the two sticks of dynamite at its base. He tied their fuses together and stood back.

You have to hurry, Matty, Jen said. *As soon as she realizes what you're up to...*

"I know. She'll be coming."

And then some. Get a move on, baby.

He retraced his steps to the front of the room and nudged the door to Mitchell's office. It was locked and frozen in place. He reached for the knob before he thought better of it. He pulled at the wastebasket next to the door, but it was welded to the floor with ice. Anderson kicked at it. Chips of ice flew in all directions. It was difficult to keep his balance but somehow he remained upright. He lost count of how many times he smashed at the ice with his foot but he managed to loosen the wastebasket. He tore it from the floor and hurled it at the office window.

The glass and ice exploded into the office. It bounced off the walls and Mitchell's desk. The basket skidded across the floor and came to rest against the opposite wall. Anderson did not wait for the glass and ice to stop ricocheting around the small room. He climbed through the window and went straight to Mitchell's desk.

A small calendar labeled *Courtesy of Your Friends at Deacon's Landing Banking Center* was frozen to the desktop. The top page showed the month of October 1985. Framed photographs of Mitchell's wife and children stood at strategic points around the desktop. A large glass ashtray sat to one side.

Anderson tore open the top drawer and was rewarded immediately. Mitchell's leather cigar case rested atop a few notebooks. Next to it was his old Zippo. Anderson picked it up and ignored the pain of the icy metal in his palm. He opened it and flicked it. Nothing happened. He tried again and received the same result. "Are you fucking kidding me?" he asked the empty room. He tried it again. The flame did not appear. "I don't suppose you have a lighter that works."

Sorry, babe. I didn't smoke.

"I know. I had to try."

He closed the lighter and shook it rapidly. He counted to ten before he opened it and tried it again. A tiny flame sputtered to life. "I got it, hon, I got it." He gasped with delight and made for the shattered window. He checked the flame again when he was once more in the locker room. It remained alive but it was small and weak. "No, no, no," Anderson whispered. He cupped the lighter with his free hand and moved as quickly as he dared to the dynamite.

****

Holly watched herself watching Dark Annie glide slowly toward her. The dead woman paused long enough to look over the dead people in the last row. Her eyes blazed with hatred of them and she seemed quite satisfied with their present state. After a moment she returned her attention to Holly.

Holly could not move. Her legs felt as frozen as her left arm. She stood in the center aisle and awaited the cold touch of the ghost woman. She wondered absently if it would hurt when she died. She thought of Cassandra and hoped she was safe. Holly's mother would take the girl in, of course, and she would have a shot at a normal childhood. She was still young enough that she might be able to shake off the loss of her mother. *Assuming Anderson succeeds.* She hoped he would. She hoped the explosion would be powerful enough to bring down the entire building. The thought of smoke rising from the ruins of Deacon's Landing Elementary School warmed her and made her smile.

Dark Annie stopped in front of her. *You tried to take my children from me.* She opened her mouth wide and leaned in to Holly.

Holly closed her eyes and awaited the end.

Dark Annie screamed in rage.

Holly opened one eye and saw the apparition shoot straight up perhaps ten or fifteen feet. She pirouetted and dove for the floor at a high rate of speed. She vanished through the floor of the auditorium. Ice formed on the carpet around the spot.

Holly stared at the ice for several moments before she said, "Matt." She exhaled long and loudly and her shoulders slumped. She found she could move again. She ran from the auditorium.

The corridor was silent save for the drip-drip of fluids leaking from the ruined Chevelle. Holly heard a commotion from outside. She could not see the children but she could hear them quite clearly. *So Matt's done his job.*

She paused at the threshold and looked again at the Chevelle. She spared only a moment for it before she was running as fast as she was able for the front entrance. She was shouting her daughter's name even before she made it outside.

****

Anderson knelt beside the dynamite and held the lighter to the fuse. The flame had diminished considerably from when it first sprung to life in Mitchell's office. He could barely see it and it provided no warmth. He held it to the fuse and whispered, "C'mon, c'mon." The fuse showed no hint of an interest in igniting.

He picked up the dynamite and rubbed the end of the fuse with his fingers. He twisted the end as best he could and held the flame to it again. The fuse sparked but did not catch. "C'mon you piece of shit, light." He held the flame against the fuse and swore and prayed. He tried to ignore the numbness creeping into his fingers.

He nearly dropped both the lighter and the dynamite when the scream pierced his ears. He spun in time to see the dead woman emerge from the far wall in Mitchell's office. She flew through the shattered window and dove for him.

Anderson threw himself to the floor. The lighter flew from his hand and skidded beneath a row of lockers. Dark Annie passed over him close enough to freeze the hair on the back of his head. She vanished into the wall in front of him.

He stared dumbly at the lockers which had swallowed the lighter. He pressed his cheek against the floor and ignored the searing pain and tried to locate it. It was too dark to see anything and he swore.

He became aware of the smell of sulfur and was honestly confused. He looked about the room until his eyes were drawn to the two sticks of dynamite in his hand. The fuse was lit and burning fast. He yelped and planted the dynamite against the wall. He was on his feet and struggling to make it to the door. His feet slipped and he went down. The breath was driven from his lungs. He gasped and clawed at the floor and succeeded in getting back to his feet.

He looked at the fuse and saw it had already burned past the separation point. Both fuses burned quickly. He looked at the door and realized he would not make it. He ran for the other side of the room.

Dark Annie emerged from the wall. She looked down at the dynamite and screamed with rage. She flew at Anderson, arms outstretched and murder in her eyes.

Anderson threw himself through the window to Mitchell's office. He hit the floor hard and his momentum carried him into the far wall. He rebounded off the wall with a grunt and scurried beneath Mitchell's desk. He curled into a ball and covered his head with both hands.

The explosion was both violent and deafening. Flames and dust and debris filled the locker room. The lockers in front of Mitchell's window toppled over. Drywall from above and pieces of cinderblock and dust invaded the office. The desk saved him from being pelted with debris. The left side of the desk collapsed when something heavy landed on it. He pressed his hands more tightly to his ears and gritted his teeth and felt the rapid temperature change within the room. He remained curled into himself until he felt the familiar sensation of Jennifer's arms around him. He felt her press her body against his. It should have been impossible given the smoke and dust but he recognized her perfume and it made him cry. He managed to free one hand and he used it to clutch her arm and hold it tightly against him.

The cacophony around them began to lessen before it faded away completely. He smelled smoke and felt the ice melting beneath him. He heard the flames consuming the wood benches and drywall around him. He kept his eyes closed and his hand wrapped around Jennifer's arm. The pressure of her body against his reminded him of every night they spent as a married couple. His tears became sobs and he would have remained that way forever were it up to him.

After a few moments he became aware that he could no longer feel Jen behind him. He opened his eyes and turned his head. He was alone beneath the partially collapsed desk. Dust continued to drift around the room and the smoke was thick near the ceiling. He crawled out from under the desk slowly, tentatively. He found Mitchell's desk calendar on the floor amid the shattered and melting ice. He knocked it away and climbed to his knees.

A heating duct had fallen through the ceiling and landed on the desk. He grabbed onto it and used it to haul himself to his feet. The door to Mitchell's office hung from its top hinge. The outside of the door was blackened and cracked. He peered through the window into the locker room. The lockers had fallen into each other like a series of dominos. The nearest row had landed on the wooden bench and destroyed it. Chunks of cinderblock, some nearly complete, littered the floor. Much of the ice was melted and his feet splashed through puddles as he entered the locker room.

The ceiling fluorescents were mostly gone. One remained intact and flickered. The door to the locker room had vanished completely. He peered around the lockers and saw the wall where he had left the dynamite was gone. He approached it slowly. He waved away some smoke and peered through the new opening.

There was a small room on the other side of the wall. It appeared to be no more than two or three feet wide. It contained no door. The wall on the opposite side bore the cracked and pockmarked scars of the blast. Small pieces of debris lay scatted about the enclosed space. The room was empty save for the woman lying in its center.

Anderson thought at first she might be alive. The body showed no sign of decomposition. Her long black hair partially concealed her face but he could see enough to notice the mascara which had run down her cheeks. Her black dress was covered with dust and bits of cinderblock but appeared otherwise intact and new. He caught sight of the bruises on her neck. They looked disturbingly like fingers. Her own fingers were raw and caked with dried blood. On the wall above her head, scratched into the cinderblock, were two small words: *Help me.*

Anderson swallowed and waved away more smoke. He looked again at the locker room. The small fires were already dying out. The walls dripped water and most of the ice had already melted. He looked again at the corpse before he turned away. His feet splashed as he limped slowly to the open doorway and the corridor on the other side.

He heard a slight rustle from behind before he took his first step outside the room. The frostbitten handprint on his arm suddenly upped the wattage. He gasped and moved to cover the wound with his hand. The hair on his arms and neck stood straight up. The rustling repeated itself. Anderson closed his eyes and swallowed hard. Slowly, almost against his will, he turned.

The woman peered at him through the hole in the wall of her room. She was on her knees, hands draped over the broken cinderblock that remained of the wall. Her hair was wild, her expression more so. She turned her head and her eyes fell on Anderson. "My children," Ann Carlson hissed. Her features twisted into a mask of hatred. "You won't take them from me."

Anderson looked wide-eyed at her. He took an involuntary step back, out of the locker room. He could not look away. Her eyes were the blackest shade of black Anderson had ever seen...and they were focused entirely on him.

But there was something else. She already appeared differently from a moment before when Anderson first saw her body. Her black hair was thinning. The exposed skin on her arms had become gray and appeared to have pulled tightly against her bones. The bruises on her neck had turned black. Her face, once beautiful enough to seduce her male students and their fathers, was ashen and riddled with varicose veins. Her elegant dress became a tattered rag.

She continued slowly toward him. Skin sloughed from her arms and splashed bloodlessly into the receding water on the floor. She did not appear to notice. Her eyes, still focused on Anderson, turned gray and receded into her skull and then vanished. She planted her right hand on the floor and her arm snapped off at the elbow. She splashed onto her stomach. She lifted her head and regarded Anderson with blind fury. She reached for him with her remaining arm. Her jaw dropped open but she made no sound. Her skeletal fingers caressed his shoes.

Ann Carlson, little more than a skeleton wrapped inside a black dress, collapsed completely to the floor.

Anderson stared at the corpse.

His initial emotion was exultation that he was still alive. The second was relief that it seemed to be over. These were followed quickly by something approximating pity. Whatever Ann Carlson had been in her life she did not deserve what happened to her. He thought of the message she scratched into the wall of what would become her tomb. What were her last hours like? Had she heard the men working in the spaces around her or the sound of children in the locker rooms? No more than a few feet from her but oblivious to her presence? He did not want to speculate and so he pushed those questions away.

Then he thought of the corpses in the auditorium and the ruins of the police station and what happened at the fair and his sympathy for her evaporated. He backed away from the corpse and toward the door.

What he at first mistook for wind blew through the locker room. Later, he would come up with what he thought was a more accurate term for what he felt: A *wave*. It made him grab onto the doorframe to stop from falling over. The locker room itself seemed to ripple. The fallen lockers shifted from baby blue to dark green. Mitchell's office disappeared completely. When the wave passed Anderson blinked and looked at the locker room. The results of the explosion were still present, but the room had changed completely. He guessed it was now the boys' locker room of Deacon's Landing Magnet School.

He looked again at the corpse of Ann Carlson. He lingered for only a moment before he retreated into the corridor.

It was different as well. The drawings created by children who were now likely parents themselves were gone from the walls. The floor tiles were a different color. The end of the corridor now contained two side rooms. Anderson noted with some unease the dynamite above the exit door was still present. He made for the cafeteria.

It was largely the same, although the lunch counter had moved across the room. The exit doors were where he had last seen them. The blue SUV remained parked outside. Anderson walked slowly across the cafeteria and exited Deacon's Landing Magnet School.

****

The sun was high when Anderson stepped out of the state police barracks. He walked beside the trooper assigned to drive him home until he spotted Holly and Cassandra in the parking lot talking and leaning against a red Camry. They waved and smiled when they saw him. He waved back and looked at the trooper. "I think I have a ride waiting for me."

"You sure?" the trooper asked.

Anderson nodded. "Yeah, I'm good. Thanks."

The trooper nodded and returned to the building.

Anderson walked toward Holly and Cassandra. The girl looked excitedly at her mother, who nodded. Cassandra ran to Anderson and wrapped her arms around his waist and proceeded to squeeze with all her strength. "Whoa, whoa," Anderson said. He laughed and hugged her back.

"Thank you, Officer Anderson," Cassandra exclaimed. "Thank you, thank you, thank you!"

"You're very welcome, honey," Anderson replied.

They walked arm in arm to Holly. When they reached her Holly smiled and hugged him and he hugged her back. They remained that way for several moments before Cassandra cleared her throat and they separated.

Holly was beaming. "I can't thank you enough, Matt."

"All in a day's work," he said and smiled. "How's your hand?"

Holly held up the bandaged appendage. "Frostbite is healing, but it'll be a while before I can play the piano again." She smiled wryly.

Anderson looked at the Camry. "Where'd this come from?"

"It's my mom's," Holly replied. "She's letting me use it until I can find another one." She inclined her head in the direction of the barracks. "How'd it go in there?"

He looked back over his shoulder. "They still don't have any real ideas about what happened. When Dark Annie—" He looked at Cassandra and chose his words carefully. "When she ceased to be among us the school building reverted back to what it is now. They think it was all Atkins and his buddy, Fisher." He shrugged. "That looks better on an official report than what really went down."

"But they have her body, right?"

Anderson nodded. "Yeah. What's left of it. They have the state examiner on his way here to determine cause and time of death. I could have told them, but they wouldn't have believed me, anyway."

Cassandra tugged on Holly's arm. "Mommy, you said we could get cheeseburgers after we pick up Officer Anderson."

Holly smiled and patted her daughter's head. "That I did, munchkin. We'll go in a minute. You can get in the car. And put on your seatbelt, please."

Cassandra said, "Yes!" and hopped into the Camry's backseat.

Holly closed the door for her and turned back to Anderson. Her expression sobered. "What did they say about Murph?"

"Actually, I think they're pretty close to the truth about how that went down. Atkins wounded him fatally. Before Murph died he ran Atkins down with the car." He paused. "They were a little hard-pressed to explain how the car got stuck inside a wall that seemed to have grown around it. Guess the floor plan of the new school is a bit different from the old one."

"Yeah." Holly looked away and a shadow passed through her eyes. She brushed at a stray strand of hair.

"Whoa," Anderson said and leaned in closer to Holly. He took a lock of her hair between his fingers. "When did this happen?"

"Hmm? Oh. That. I didn't notice it myself until I got out of the shower this morning. Do you like it?"

Anderson smiled. "Jerry Garcia said it best. 'The touch of gray kinda suits you, anyway.' Besides, now you look a little more like me." He smiled again and indicated the new gray at his temples. He laughed honestly and after a moment she joined him.

"C'mon, let's get some lunch," Holly said. "On me." She walked around the car and opened the driver's door.

"I was thinking more along the line of dinner. On *me*. What do you say?" He looked hopefully at her.

She smiled and stepped into the car. "I say it sounds wonderful." She started the car and closed her door.

Anderson slid into the front seat and buckled his seatbelt.

I'm so proud of you, baby, Jen said. Her voice was both sweet and distant. It was the first time she had spoken to him since the locker room. *See ya around.*

Sudden tears welled in Anderson's eyes, but he blinked them back. "See ya," he whispered.

Holly turned to him. "Did you say something?"

After a moment of silence Anderson turned to her.

"Nah. It's all good."

Holly smiled and squeezed his leg. "Okay, then. Let's go."

She guided the Camry out of the parking lot.

The author wishes to thank:

Detective Kevin Macharelli, Milford P.D.

Lyn Avery

Theresa Gumpert

Elizabeth Fortin

Author photograph by Taria A. Reed

Joseph J. Christiano is the author of

The Last Battleship and *Moon Dust*.

He resides in Connecticut.

Thank you for purchasing this Tell-Tale Publishing Group publication. We appreciate your patronage and feedback. Feel free to post a review or leave a message for the author on our website. Also, if you would like to read more by this or other wonderful TT author's please visit us at:

http:/www.tell-talepublishing.com